1.25

Grippi...
a...
Signet Double Mysteries

The Last Score
&
Beware the
Young Stranger

The Last Score

AND

Beware the Young Stranger

———•———

by

Ellery Queen

A SIGNET BOOK from
NEW AMERICAN LIBRARY
TIMES MIRROR
Published by
THE NEW AMERICAN LIBRARY
OF CANADA LIMITED

*NAL books are also available at discounts in bulk quantity
for industrial or sales-promotional use. For details, write to
Premium Marketing Division, New American Library, Inc.,
1301 Avenue of the Americas, New York, New York 10019.*

Published by arrangement with Frederic Dannay and the late Manfred B. Lee.
The Last Score and *Beware the Young Stranger* also appeared in paperback
as separate volumes published by The New American Library.

First Signet Printing, October, 1978

1 2 3 4 5 6 7 8 9

 SIGNET TRADEMARK REG. U.S. PAT. OFF. AND FOREIGN COUNTRIES
REGISTERED TRADEMARK — MARCA REGISTRADA
HECHO EN MONTREAL, CANADA

SIGNET, SIGNET CLASSICS, MENTOR, PLUME AND
MERIDIAN BOOKS are published in Canada by The New
American Library of Canada Limited, Scarborough, Ontario

PRINTED IN CANADA

COVER PRINTED IN U.S.A.

The Last Score

Cast of Characters

One

Reid labored (for the sake of public relations) and produced a smile. To sit there and see his client's chair actually occupied by a Gibson should have given him that old steak-and-potatoes feeling. Instead of which, he had to tell the client—politely—that he wasn't hungry, which was sheer Texas brag.

May Gibson was an original. Around forty-five, the TV hair-rinse age, she left the touched-up gray syndrome to the lesser women of Greengrove. Her hard beauty might be shatterable, but it was not to be dented. Everything about her was understated and unique, like the black Givenchy suit and the emerald solitaire burning her finger.

Reid glanced over at the checkbook lying lasciviously open on her lap and thought of his office rent, the payment due on his three-year-old Dodge, the bank loan, and other disagreeable facts of his life.

"You've come to the wrong man, Mrs. Gibson."

Her eyebrows went up with the sweep of longhorns. "I thought you were a travel agent."

"Not in the ordinary sense."

"Then what does that sign on your door mean?"

He cautiously shifted the bones of his bottom on the lumpy chair and looked past her head at the reverse lettering on the frosted glass: REID RANCE TRAVEL SERVICE.

Well, you had to wear a label, and you had to get used to people never seeing beyond it. He had worn the Reid Rance label for 32 years, but who knew him? They saw a male American: height, six feet, two and a half inches; weight, one hundred and ninety-two (he weighed more and enjoyed it less when he was hung up in the office); eyes 20/20, blue, with permanent wrinkles at their corners from squinting at the south Texas sun (which gave him that probing Texas look that really came from staring into the mirror and not liking what he saw); hair, Indian black (with smudges of gray above the ears that he carefully encouraged); complexion like brown shoe polish, free of blemish except the scar received, not in a knife fight with a desperado, but by falling on a sharp rock at ten); a face that he had been told didn't frighten women away (they frequently frightened him); mental condition, coolly sane (he often doubted it).

He had one way of getting back at the surface-lookers: he never accepted a client he disliked. This, he kept telling himself, spelled integrity.

"The sign means what it says, Mrs. Gibson. I sell a travel *service*. A rather special kind."

"Well, that's precisely what I want," she snapped. "And I'm prepared to pay for it." She riffled her checkbook.

Reid felt his neck warm up. So that's what *she* saw behind the label—a man who'd do anything for a price. She'd probably got the idea from his office, the barren waiting room outside, and the ancient receptionist he shared with an insurance agent and a seedy lawyer. Reid's carpetless cube of an office was furnished shabbily; it had a wheezing air conditioner and a single window that had been stuck for the three years of his occupancy which offered a grimy view of the Greengrove railroad yards.

Reid paid little attention to his office; the men who came there to hire him seemed to like it the way it was. They looked at the bullfight posters, the press clippings, the photographs tacked to the walls; they stroked the jaguar pelt draped over the threadbare sofa; they fingered the multiple rows of a shark's teeth set in jaws the size of a bushel basket; they rubbed the obsidian nose of the pre-Columbian *mono* he had dug up in the mountains of Guerrero; they hefted the rifles which gleamed in the wall rack and tested the business end of a six-foot spear gun with slackened cables which stood in a corner. His clients measured him in terms of swamp, jungle and sea; to them, as to him, an office was a place to hang one's hat, pick up mail, maybe chew the fat. Only a woman like May Gibson would demand more of it.

"Money is beside the point, Ma'am. I don't feel qualified to escort a high school girl on a three-week tour of Mexico."

"My daughter is not a high school girl, Mr. Rance. She graduated this spring."

Reid sighed and wondered how to terminate the interview. He glanced over at the window where the girl was a small silhouette against the brilliant morning. She had been standing for ten minutes without joining in the dispute. A pale blue suit jacket sheathed her back and narrow waist closely and ended at the flare of feminine hips. May Gibson had introduced the girl as her older daughter Karen. The relationship was self-evident. Karen had the same dark eyes and hair, the same fine-edged looks, the same straightforward, let's-stick-to-business air. Reid wondered what the younger daughter was like, the one who wanted to go to Mexico.

"I still can't take her, Mrs. Gibson."

"Why not?"

He held out his hands, palms up, a Mexican gesture he caught himself using more often than he liked. "For one thing, I'm a bachelor."

"I know that, Mr. Rance."

"For another, I'm not old enough to play father to a restless adolescent."

"You'll find Leslie quite mature."

"Lez-lay?"

"*L-e-s-l-i-e.* She's really a completely self-sufficient girl. She's toured Europe———"

"Alone?"

"No. But she could."

"Then let her go to Mexico alone. I'll arrange transportation, hotels, guides——"

Her lips vanished. "That's exactly what I won't permit."

"Then you go with her."

"That's exactly what she won't permit."

"Her sister——?"

"I work," interrupted the sister, still staring out the window. May Gibson's older daughter *worked?* And what the devil was fascinating her out there? There was nothing to see but the railroad tracks and the flat cotton lands of the Rio Grande Valley stretching twenty miles south to the river and, beyond, the brush-and-thorn wasteland of Tamaulipas. Was Karen the reserves—waiting to jump in and finish him off after her mother wore down his resistance? It sounded silly—it meant a planned campaign and he couldn't possibly be that important to them.

"Why not hire a traveling companion, Mrs. Gibson? Or I could arrange for a responsible Mexican duenna——"

"Leslie won't hear of a woman," May Gibson said.

Reid felt the warning stomach flutter that signaled the onset of exasperation. What the hell was this Leslie, anyway? A spoiled rich darling whose every whim had to be satisfied? A teen-age nymphomaniac? Or what? He began to think that what Miss Leslie Gibson needed was a good smack in the panties.

He told his stomach to behave, and after a moment it did. After all, he had no intention of becoming involved with the brat, and there was no point in getting on the wrong side of a Gibson. He still had to live in Greengrove.

"Tell me, Mrs. Gibson," Reid asked, leaning forward companionably, "what does your daughter want to do in Mexico?"

"Quote: 'Dig it.' " Mrs. Gibson barely smiled; it made her look sad and, for a moment, human.

Reid felt sorry for her, but the flutter was starting again. "Okay, so Leslie wants to 'dig it.' It's true that it's the dig-people who come to me, Mrs. Gibson, but, the trouble is, they're all men. I mean, you dig? Businessmen, professional men, retired men—men who like to squeeze out from behind their desks or climb out of their holes once every year or so to prove that they're still *macho*. Some want to make the bullfight scene. All right, I take them down, give them a look from the inside, police a tequila bust with some of my *corrida de toros* friends, take them out to a ranch where they can wave a *muleta* at some tottering old bull and make believe they're the reincarnation of Manolete, and so on. Would Leslie dig that? Does she dote on Hemingway and Tom Lea?"

"I don't think so. She's sensitive about animals."

"All right, how about this?" He pushed up and went over to the wall, where an 8 x 10 glossy showed him kneeling beside a five-hundred-pound jewfish. "I went down seventy feet off La Paz to spear this baby." He fondled the open jaws of the shark. "These teeth came out of a white shark that made a very serious pass at one of my clients off San Blas. That hide over there is off a four-hundred-pound jaguar I shot in Chiapas. Do you think Leslie would like to go for cat? Or would she rather shoot alligators in Quintana Roo?"

Karen half turned from the window. Her dark eyes were cold. "You do the sarcasm bit very badly, Mr. Rance."

"My apologies, Miss Gibson. I didn't mean to sound superior. It's just that I'm trying to convince you ladies that I'm not set up to escort little girls on shopping tours." He went back to his chair, but he did not sit down; maybe they'd take the hint. "I couldn't even show Leslie where to buy a serape—I mean the kind you'd let her bring into your home."

"I can't believe," May Gibson said, not stirring from the client's chair, "that you limit your services to giving your male clients a cheap thrill with a harmless bull or saving the fools from sharks."

"No——" Reid sat down, stifling his sigh. These women didn't give up; maybe that's because they were Gibsons. "If a client is stupid enough to want it, I can take him where the wheels are running in Acapulco. Or I can show him—provided he isn't a cop—acres and acres of marijuana under cultivation. I once took a doctor to Oaxaca to sample *teonanacatl,* the sacred mushroom of the Aztecs; I held his head in San Luis Potosi when he insisted on trying peyote and threw up all over the place. I remember once arranging for a client to see a fellow in Mexico City who claimed he could arrange anything for a price. My client had told me he wanted to see a fight between a mongoose and a bushmaster. It turned out that what he really wanted was to arrange a little friendly killing. I left him on his hands and knees picking up the money he had paid me. So, you see, even with male clients I have my limits." Smiling, Reid reached for his phone. "Why don't I put you in touch with Interamerican Tours? They have a couple of dozen reliable men——"

"They wouldn't do," said May Gibson.

He settled back slowly. So that was it. "And *I* would. Reid Rance, or you don't play. Why, Mrs. Gibson?"

"I'll answer that, Mama."

Here come the reserves, Reid thought. He turned toward the girl. "All right, Miss Gibson. Why me?"

"You were a police officer once," the girl said.

He was surprised, but he kept his face blank. "How did you know that?"

"I work for the *Houston Post.* I asked the *Greengrove Leader* about you, Mr. Rance, and they let me look at your folder in their morgue. In it—among a lot of other things—I found a photo of you being sworn in as a policeman."

"I'm flattered at all the trouble you've gone to," he said dryly.

"You've had quite a career," Karen said, but not as if she admired it. "Calf-roping. Brahma-riding. Stunt-driving. Even bullfighting, Mr. Rance. And other gay, mad adventures on land and sea. I'm sure you've been bored sitting around this office for the past two months."

So Girl Reporter knew about the last two months, too. He looked at her, not concealing his resentment; she looked back at him quite coolly. He found himself fighting the impulse to tell her that autumn was his slow season, that the summer had been full, that December would bring more business than he could handle. He won, and turned back to her mother.

"My police career didn't last very long, Mrs. Gibson. I like my own freedom too much to enjoy locking other people up, even those who deserve it. I was a rotten cop and I haven't improved since. If it's a bodyguard you're looking for——"

"Not exactly a bodyguard, Mr. Rance."

"I sit corrected. Just a guard."

May Gibson lost her poise for the first time. She flushed and fumbled with her checkbook. "I just think Leslie would be less likely to . . . well, get away from you, Mr. Rance."

"Oh," Reid said slowly. "Now I get it. Leslie wants to solo on this flight, and she'll do her damnedest to give the slip to anybody you send with her. Well, Mrs. Gibson, you couldn't write a check big enough to send me out with a thrill-happy girl handcuffed to my wrist. I'm sorry."

"But if I pay you far more——"

"Mama, put your checkbook away." Karen came away from the window with a businesslike tap-tap-tap of her heels on the uncarpeted floor. She took up a position beside her seated mother and looked down at Reid. It was the kind of look, he thought, that she might have given the boy who sacked her groceries at the supermarket. "Mr. Rance, would you please leave us alone for a few minutes?"

He went out into the waiting room and through the door marked: HAROLD CHESNEY, GENERAL INSURANCE. Chesney was a thin, bald man with a sad voice who would have been type-cast in Hollywood as a mortician. Reid usually took his morning coffee break with Chesney, chiefly for the pleasure of listening to the insurance man's condemnation of the marriage trap or his laments over Reid's barren bachelor existence, as the case might be. It all depended on whether Mrs. Chesney had got up in time to prepare his breakfast.

Hal started to rise eagerly, but Reid waved him back. "Coffee later, Hal. I've got some people in my office."

"Like clients?"

"Like May Gibson, for one."

"My God!" The insurance man looked positively funereal. "Is she evicting?"

"That's right, I forgot!" Reid exclaimed. "She owns the damn building." He sank into a chair. "Man, that's all I need just now. She's made up her mind that I'm to take her daughter Leslie to Mexico. Now what the hell do I do? I owe her a month's rent."

"What's the problem?" jeered Chesney. "If li'l ol' May Gibson wants you, Reidy-boy, you can write your own ticket. That Leslie means more to her than her left one."

"How do you know so much about them?"

"My daughter Betsy. She and Leslie graduated from high school together."

"What kind of brat is this Leslie?"

"Well, you remember her old man?"

"No, I've been out of touch with Greengrove society."

"You know May's had three husbands, don't you?"

"No."

"You haven't been out of touch—you've been *daid*. Want me to brief you, boy?"

"Looks as if I'm in for it," Reid said glumly. "I guess you'd better."

Hal Chesney made a comfortable arch of his fingers

and leaned back in his swivel chair. "You take May's family. Just folks—came here with the railroad, never amounted to much. I don't think there's any of 'em left. Well, May was twenty when she got hitched the first time. To Jim Frankel, a sharp young lawyer who'd just got started in practice. Then the war came. Jim made lieutenant at Fort Bliss, and the first thing you know, an artillery round fell short and wiped out a dozen of Jim's platoon, including him. Karen was two years old; I doubt if she remembers him.

"Well, May played the chin-up young war widow till after the war—you could almost hear the violins. Then she started dating Bradley Gibson, and the tune changed so quickly you'd have thought she'd opened a parlor house.

"Brad was four years younger than May. His dad was old Nate Gibson—the first man in the Valley to think of bulldozing off the mesquite and planting cotton. Nate wound up owning half the county. Brad was his only son, a wild kid, moody as a bull in season. Smashed up a car every six months. He had a little Bonanza he flew to Dallas or New Orleans when he got tired of Greengrove. Good flier, Brad—I've seen him make a perfect landing and then have to be helped off the field because he was too drunk to navigate by himself.

"When he married May, Brad seemed to settle down. After Leslie was born, Brad went into business with old Nate, and everything looked cosy. Then, one day, while Brad was flying a duster, sober as a judge, he hooked his wheels in a high wire, the plane flipped over and burst into flames, and that was the end of Brad Gibson. Am I boring you, Reid?"

"No, indeedy," Reid said. "I'm just on edge, thinking of May Gibson sitting in my office. Better speed it up, Hal."

"May moved into old Nate's big ranch house and started working for him as a kind of unpaid private secretary. 'Just for something to do,' Nate used to tell people. He was sure fond of his son's widow. Well, Nate had a stroke, and May took charge right off. Did such a bang-up job that, when Nate had the second stroke, he married her. Must have been a tax gimmick, because he wasn't good for anything any more—couldn't even sit up for the ceremony. When he died, May came into a hell of a lot of money—I don't know how much. I do know Leslie gets about two hundred thousand of it when she's twenty-one."

"How about this Karen?" Reid asked.

"Karen got frozen out—or more likely froze herself out, if I know Karen. She's smart and prickly and independent as a bronc at its first sight of a tailgate. She sure gave the Greengrove bucks a hard time—any boy who forgot there were brains behind that pretty face slunk off holding his crotch. She took off after two years of college and got herself a job on that Houston paper. She's got a by-line now, and I don't figure she's long for Texas. Sharp as a whip, Karen. Not a bit like Leslie."

"Leslie's wild?"

"I wouldn't say 'wild,' exactly," Hal Chesney remarked critically. "More like . . . well, my wife dragged me to a school do once—Betsy played a clarinet solo, and Leslie read a poem she'd made up. The poem had words in it that . . . well, the school superintendent looked like he'd been hit over the head with a singletree. I thought, uh-uh, bye-bye, Leslie. But when Leslie finished, she said in a shy voice that she was sure she hadn't *shocked* anybody, because she'd only used four-letter words that people saw on the walls and sidewalks of Greengrove every day. About all that happened was the PTA sent a delegation to the mayor, and the mayor put the tenants of the city jail to work painting out the dirty words." The insurance man grinned. "That give you a picture of Leslie Gibson?"

Reid groaned as he rose. "I've got to get back, Hal."

"Don't forget the Mann Act. Make the kid's old lady put everything in writing."

"Maybe they've left."

He was only half right. When he re-entered his office, he found Karen alone; apparently she had talked her mother into leaving the mop-up operation to her. The girl had her hands behind her, patent-leather purse dangling. She was studying a newspaper clipping framed on the wall.

"Is this really you, Mr. Rance?" she asked without looking around.

Reid stopped just inside the outer limits of her perfume. Even in her heels, Karen stood no higher than his nose. The glistening black hair strained against the severe upsweep of her coiffure; a wisp had fallen free and straggled down the nape of her neck. For some reason, this atom of disorder pleased him.

"Yes."

The four-column bullfight close-up had been brought into gory focus by a telephoto lens. Reid lay on his face in the sand; two inches of horn had been buried in his back, the bloodstain spread widely over his *traje de luces*. That *coronada* had left him with a deep puckered dimple in his back and a slight droop to his left shoulder.

"It happened eight years ago at a small *corrida de toros* in Puebla. I turned my back on the bull during a *quite,* thinking I had him immobilized. I thought wrong."

"Weren't you a good bullfighter?"

"Well, I took some powerful risks," Reid drawled, "but I was too big to be a crowd-pleaser. I made the bulls look scrawny. There was always some hundred-pound Mexican kid pulling the big money."

"But, of course, you didn't care about that, did you? You did it for the risks—isn't that right?"

Karen faced him suddenly with an unlit cigaret between her lips. Reid found himself looking deeply down into a pair of unwavering, large dark brown eyes. After a moment, he said, "Oh, excuse me!" cracked a match-head with his fingernail, and held the flame up to the cigaret. She puffed and nodded, still examining him.

"I don't know, Miss Gibson," he said, and blew out the match. "I wouldn't say I did it just for kicks. The kicks and the money sort of go together. If people have to pay somebody to do what they're afraid to do themselves, the pay makes the risks sweeter—and there's more of it. Pay, I mean."

"Afraid?" The girl raised her brows. Nothing longhorn about *them*. Delicate. She turned away, walking toward his sagging sofa. "Or just sensible?"

"You don't know much about people, do you?" Reid asked pleasantly.

She stopped in her tracks. Then she was facing him again, taking the cigaret from her lips with a steady hand. Nice control, Reid thought with admiration. "What makes you ask that, Mr. Rance?"

"I didn't mean to get you angry."

"I'm *not* angry!"

"Sorry. What I mean is, fat cats can afford to be sensible, Miss Gibson——"

"That's the third or fourth time you've called me 'Miss Gibson,' " the girl said icily. "My name is Frankel. Of course, you couldn't know. And I'm *not* a fat cat. I work for a living—just as you do, Mr. Rance."

"With one difference, Miss Frankel," Reid said dryly. "If you should lose your job, or become incapacitated through illness or an auto accident, you can always go back to mama's millions. I can't."

"We're getting off the subject——" She was flushed.

"One minute more, and we'll get back on it. The first money I ever earned, outside of delivering groceries for my dad's little store, was collecting snake venom. I was twelve. This guy gave me a bottle with a thin rubber cap and told me how the rattler was supposed to sink his teeth through the cap and squirt his venom into the jar. I hunted through the brush for a week with a stick and a bent rod. When I found a rattlesnake, I pinned his head to the ground, grabbed him behind the jaws, and milked him. The little prairie rattlers gave only a thimbleful, but man, those big diamondbacks! Two of 'em would fill the bottle. So you see, Miss Frankel, even at the age of twelve I'd already learned what you'll never know—that the bigger the physical risk, the quicker the money. No, I wouldn't say I took that horn in my back just for kicks. I was broke."

She was over at the sofa now, rubbing her palm absently over the pelt of the jaguar. Her left hand was ringless, he noticed. He felt a momentary satisfaction and wondered why.

"If you're so interested in money, Mr. Rance," Karen murmured, "why not take Mama's offer?"

"Because it's not my kind of risk. Hasn't it occurred to your mother—or to you, for that matter—that I'm young, male, and have never taken the vow of celibacy?"

"Oh, that," she said. "Mama's willing to risk *that*. I mean, she's looked you up, and you have a good reputation personally, and . . . well, I mean, she wishes Leslie would act like a normal girl. Mama has some idea that Leslie's a freak. I keep telling her that there's no such thing as a 'normal' teen-ager and never was—that they've always been little bundles of receptor nerves responding to stimuli. In Mama's day, it was gin and roadhouses and dancing all night. Now it's folk music, poetry and pot. The trouble is that today they can go way out where nobody's ever been. Like picking up on pills, saggies and bennies and dexies, or dangerous barbiturates like redbirds and yellow jackets."

"Is Leslie a *pillhead*?"

"She's not hooked, but she's been high. Mama tells me she'll come home with her eyes out of focus and a goofy smile on her face, but nothing on her breath. Once Mama smelled ether in the house for two days. She didn't realize it was coming from Leslie. Ether-sniffing is a hundred years old, but these kids think it's a brand-new kick. Marijuana, peyote, mescaline . . . they think they invented it."

Reid leaned back against his desk. In Mexico, you could walk into a pharmacy and buy almost any drug except cocaine, heroin, paregoric or marijuana. No prescription needed. He began to understand why Leslie dug Mexico.

"Who picked me, Miss Frankel? You or your mother?"

Her chin came up. "I'd rather you called me Karen. Men can't say 'Miss' without condescending."

He smiled, letting his eyes trail downward. She had perched on the arm of the sofa, one knee raised slightly higher than the other; he could see the lacy edge of a black slip under her skirt. "If you don't like being a woman, Karen, why do you dress like one?"

She reddened, but he noticed that she did not move. "Since I live in a man's world, I intend to exploit whatever advantage my sex offers."

"Why not play your advantage to the hilt? Get married and have kids."

"Naturally, you'd be one of *those*."

"One of what?"

"Those great big hairy-chested men who say the only way to handle women is to keep them pregnant and barefoot."

"Do I remind you of somebody you hate?"

The red deepened; for a moment she seemed confused. Then she began hunting through her purse. "You asked me who picked you——"

"It's not important."

"It's very important. It's Leslie who picked you. She says if she has to go with somebody, it's got to be you. Otherwise, she threatens to take off on her own."

"But why me?" Reid frowned. "She doesn't even know me!"

"She reads the papers. She had this stuck in her vanity mirror."

Karen handed him a ragged clipping. The headline read: SOLE SURVIVOR OF SEA DISASTER. The cut showed him in a hospital bed, almost hairless, his face a hollow black mask against the pillow. Reid winced, recalling those thirty days adrift on a sea of burning gunmetal . . . the rough lump of his tongue scratching his mouth, gums turning spongy, skin sloughing off like a boiled potato's, eyesight going bad from lack of food. He had watched his three companions roll up their eyes and sink into death. When the tanker picked him up, his rescuers later told him, he was croaking over and over: *"Stay alive, stay alive, stay alive."*

"I don't see how this turned her on, Miss Frankel—oops! Karen."

"Leslie admires people who risk their lives for a cause. You were hauling supplies to the rebels in the hills——"

"I didn't dig the rebels' cause one little bit. Like a lot of revolutionary cliques, what they were really after was their turn at the public trough. They needed guns and supplies, and I went in with three other guys and we bought a sloop. The rebels had agents buy the stuff, and all we had to do was load it under cover and haul it without getting caught. There was big money in it. But somebody got drunk in the wrong place and shot his mouth off, and a coast patrol boat was laying for us. We had to run for it—straight out to sea. Then a tropical storm with the pretty name of Irma twisted the drive shaft off our auxiliary engine, tore away our canvas and rigging, and split a hundred seams. To keep afloat we had to throw the guns and supplies overboard. We drifted for a month, my three partners lay down and gave up the ghost. I was stubborn and stayed alive till that tanker found me. And that was the end of my gunrunning career. No blood on the flag, no heroics—just a business venture that went sour."

Karen got up. "All right, Mr. Rance. I'll tell her that."

Reid frowned. He remembered a bronc rider he had once esteemed as the greatest human who ever threw candy bars at the boys hanging around the rodeos, and how bewildered and hurt he had been when the man was sent to prison for armed robbery. He had known with infinite exactitude after that what the kid had gone through who begged of Shoeless Joe Jackson, *Say it ain't so.*

Karen was offering her hand. "And thank you for listening to me. I know you didn't have to."

Oh, didn't I? he thought. Or maybe you don't know who's the landlord of this building.

She gave his hand a quick, impersonal squeeze and tried to withdraw hers. He held on. It immediately went dead; softly female, but dead. Nevertheless, he kept holding on. "What are you going to tell your sister?"

"That you're an unromantic coward and an unsuccessful mercenary and she'd better look for a normal, healthy relationship with someone else."

"Oh, blackmail, is it?"

She smiled. The smile created a dimple in each cheek. "Or you could tell her yourself."

"Where is she?"

"Downstairs in the coffee shop. She's wearing——"

"I'll know her. Are you coming along, or did you and your mother set it up for me to see her alone?"

"You're horrible," Karen laughed. "Alone."

The coffee shop was crowded by the midmorning break. Reid looked over the clusters of office girls at the tables—big and small, fat and thin, homely and pretty, but all managing to look as if they had just been produced on an assembly line, each with a pile of swirled and convoluted hair stiff with spray, each with electric blue eyelids, each with iridescent fingernails and not quite clean fingers. One girl was sitting alone, staring into a coffee cup as if she saw something sadly amusing there.

He walked over to her table. "Leslie Gibson?"

She looked up slowly, her brown eyes distant. She was pretty enough, but that was not what startled him. It was her hair. Her hair was . . . *vivo*. Where the other girls carried on their heads stony masses, like garden urns, Leslie's hair fell in glinting waves to her shoulders, great combers in a dark brown sea that seemed to be in motion even when it was still. The illusion of vital movement extended to the rest of the girl's body. The fashionably loose yellow frock could not contain what it covered . . . *vivo, vivo* . . . a vibrancy that unified her parts . . . so that her lack of a brassière, for example—and her lack of need for one, Reid thought—was not apparent at first; it became so only after a while. He almost whistled. Quite a punkin!

With a bit of artfulness she could have turned herself into the girl on the billboard, the face on the movie poster, the figure in the bathing suit ad, or any of a dozen other commercial stereotypes. He decided at once that he liked her just the way she was. But what she must do to the boys!

"If you are," Reid said, "I'll sit down. But I know you are."

The distant look went away. "Then why don't you?" When he promptly pulled up a chair she said, "Your voice is a surprise. I expected you to squeak."

"Me, squeak?" He offered her a cigaret. "Why?"

"I don't smoke tobacco, thanks. Why, because your voice is the only thing I didn't know about you. *Something* had to be out of character. There always is. I'm so pleased, Reid."

So it's 'Reid', is it? "Generalizing is a bad habit. That's your first lesson, Miss Gibson. It is Gibson, isn't it?"

"Of course. Why do you ask?"

"Your sister chewed me out for not knowing her name is Frankel."

"Oh, Karen. Of course, she had a different father. Anyway, call me 'Leslie'."

"Not 'Lez-lay'?"

"Not 'Lez-lay.' I *loathe* 'Lez-lay'."

"So do I."

"Then we're off to a flying start."

"Whoa!"

Her big eyes opened wide. "But isn't everything set?"

"Nothing is set."

"That's all right," Leslie Gibson said calmly. "I like it with nothing in front. We can split now, this afternoon."

Reid pulled his nose. This would make his third refusal—somehow, the toughest of the three. "I told your mother I wouldn't take you."

"Oh?" She looked down, smiling her secretive smile. "Mama never accepts *no*. That's why I never say it. I let her go ahead and make all the arrangements, then I do what I want. I mean, it's my life and I'll live it my way." She looked up suddenly. "You've got another client, is that it?"

He was tempted to grab the excuse. But his experience was that the easy way usually turned out to be the hardest. "No, that's not the reason."

"I know, you think I'll bore you. That you'd have to stand around yawning while I buy silver in Taxco, bells in Oaxaca, sweaters in Toluca—load my camera for me when I swoon to photograph a bunch of stupid churches——"

"Wouldn't I?"

She laughed, a low throbbing sound. "Do I really look like the tourist type? Man, if I wanted to pick up on that, I'd take Mama." She leaned forward. "Look at me, Reid. I mean, *look*. What do you see?"

Her eyes were on fire. Reid thought: For all her sophisticated airs, she's still just a kid putting her head down and charging at life, with no responsible back-ground to rein her in. She thinks she's going to rip open Mexico's seams and find what they're hiding from the squares. He felt a vague alarm. This kid could get into trouble. Real trouble. And her mother and sister knew it.

"What do I see? I see a seventeen-year old girl——"

"That," said Leslie, "is a temporary condition."

"—who thinks she's wearing a beard and riding an old nag named Rosinante."

"A *romantic?*" she exclaimed, as if he had called her a dirty name. "My God, you're like all the rest!"

"You've looked around from your long observation post of seventeen years and you've asked yourself, 'Is this all there is to life?' And you figure it can't be—they're hiding something——"

Leslie sniffed. "They only think they are."

"The fact is," Reid said, "They're all asking the same question you are: 'Is this *it?*' The girl with the muscles on her fifteenth parachute jump, the burned-out boy on his fiftieth drag race, the movie star with her fifth hus-band——"

"So let her take number six. Maybe she'll make it with him."

"If she's smart she finally admits, 'Yes, this *is* it.' The hash-slinger, the notions salesman, the guy in the teller's cage, everybody has to learn to settle down and make the most of what he is and has in a large economy-size world that holds no mysterious gifts, only a little plastic doodad worth about a twentieth of a cent."

"A philosopher, too," the teen-ager laughed. "Look, philosopher, I'm a chick who comes into two hundred thousand dollars at the age of twenty-one. How do I make the most of those apples?"

"Learn how to use it."

"Like practice with stage money?"

"Like don't hit people over the head with it."

"The way Mama does, huh?" Leslie set her little jaw.
"Fear not, I'll play it cool when I collect. Meanwhile,
there's four years to get through."

"A long time to live for kicks."

She frowned at that. "This is getting us nowhere. All
right, I'll dig Mexico alone."

"No," Reid said.

"No, Papa?" she gibed. "What makes you think I'd
listen to you? Any more than if you *were* my father?"

Reid tottered on the brink, trying to pull back. Then,
without really knowing why except that somebody had
to do it, he said, "if you're going with me, young lady,
you'd better listen."

Her mouth opened like a little girl's at the sight of a
new doll. Then she was up and around the table and gone
like a spring breeze, leaving him with a soft tingle on his
cheekbone. A minute later, she came running back with
her mother and sister in tow. Reid got up mechanically
and held chairs for them, feeling like an exhausted bear
finally treed by three hounds. Karen's face showed nothing; she was wearing her neuter mask again. Mama's
face showed nothing—her checkbook showed it for her;
she had it out and was unscrewing the cap of a gold
pen.

"I ask only one thing, Mr. Rance," May Gibson said.
"You're to call me every evening at seven. I'll feel
better if I can speak to Leslie."

Leslie made a face. "Mama, don't start spouting conditions."

"I'm talking to Mr. Rance, dear."

Leslie muttered something.

"It's your money, Mrs. Gibson," said Reid. "But suppose we go where there are no telephones?"

"I prefer that you don't," she said coldly.

Reid shrugged. Telephones were the exception, not the
rule, in most of Mexico; didn't she know that? Well, he
would fight that battle when he came to it.

"Now about the financial arrangements," said May Gibson. "What is this going to cost me, Mr. Rance?"

"I'll use my own car. It has six-ply tires, extra road clearance, and it's equipped for long trips. Fifty a day for expenses; I'll refund what we don't use. Assuming a twenty-day trip, that would be a thousand dollars. My fee is two thousand. In advance."

She stared at him. "It seems to me that's very high, Mr. Rance."

"It sure is," said Reid. "Double my usual," and gave her back the stare. Go ahead, he thought, do me a favor and turn it down.

"Oh, give it to him, Mama," Leslie said impatiently. "Apply it against my trust fund, or something."

The stare switched to Leslie, and something in it made the girl subside. Mrs. Gibson began writing a check. As she wrote she said crisply, "I'll pay a thousand dollars of your fee now, Mr. Rance. You'll get the other thousand when you return Leslie safely."

Reid counted to ten in his head. "Mrs. Gibson, you either put your daughter in my charge with confidence, or keep her. I intend to bring her back undamaged, barring acts of God. Retaining fifty percent of my fee isn't going to make me fifty percent careful. Or would you rather have me operate on that basis?"

She stopped writing. "But there are special dangers for a girl of seventeen——"

"Suppose you give me a rundown, Mrs. Gibson?"

She colored slightly. "I'm sure that's not necessary."

"I'm sure it is, since I don't know what you're talking about. Is it the *Indios?* They quit sacrificing young virgins a long time ago."

"For God's sake!" said Leslie. "Who says I'm a virgin?"

"*Leslie.*"

"Mama, were you a virgin at seventeen?"

"*Leslie!*"

Karen's neuter mask came alive with feminine amusement. "You'll have to give Mr. Rance what he asks, Mama," she said. "You either trust him or you don't, as he says. Once they take off, he's your proxy."

"I suppose that's so," said May Gibson reluctantly. "Very well." She tore up the check, stowed the bits in her purse, and wrote out another. "Here you are, Mr. Rance. Three thousand."

She had written something on the back of the check. He turned it over and read: *Fee $2,000.00—Expenses @ $50 per day—Any Unused Funds Returnable.*

"How long will it take you to get ready?"

"I can leave any time, Mrs. Gibson. Any supplies we need I'll buy in Mexico."

"Then you may pick my daughter up Thursday morning."

"*No,*" Leslie said. "Tomorrow morning. You know I'm practically all packed. And," the girl said to Reid just as his mouth was opening, "that gives you all the rest of today to go to the bank, get your gear together, or whatever. Right?"

Reid shut his mouth.

"But, dear," May Gibson said weakly—how often did she say anything weakly?—"we have so much to talk about first. . . ."

"Mama, for heaven's sake. I'm not going to the moon. Anyway, didn't you say yourself we'll be talking on the phone every night?"

There was a glint in Leslie's eye, Reid observed; the girl knew perfectly well that much of the time they would be in places where no telephone service was available.

"Oh, all right." Her mother suddenly looked quite old. "Then we'd better go home now, darling, and get you ready."

"You and Karen go on," Leslie said carelessly. "There are a few things I want to pick up at Snider's. And some of the kids to see and stuff. And I want to get better acquainted with this cat."

Greengrove's wealthiest woman labored and (thus history turns its tables, Reid said to himself) produced a smile. So in the end, he thought, snoot-faced Lady Gotrocks is just like all the mamas. Talk about Achilles's heel! He was rather relieved when Leslie embraced her and gave Karen a peck.

A moment after Mrs. Gibson and her elder daughter disappeared, Leslie had his arm in hers and was pressing it against her full, firm young breast enthusiastically as she began chattering away.

What had he got himself into? Remembering the amalgamated look of amusement and pity on Karen's face when she gave him a casual handshake, he had to bolster his sinking stomach.

Two

Reid drove slowly along the pitted road south of Montemorelos, passing an occasional high-wheeled buggy. The red aurora of the setting sun flared up behind the jagged sierra to the west. A smell of oranges came through the open window.

"Ohhh. You feel it?"

Leslie sat beside him with her long legs drawn up beneath her. She was wearing the brown slacks and blouse she had put on after they crossed the frontier. There was a language guide on her lap. She was looking out the window.

"Feel what?" Reid asked.

"The breathlessness in the air. How *swollen* everything seems." She drew up her breasts. "Something glorious is going to happen."

Reid wondered why he felt disquieted. Leslie was proving far more tractable than he had expected. He had let her take the wheel on the little-used road between China and Montemorelos, and she had driven with confident competence. At lunch in a little fly-infested *café* in General Bravo, she had reacted with none of the nose-wrinkling that annoyed him in most tourists. Eating her beans and enchiladas with one hand, she had used the other in true Mexican fashion to wave away the flies. So far she was an exemplary client.

It seemed impossible to discourage her enthusiasm for Mexico. During the drive south from Reynosa, after miles of dry brown hills relieved only by occasional adobes, he had remarked that the scenery would improve.

"But it's beautiful now!" she said. "No *billboards*. You don't realize what they've done to the States until you see a place that hasn't felt their grubby commercial fingers."

Now Leslie suddenly turned on the radio. The car thumped and blared with Mexican rock-and-roll. Reid cringed; maybe his optimism had been premature. If he had to spend three weeks with this banging in his ears . . . .

Abruptly she turned it off. "Same old stuff with a cha-cha beat. No counterpoint, no melody."

She bent to her language guide, her lips moving as she ran a finger down the page.

"How come you didn't learn Spanish in high school?" he asked.

"Mama wanted me to go to one of those finishing schools where you get French, horseback riding, flying, art appreciation, modern dance and the psychology of marriage. We compromised—I learned French in Greengrove and she forgot the finishing school." She glanced at her watch. "Talking about Mama, it's nearly time to punch the clock. Where's the nearest phone?"

"It's twenty miles to Linares. We'll call from the hotel."

"Where do we go from there?"

"Where do you want to go?"

"*Quién sabe?* Did I pronounce it right, Reid?"

"You're supposed to shrug and roll back your eyeballs."

"Like this?"

Reid glanced at her and grinned. "You look as if you're going down for the third time."

"I'll practice. I can also ask *'how much?'* and where the john is."

"Fine. Now where would you like to go in Mexico besides the john?"

She pouted. "Don't make me schedule all the fun out

of it! I want to go where it grooves me. How will I know till I get there?"

"Well, I'll give you a thumbnail travelogue. Going straight south from Linares, you've got a hundred and fifty miles of country about the same as this. You can take the cutoff to Tampico, but that's a hundred miles of brush and hemp and a hundred back. Tampico's an oil town. Takes you a couple of days to stop smelling like rotten eggs. And there are blobs of oil on the beach at Madero."

"You make it sound delightful."

"I can live without Tampico. But if you want to see it——"

"You've unsold me. Where else?"

"If we pass the cutoff, we'll go through the mountains around Tamazunchale. Beautiful, but it's a back-breaking drive. And they aren't the only mountains in Mexico."

She smiled at him like a kitten. "Reid, you don't have to keep up the fiction that I'm in charge. You lay it down, you're boss-man."

"Okay, we'll try the new road going west from Linares. It takes us onto the central plateau and joins the Piedras Negras-Mexico City route. You'll see two hundred miles of saguaro and yucca before you hit anything interesting, but it's a fast road. The farther I get from the frontier, the better I like Mexico."

"Then that's it," she said, and turned back to her book. He was pleased.

At Linares, Reid got May Gibson on the phone and turned it over to Leslie. He supervised the bellhop who carried in their bags, returning to the desk as Leslie finished her call: "I won't forget, Mama. 'Bye." She turned to Reid. "I'm suppose to drop halezone tablets in everything I drink. Remind me one of these days." She frowned at the bags. "Do we have to stay here? It's so . . . state side."

"We'd better enjoy innersprings while we can."

"I'd rather get off the beaten track."

"That means filth, no plumbing, no screens, doors you can't lock, straw mattresses, bedbugs, rats——"

"Cool."

He shrugged and picked up the bags. "Okay, you may as well learn right off."

In the falling darkness he drove upward between the deep canyon walls of the Rio Linares. Passing the town of Iturbide, newly ablaze with electric lights, he turned onto a narrow asphalt road. It climbed toward steep mountain peaks. Outside Galeana, which nestled in a crater of a valley, he pulled off the road.

"Better jump in back and put on your dress."

"Don't be *Victorian*."

"Leslie, in Mexico only bad girls wear slacks. A bad girl in a Mexican movie is as recognizable by her slacks as a bad guy in an American Western by his black shirt and hat. Take my advice and you stand a reasonable chance of not getting your bottom pinched."

Grumbling, she crawled over into the back and changed with a rather hasty rustle of clothing. Reid smiled to himself, thinking that the rare moments when she acted her age would have been refreshing if they didn't make him feel so old.

He drove twice around the central plaza before he saw the word HOTEL in letters not much larger than the middle line of an optometrist's chart. The entrance led to a "restaurant" with a grand total of three oilcloth-covered tables. A kitchen at one end gave off a smell of charcoal, fried beans and overripe meat. A pair of swinging doors beyond opened into a *cantina* with a sawdust floor and a high, brass-railed bar. A bubbling, throbbing Wurlitzer disgorged a Mexican ballad at full volume. A third door led into a flower-filled patio hemmed in by the two-story hotel.

Reid arranged for adjoining rooms with a smiling

señora whose round belly jiggled beneath a grimy apron. There was no bellboy, so Reid carried their bags up the stairs and along the wooden balcony overlooking the patio.

"Why did you say I was your sister?" Leslie demanded.

"To explain the separate rooms and still account for our traveling together," Reid explained patiently. "As my sister you're under my protection and nobody will bother you."

She made a face. "I'm older than *they* are, and I don't see any 'brothers' around."

Two girls were lounging outside a door on the ground floor. Their heavily rouged faces were so young they looked like little-girl dolls—dolls with plumply swelling breasts under low-cut blouses.

"They don't need protection, Leslie. Being bothered is their business."

"They're *prostitutes?*" Leslie looked thoughtful.

He opened the door to her room. It was what he had expected: unpainted walls, a forty-watt bulb dangling from the ceiling, calendar showing a garishly blonde girl being serenaded by a young man in an embroidered *charro* costume, both generously pocked with flyspecks. Music from the *cantina* seeped up through the cracks in the wooden floor.

Reid walked over to the tarnished brass-poster, jerked the quilt away, turned out the seams of the gray mattress cover, and examined them closely. After a moment he said, "High class. No bedbugs."

Leslie pointed her toe at a white enameled vessel with a flaring top. "Is that what I think it is?"

Reid nodded. "The facility. *El servicio.* If you want a bath, I'll have the *criada* heat some water."

"Let me try. May I?"

"*Andale pues!* Go ahead."

A half hour later, with an earthenware *olla* of steaming water beside him, Reid stripped off his shirt and dampened a facecloth. Splashing sounds came through the flimsy wood partition between his room and Leslie's. A few moments later he heard her sing in a teasing voice: "*The eyes of Texas are upon you. . . .*" He turned quickly and saw a shadow move across the wide crack in the wall. He hung his shirt on a nail above the crack.

"Don't forget, Brown Eyes, a peephole works two ways."

"Oh, you're not the peeping type. Anyway, I'm already dressed."

He joined her on the balcony ten minutes later. She was wearing a beige wrap-around skirt and cashmere sweater. He took her arm and walked her down the stairs and around the plaza. He bought her some *tostadas* and hot peanuts and kept stifling yawns until she began to shiver and said, "I guess I'll go to bed." He waited on the balcony until her light went on.

After a half hour of trying to shut out the banging music from below, Reid got out of bed, slipped on his trousers, stuffed his pajama top inside, and stepped onto the balcony. Leslie was standing at the railing with her back to him. She was talking to a small Mexican with a straw sombrero tied under his swarthy chin. At sight of Reid, the man made an abrupt bow to Leslie and walked swiftly away, high heels doing a tap dance on the balcony floor. One shoulder sloped lower than the other, Reid noticed, and the Mexican wore a gun in a belt-clip holster.

She was staring after the man in perplexity when she saw Reid. He walked over and leaned on the railing. He tried to make his voice casual. "Who's your friend?"

"Antonio something. He's a guard at a mine back in the mountains, or something like that." She looked at him, frowning. "You're scowling. Did I do something wrong?"

He studied her in the poor light. Her mammary development was sharply etched by the cashmere. He had begun to doubt that her aversion to brassières, which he had put down to her generation's rebellion against restraint, was as ingenuous as it seemed.

"What were you doing out here, anyway, Leslie?"

"I couldn't sleep."

"You hadn't even undressed."

"I knew I couldn't."

"You're not half as naïve as you pretend."

"Do I act naïve?" She tossed her wealth of hair. "And you haven't answered my question, Reid."

"All right, I'll pretend, too. Nice girls don't talk to strange men on Mexican balconies. Not if they want to stay nice."

"Don't be ridiculous." She laughed and moved closer. "I told him I had a very strict brother."

"Not strict enough, he's saying to himself right now. No doubt thinking about the friendly gringo chick in Room One while he tosses a few tequilas down his gullet in the *cantina*. And pretty soon he'll be deciding you're worth a little risk. You'd better turn the key in your lock."

Leslie laughed again. "All right, *hermano mio*. If you're really so worried, why don't you curl up outside my door?"

He did not answer. Instead, he lit a cigaret and stared out over the patio without seeing it.

After a moment, Leslie made an impatient little sound. "Will we be passing anywhere near Acapulco?"

"Why?"

"I think I'd like to see it."

"You don't pass Acapulco, you make deliberate plans to go there. I thought you wanted to stay away from the tourist places."

"Well, everybody goes there. There must be reasons."

"Plenty. The beaches are out of this world. The food is the best in Mexico, and you can get whatever cuisine your taste runs to—German, Italian, Yucatecan, French, Chinese, almost anything. The night life is one continuous

Mardi gras. The beach boys are the brownest, the girls are the readiest, and they both come in all shades. Even fly in over the North Pole from Stockholm if you get tired of Latins. Whatever you dig, you can find it in Acapulco." He squinted through the smoke at her. "Come on, now. What's this all of a sudden about Acapulco?"

She was looking into the patio. "Like I think it might groove me."

"Like you've set this up so you can meet somebody beyond the end of Mama's arm?"

That brought her head up. Then she giggled. "It must be that nasty police training." So she knew about that, too. "No, Reid, I'm not meeting anybody. Can't I just say 'Acapulco' without getting the rubber hose?"

"All right, don't tell me. You know I'll find out."

She was silent. Then she shrugged. "Oh, hell, deception's such a drag. Did you ever hear of Acapulco gold?"

He was puzzled. "The sand?"

"No, a plant."

A warning bell jangled. He kept his voice level. "Marijuana?"

"A particular kind."

"Who told you about it?"

"The word is out, man. It's supposed to be the most. Jet service to the top floor."

His abdominal muscles tightened. A faint memory out of his past mingled with the earlier foreboding. "Marijuana grows the same there as anywhere else, Leslie. The difference is in how it's cured."

"You know how?" the girl asked eagerly. "Tell me!"

"It grows big and rank on the flatlands twenty miles south of Acapulco. They strip it green and take it up to the mountains where the air is cool and dry. They hang it in a shed with open sides to let the air circulate around it. Like a tobacco shed. The slower the curing, the more resin is drawn into the marijuana leaves. That's the active principle, the resin. Cured too fast, it comes out green and fairly mild. Cured slow, it's brown dynamite. 'Gold?' I've never heard it called that."

"Can you get me some, Reid? Reid, please?"

"I don't plan to try. I'm being paid to keep you out of trouble, not get you into it."

"But I've never turned on, man! I sit around like a lump when the kids talk about pot."

"Turn on when you get home. Here, with me, it's out."

She turned peevishly to look out over the patio again. From the *cantina* came the thrum of a guitar. A high voice sobbed a Mexican hillbilly song. On the lower floor, a door burst open. A girl in a thin slip shrieked and started running around the patio. A man ran after her, shirttail flying. He caught her and snatched her up, giggling softly, and lugged her back to his room. The door slammed.

"Crazy!" Leslie cried, delighted. "They play at sex like little kids."

A shot burped in the distance, followed by a man's faint whoop of glee.

"They play with guns like little kids, too," Reid said. "Only the guns shoot real bullets."

"You're just an Eeyore, you know that?"

"A what?"

"Oh, never mind. A *poop-out*," she said crossly, and pushed away from the railing. "I'm sacking in. Good *night*."

"Don't forget to lock your door."

She screamed. Reid was across the balcony in one bound. Leslie shrank into his arms, pointing a quivering finger at her bed.

"My God, Reid, I . . . I *touched* it."

There was a big rat on her bed. Disoriented with terror, it was trying to climb the brass bedpost and slipping back and trying again. Reid lifted Leslie to one side and started forward. A strong hand gripped his arm.

"Dispénsame, Señor."

It was Leslie's straw-hatted friend. The Mexican shouldered past him, yanking at his revolver.

"Espérate——"

Reid was too late. The gun exploded; and so did the rat, streaking the walls and bed with blood and gobbets of flesh. The Mexican holstered his pistol and bowed to Leslie. *"Que pase una buena noche, Señorita."* Then, with drunken dignity, he lurched from the room.

Leslie doubled over with laughter. "Oh . . . perfect! Wonderful!" she gasped. Then she straightened up and gulped. "Reid, I can't sleep *here.*"

"Of course not. Use my bed. Meanwhile I'll see if I can get this mess cleaned up."

He found the *señora* behind the bar, a bottle at her elbow, her smile stupidly euphoric. She said the cleaning girls had gone home; she had to remain in the *cantina.* *"Mañana, Señor. Manana lo arreglamos."*

Reid returned to Leslie's room. He took one look at the dripping walls and walked out. Leslie opened to his knock.

"The word is *mañana,*" he said, "and I'm not going to sleep in your room the way it is. I'm too damn tired to act noble and bed down on the floor here. Suppose I stretch out on top of the covers. Okay?"

He was uncomfortably aware that her pajamas ended at midthigh and did a halfhearted job of covering the rest of her.

She seemed amused by his embarrassment. "Be my guest."

In bed, with the lights off, Reid tried again to shut out the noise from below. This time something new had been added: a clean, fresh, female scent from the girl beside him. He lay still, listening to her breathe.

When he was sure she was asleep, Leslie suddenly asked in a quite wide-awake voice, "You never married, did you?"

"No."

"Why not?"

"I wanted to be like my father. He was a bachelor. Go to sleep, Leslie."

She mumbled something. Then she was quiet. Then she said, "I never slept this close to a man before."

Reid decided not to answer.

Five minutes later she said thoughtfully, "You know, I just said that to drug Mama."

Reid groaned. "Said what?"

"When I implied I wasn't a virgin. I am."

"Good for you."

"Is it? Really? I mean, doesn't it seem sort of square?"

"To be a virgin at seventeen? I wouldn't say so. Why do everything the mob does? And that includes blowing pot, by the way. Now, how about signing off and getting some shut-eye?"

"I only told you, Reid, because you'd find out sooner or later."

At first he thought of letting it pass. But then he decided he couldn't afford to.

"Find out what?"

"That I'm a virgin."

"Leslie." He sat up abruptly. "Get this straight. This is as intimate as we're going to be. You keep on with this kind of fooling, and in twenty days——"

"——you'll have to make an honest woman of me."

"Or more likely face a charge of rape brought by your mother. I'm taking a room on a different floor from now on. If that doesn't do it, we'll stay at different hotels. You follow?"

"Oh, Reid." She laughed. "I was only teasing."

He lay back with a grunt. This time Leslie did not reopen the conversation. She turned over, and, after a while, her breathing changed to a deep, regular snuffle. The last thing Reid saw was a rat silhouetted on the windowsill, hunching slowly away. He closed his eyes, thankful that Leslie had her back to it.

The next thing he knew, the sun was warm on his eyes and Leslie was shaking him awake. She was dressed, and her face had a scrubbed little-girl look.

"Your bath is ready, *Señor*. Would you like me to wash your back?"

They breakfasted on *huevos rancheros* made with too much grease, and coffee so bitter Leslie choked. He was glad to check out.

Leslie clapped her hands as they dropped off the chilly peaks into the cool clean air of the central plateau. Leslie gasped at the vastness of the *altiplano*. The dust devils dancing like serpents on their tails delighted her. She tossed silver pesos at the women and children begging along the highway; she studied her Spanish; she napped. They settled into an easy friendliness; sometimes she talked, sometimes he did; sometimes both were silent.

The molten silver sun climbed in the sky. They stopped to swim in Matehuala, where she exhibited with cool slyness an expanse of dazzling golden flesh barely interrupted by a peppermint-striped bikini, so that when she got into Jamaican shorts and a halter afterward she seemed overdressed.

Because Leslie wanted to change from restaurants, Reid bought the makings of a picnic in San Louis Potosi and pulled off the highway beside the Rio Bagres. Here they feasted on goose liver sandwiches, baby eels in garlic, a bottle of Chianti, and Spanish peanuts.

He was sprawled on his back, in the semi-conscious aftermath of good food and wine, when Leslie suddenly asked, "Reid. How do you say *marijuana* in Spanish? I can't find it in this dictionary."

"Never mind," he said sleepily. He almost laughed.

"All right, if you won't tell me I'll ask somebody."

He popped up on an elbow. "Leslie, if you start asking these people——"

"Don't you trust me?"

"I never trust people who ask me if I trust them."

She looked at him over the rim of her paper cup. "If I have to, I'll use sign language. I'm pretty good at it."

He lay back. A *pilote* was wheeling on the rising air currents. She was right. He couldn't stop her by keeping her in ignorance, not if she had made up her mind.

"Officially, it's *cannabis saliva,* but usually they call it *mariguana,* with an aspirated g. Colloquially, it's *mota.* They sometimes call it weed—*yerba.* Users tend to have their own regional words for it."

"How come you know so much about it?"

He felt the wine beginning to curdle in his stomach. "I've used it. The last time was eight years ago."

"You?" Her startled face appeared over his. "And you never mentioned it!"

"I'm not exactly proud of it."

"Tell me about it! Please, Reid?"

She was too close; he could smell the wine on her breath and the sun on her young flesh. He rolled away, sat up, lit a cigaret.

"I was bullfighting at the time. It was a jittery business. I couldn't relax on alcohol; anyway, it slowed my reflexes the next day. And some joker got me to try pot. Pot seemed to unravel my nerves in the evening and leave me fresh and alert the next day. I could function perfectly—I thought. Also, when I got high I became detached from my problems. So gradually, pot got to be the answer for everything—fire up a joint and blow your worries away. It was cool—except for the spooks."

"The spooks?" Leslie frowned. "What's that?"

"It's a vague dread of you don't know what. One minute you're gay as a lark, the next your flesh is creeping with fear. Sometimes the fear focuses on somebody or something—the bartender, he's poisoning your drinks; your manager, he's trying to get you killed in the ring; the front wheel of your car, it's been booby-trapped. Contemplating the simplest act becomes agony, because it's going to end up in disaster. And all the time you know you're in no real danger, because all you have to do to kill off the spooks is to take another smoke. So that's what you do. You smoke another, then another . . ."

"But you can't smoke it *all* the time, can you?"

"In Mexico, you can. I knew an American beach bum who smoked three joints before he got out of bed in the morning. He smoked twenty or more a day."

"And still functioned?"

Reid laughed. "He was functioning—if you can call it that—in the Guadalajara jail last time I saw him. He'd tried to sell it and got caught."

"Can they do that—put an American citizen in jail?"

"He had a choice between Mexican jail and deportation. He chose the Mexican jail because there he can get his pot brought in daily by the jailer."

"How did you kick it, Reid?"

"It took a bull's horn in the back. In the hospital, I had nothing to do but lie on my belly and wonder why I'd goofed in the *corrida*. I decided it was the pot, so I quit."

"Was it hard?"

He squinted up at the sun, thinking back. "Right now that whole year is overlaid with a thick fog. As if it happened to somebody else. Pot gives you a different frame of reference. It wasn't until I fought my way out of the frame that I saw I'd been turning myself into a vegetable."

"But . . . couldn't you still smoke now and then?"

"What for? Once you penetrate the illusion of the weed, it's never the same again. The kick is gone. You know what's going to happen—reality shifting, time being disrupted . . . you can't help telling yourself, 'This isn't real.' Pot is for people too lazy or unimaginative to use their normal senses."

Leslie got to her feet and began picking up cans and paper plates and stowing them in the sack. "Well, at least it's an answer, for which I thank you, *Señor*. Everybody else I've ever asked about pot just did some horrified eyerolling and said to stay away from it or else."

"They probably figured to scare you. Lots of youngsters have been led to believe that it'll make them jump out of a window or go berserk with a knife. Of course, telling that to a teen-ager only makes him more afraid of chickening out when he is challenged by his peers to try some than of the horrid consequences promised by his elders. So he takes some, and he finds out that he didn't turn blue and his hair didn't fall out after all, and he decides it's all a grown-up world's plot to oppress the lowly delinquent.

"So then he starts wondering: They lied about pot; why not about cocaine, too? He sniffs some, gets high, comes down, and again finds that there's nothing in his chemical make-up that craves more. Psychologically, yes; the high is a real gas, and he'll try it again one of these days. But coke is hard to come by; since it isn't addictive in the physical sense, there's no percentage in it for the pusher. But heroin—now, that's a profitable product. In fact, an obliging pusher will even give you H for free —to get you hooked.

"So our boy—or girl—picks up on H, and that's the beginning of the end. Your whole body chemistry becomes rearranged; you've got to have the stuff or die. Going without it is like having hot water squirted up your nose and mouth with increasing pressure.

"Pot is dangerous not because it's addictive—it isn't —not because it drives you nutty—it doesn't—but because too often it starts you on the road to heroin. And that, boys and girls, is the end of today's lesson."

Reid jumped up and brushed his trousers. "We'd better hit it, Leslie. We've got a hump of mountains to cross before dark."

Leslie rode beside him in silence for nearly an hour. He had just turned into the side road which would take them through Dolores Hidalgo and Guanajuato when she said: "You said yourself one joint doesn't do any harm. That's all I want, Reid. One high, then period, *finis.*"

Reid was jolted. "So much for leveling! What if you really dug it?"

"How could I, the way you put it down?"

"I'm responsible for you."

"All the more reason for you to get some for me. You wouldn't want me to get in trouble trying to score on my own, would you?"

The dark brown eyes were unblinking. She was an armful, all right—her mother and sister rolled up into one, and then some. Automatically glancing into the rearview mirror, he noticed a deep crease between his eyebrows. He almost laughed. He looked like a father at the end of his rope.

"I'll see what I can do, Leslie." Why in *hell* had he ever let himself in for this?

"Oh, Reid, you darling!" she cried, grabbing his arm and hugging it to her; he had to wrestle with the wheel to keep it on the road. "When, Reid, when?"

"Maybe in the next town. There's a man I know. . . ."

Reid looked down at the Mexican who had just given him the bad news. The taxi driver was smiling uncertainly, obviously afraid that the disappointment of the big gringo might vent itself on him.

"You're sure?" asked Reid. "I saw Torres two months ago. He said nothing about retiring."

The smile took on a different character; it turned into the grin of a man with a private joke. "I am sure, *Señor*. The police said he must retire for three years. To the *cárcel.*"

The word *policia* made Reid tense. He concealed it by lifting his brows and narrowing his blue eyes. The Mexican switched from one foot to the other. Since his joke had fallen flat, he now looked up at Reid and spoke with deep sincerity. "I tell you the truth. *El Señor* Torres is in the penitentiary. *La Chirena. El Bote.*"

"I understand you," said Reid. He was speaking Spanish with the slurred *tejano* accent of the Texas border. "Why was Torres arrested?"

"I do not know, *Señor*," said the Mexican. In English. "I could ask the *policia*——"

Reid thought: Watch your step. A Mexican who insists on speaking English wants something. And this one seems too happy about his colleague's arrest. Maybe he helped put Torres away. Maybe he's working for the police. Maybe he's been staked out to intercept Torres's old customers.

Reid felt helplessly exposed. He looked away from the Mexican to the sunny plaza of Dolores Hidalgo. A drayman pulled his empty cart past the cabstand, his blackened feet sliding inside his straw sandals. A *zapatero* was setting newly dyed *huaraches* in the sun to dry, lining them up in a row at the curb. An old woman walked past the church with eyes averted, crossing herself. Workers were prying up slabs of sidewalk in front of the hotel. In the park old men sat on stone benches watching other old men on other stone benches.

It looked all right. Yet the sun was many degrees hotter on the back of Reid's flower shirt; sweat ran down his spine. He thought: No score in this town. Not now. Better get out of here.

The taxi driver tapped his arm. "I now have his taxi, *Señor*. Where did you wish to go?"

"Nowhere," said Reid. "Just looking around. Thanks."

He crossed the street, forcing himself to walk slowly. He walked past the plaza, gawking at the flowers and the fountain, until he came to his gray Dodge with its TURISTA sticker and Texas plates. In the reflection of the window, he saw the taxi driver watching him. I should have parked off the main square, he told himself fretfully.

Leslie gave him a questioning look as he slid behind

the wheel. Reid could have slapped her. He stuck a cigaret between his lips and stabbed the dash lighter in,
then forgot to use it. He started the engine, rolled out of
the plaza, followed the twists of a cobbled street to the
edge of town. He then turned sedately onto the asphalt
of the highway, snaking up out of the sunken city toward the mountain range that threatened it from the west.

Abruptly, Reid pulled off onto a graveled turn-around.
He killed the engine and looked back.

The highway was empty. The Independence Monument
standing behind the town looked like a rocket poised for
blast-off. The town had a sleepy, innocent look.

"Why so mysterious?" Leslie asked curiously. "Did he
lay one on you or didn't he?"

Reid leaned back and discovered his unlit cigaret. Perspiration from his upper lip had made it unsmokable. He
tossed it out the window, took another out of his pack,
lit it and inhaled, a long one. Then he released the smoke
and said, "He didn't. My man got busted."

"*Damn,*" she said. "How come?"

"He'd been operating for ten years without any trouble
at all. Had three women working for him—cleaning the
stuff, rolling it into little five-peso packets. He paid off
the local police and everybody was happy. All of a sudden—jail. That means heavy heat from higher up. I had
a bad few minutes there."

"You did?" Leslie exclaimed. "You didn't seem shook.
You don't right now."

"I long ago learned not to let anything show. It's something you'll learn, too."

She stared at him. "You're terribly vulnerable, aren't
you?"

Reid started the engine, lowered the visor to keep out
the sinking sun, pulled out onto the highway. They
drove slowly past a herd of goats.

"When I was dealing for pot down here, Leslie, I put

myself outside the protection of the law. It's a feeling
that stays with you. Sure, I'm vulnerable."

"Maybe the heat is only local. Some other place———"

He shook his head. "The only place to score is from
the underworld. And that's out."

"Why?"

"Twenty years ago, the cops here didn't bring in prisoners, they shot them where they caught them. Still do
—in the back country of Chiapas and Guerrero. Or often enough so a man never knows when he's arrested
whether he'll get to see the inside of a courtroom. Or,
suppose he's lucky and they don't shoot him out of hand,
just send him up. It's a three-years jolt for selling pot, usually more—and if you kill a man, maybe you get off
with four years. It makes the pushers kind of rough, dig?
They just don't care. If I got hung up with the Mexican
underworld of pimps, thieves, *pistoleros,* God knows what,
they might decide to go for all I've got. And that includes
you, my little chick. Especially when they find out you're
a virgin."

It was brutal, but he was angry. Leslie said nothing; she
merely bit down on her lip.

She maintained her silence during the awesome climb
to the peaks—around hairpin turns, on the edge of thou-
sand-foot cliffs, up to the thick pine slopes of the sierras.
He topped the summit.

Two thousand feet below lay Guanajuato, a tinted
jumble of adobe and stone. It looked like the debris of
a landslide. The setting sun lit up a few domes and spires;
the rest of the city was shrouded in purple shadow.

"It's got two main streets," Reid said, trying to arouse
Leslie's interest. "Both barely wide enough for one traffic
lane—a single burro can tie up the entire town. When
we get down there, you'll see the scars on the sides of
the buildings where the trucks and buses have gouged
out their own passing room."

"I'm fascinated," she said sullenly. "Will you try again down there?"

"No."

She leaned forward and turned on the radio.

"And if I catch you trying to score on your own, I'll take you home."

She gave him a sidelong look. "Sure, man. You didn't have to tell me that." Her tone was hostile.

Reid touched his brakes delicately as he approached a hairpin curve. He felt the bird of ill omen clawing at his belly again. It was likely the end of a beautiful friendship, but the hell with it. Leslie would have to be watched.

Three

There was trouble with Mama that night. Reid placed the daily call immediately on checking in at the Posada Santa Fé, but the lines were busy. Not until an hour later, when Leslie and he were at dinner, was she called to the phone.

Leslie returned in ten minutes with red in her cheeks. She sat down and pointed at Reid's order, which had just arrived. "What's that?"

"*Quesadillas.* Try one."

She seized a brown cylinder in her slim fingers and bit into it. "Cheese—good! Oh, Mama wants to talk to you."

Reid dropped his fork. "Why me?"

Leslie reached for another *quesadilla.* "She called the hotel in Linares after we left. She's all shook up. I tried to explain, but you know Mama. Or do you?"

Reid approached the desk with dread. This was going to be nasty. He found the phone receiver in its cradle.

"Wasn't there a call?" he asked the clerk, who was sorting mail.

The clerk, a fat man, looked up and blinked behind rimless glasses. "The *señorita,* was she not finished?"

"No. She went to get me."

At that moment the desk phone rang. The clerk answered, then looked up. "*Señor* Rance?"

Reid took the phone from him and managed one syllable. May Gibson's voice knifed through it.

"What did you hope to accomplish, Mr. Rance, by hanging up?"

"I didn't, Mrs. Gibson. The clerk misunder——"

50

"I'm not going to bandy words with you. Last night I had a feeling something was wrong and I phoned Leslie. It was one A.M., Mr. Rance, and she wasn't in her room! Where was she?"

Oh, brother, thought Reid. Suppose I tell this woman her precious teen-ager was sleeping in my bed—with me? Because of an exploded rat!

"The room she'd been given, Mrs. Gibson, turned out to be full of bugs. I had to get her a different room."

"And the management didn't know it?"

Reid sighed. "It must have been a night man, or somebody, who didn't know of the change. Mexican hotels aren't like——"

"Mr. Rance, you're lying to me!"

"Look, Mrs. Gibson," he said. "You put your daughter in my charge, so you must have trusted me. If you don't trust me any more——"

"I most certainly do *not*. For some reason, Leslie's infatuated with you. I was insane to allow this jaunt. Girls will lie to their own mothers when they get that way— especially to their mothers! Unless I can get adequate assurances——"

Reid held the blatting membrane away from his ear as May Gibson ran on and on. She would stand for no repetition of last night's . . . whatever-it-was. She was going to phone the Posada Santa Fé tonight—never mind what time!—and if she didn't find Leslie in. . . . Reid gathered the impression that the provisional result would be immediate recourse to the American consul, the American ambassador and the United Nations. She had friends in high places, she would have him understand, and at the least suspicion of hanky-panky. . . .

"Mrs. Gibson," Reid put in.

"You're not going to turn my child into a—a Lolita!"

"Be quiet for a moment."

There was a gasp in the receiver, then silence.

"I haven't seduced your daughter and I have no intention of seducing her. And if you persist in these conditions, Mrs. Gibson, I have even less intention of continuing this trip. I'll refund the fee and the unused expense money and return home."

"Just you try and come back to Greengrove without Leslie," May Gibson screeched, "and I'll have the law on you, I'll make you wish you'd never heard the name Gibson——"

He set the phone on the cradle gently, a considerable feat of self-control, and leaned against the desk to simmer down.

It was interesting that the woman had leaped to the conclusion that he was threatening to abandon her daughter in mid-tour. He had never left a responsible client stranded, much less an irresponsible one seventeen years old. But that's what May Gibson was afraid of—Leslie's being left on her own in Mexico. Well, let Mama stew about it; maybe she'll start behaving herself. He wouldn't abandon Leslie; and he wasn't sure he could persuade her to let him take her back to the States until the three weeks were over—if then.

Reid went back to the dining room.

Leslie had company.

The man who stood behind Reid's empty chair, talking across the table to Leslie, was a stocky young Mexican in a patched green corduroy jacket. Leslie was eating and she had apparently taken Reid's warnings seriously, because she was paying no more attention to the Mexican than if he had been part of the heroic murals on the dining room walls.

He started away as Reid came up, but Reid said, "One moment. You wanted something?"

The young man turned and touched his finger to his forehead. *"Soy un chófer. Salvador, a sus ordenes."*

Reid stared after him, memorizing his catlike walk, the small ears set close to his head, the way his oiled black hair curled at the back of his neck. Had he sounded a bit smooth for a Guanajuato cabdriver? But then it was a fair-sized city, and it had become tourist-wise in recent years. . . .

Reid frowned and sat down. He sank his teeth through the crisp casing of a *quesadilla* into its tart cheese filler without appetite.

"Hello again," said Leslie, smiling. "Did you catch hell from Mama about last night, too?"

Something in her voice sent a chill through him. "Leslie. Did you tell your mother that I— that you spent the night——?"

"Are you out of your mind? There'd be a Red Alert at SAC right now. How did you weasel out of it?"

"Let's not talk about it now. I want to enjoy my dinner."

"Which reminds me. How about ordering a bottle of wine, Reid? I mean, if Mama didn't put it on the proscribed list."

He signaled the waiter. *"Por favor. Vino tinto.* And by the way, Leslie, go easy on the *vino.* All I need now is for you to get lushed. Your mother is calling you again tonight, late."

She laughed. "Mama's so square she thinks nothing can happen past midnight. She'd never dream I could make innocent little yes-Mama noises over the phone while lying in your arms——"

"Cut that talk out. I mean it, Leslie."

"Sure, baby," she cooed. "Who needs talk?"

He put down his fork with a little bang. "What's behind this sexy come-on, Leslie? Don't you realize how unbecoming it is? Why don't you start growing up?"

She flushed.

"Or is this some new strategy to get me to score for you?"

"I'm sorry, Reid," she said submissively. "But that's not true. You tried, you didn't make it, and you've said you won't try again—okay, I accept it. As for growing up. . . ." She gave him a little-girl smile. "Let's not let Mama get us down, Reid. How about some fun?"

The waiter's appearance saved Reid from answering. He filled their wine glasses and Leslie proposed a toast to Alexander Graham Bell, "inventor of the long-distance umbilical cord." That made him grin.

They were on their second glass when Reid asked casually, "What did the taxi driver want?"

"Who?" Leslie asked.

"That Mexican I found talking to you."

"Oh! From what I was able to gather, he was trying to sell me on a tour of some mummies tomorrow."

"The Catacombs? I'll take you if you want."

"I don't know, Reid. A lot of crumbling skeletons——"

"They're not skeletons. Something in the soil here has preserved a few dozen bodies in almost perfect condition. You see them as if they just died yesterday—bullet holes, knife wounds, graphic expressions of terror, agony, a regular Grand Guignol, only for real. One woman apparently had been buried alive in a cataleptic trance. You can tell she woke up later——"

"Reid, stop!"

"You come out wanting to forget what you saw, but you can't. You keep remembering that the mummies have living relatives—people right here in the city. You suddenly recall that the Aztec priests used to flay human beings and wear the skins like long underwear. You go over to the Alhóndiga de Granaditas—it's a fort I'll show you —and wonder how the Hidalgo forces ever thought they could storm it; then somebody points out the corners where the heads of Hidalgos, Allendes and Aldamas were stuck on spikes. And that leads the talk around to Jalisco, where, for a time, the favorite decorations on telegraph poles were the rotting bodies of crucified priests. And so on. It's pretty hard after that to think of Mexico as the land of glorious sunshine and the smiling *peón*. Do you want to take in the Catacombs?"

Leslie shuddered. "No, *thank* you."

He talked her out of drinking any more wine, and they left the dining room. He made her sit through a concert in the *jardin* outside the hotel, then took her for a drive around the cliffs which overlooked the pocketed city.

He parked at the pink stone monument to Pípila, the *Indio* hero of Guanajuato. Leslie looked up at the immense spotlighted statue. "What a kookie monument! He looks like a deodorant ad, with his arm in the air that way. Who was he?"

"An Indian volunteer who, the story goes, got the Hidalgo forces to place a huge stone slab on his back during the storming of the Alhóndiga and, bent double, rushed the entrance to the fort and cracked it."

Reid walked to the railing and looked down at the city. A string of lights wound through the canyon like a jeweled serpent. From below came a sleepy hum, as if a beehive were settling down for the night. Now and then a radio struck a dissonance. A dog barked, and the answering yap traveled around the cliff city like a canine night watch calling the "all's-well."

Leslie took a deep breath. "Man, this I dig."

"It's not a bit better on pot."

"Pity I'll never know," she replied in a flat tone. She peered at her watch in the light from the statue. "Midnight. Mama will want to know if I've got my chastity belt on tight."

She was being paged as they entered the lobby. Reid went on to his room, showered, and climbed into bed. He was just dropping off when Leslie tapped lightly on the door and he had to get up to open it. In the pale light from the window, he saw that she was wearing a sheer black negligee. It was about as concealing as a cobweb.

Here we go again, he thought. He shut the door against curious eyes, and when he turned around Leslie was stand-

ing between him and the window. On the pretext of getting a cigaret, he went over to the bureau. He did not put
on the light.

"Everything all right on the Greengrove end?"

"Of course not," Leslie said. She drifted over toward
his bed. "Mama's positive I suffered a fate worse than
death last night. If she only knew how safe my honor is!"

"It'll be a lot safer if you get out of here right now."

"Oh, goodie! Do I tempt you?" She whirled around,
laughing.

"Go back to your room, Leslie."

"No." The bed sagged as she sat down on it. "Look,
Mama's convinced you deflowered me—that's her word—
so why not do it?"

"Because I prefer not to. Go back to your room."

"Man, don't come on noble. It's bound to happen."

"Pick on somebody your own age."

"*Boys?* They either turn arrogant and act as if they own
you, or they're eaten up with guilt because they think
they've maimed you for life. I want a mature man who's
been around."

"There are plenty of those available."

"You mean that, Reid? You really want me to start
my experience with somebody else?"

He looked at her. The dark eyes were wide with excitement. He felt old, battered and corrupt, conscious of
a regret he could not identify.

"Let me put it in your language Leslie. The initiation
ceremonies are a drag. It's something I don't go for.
And I especially don't want it with you. And, no, I don't
want you to have the experience with somebody else. Not
now. I don't think you're ready for it. However, that's
your affair. But while you're in my charge—regardless of
what your mother thinks—you're going to remain lily-
white and clean-o."

She was silent. Then she tossed her hair and asked,
"You really don't want me, Reid?"

"I really don't want you."

"Suppose it were my sister Karen you were squiring around Mexico. Would you feel the same way?"

He squinted, picturing Karen Frankel. "No, I don't think I would."

Leslie jumped off the bed. "I guess that's it. May little sister kiss you goodnight?"

Before Reid could evade her, her mouth was searching, finding his, her body pressing, warm and moist. He seized her shoulders and shoved her away, and she padded demurely to the door.

"Don't worry about me, Brother Reid. *Hasta mañana.*"

He lay on his bed for a long time after she left, watching his smoke spirals drift to the ceiling like ghosts. Pull out of this, he kept telling himself. This kid's a walking fire hazard, shooting live sparks in all directions.

Gradually, he became aware that he was uneasy. Why? He probed. Something was wrong, but what? He decided after a while that it was something Leslie had said. It hovered just outside his consciousness, tantalizing him. He began to think over their talk. . . .

"Don't worry about me. . . ."

That was it. Why should her having said those words on leaving bother him? It seemed a natural thing to say after his turndown. On the other hand, it might mean. . . .

He got out of bed and reached for his trousers. Barefooted, he hurried out of his room and up the corridor to Leslie's door and knocked. There was no answer. He tried the knob; it turned in his hand. He opened the door. "Leslie?"

The bed was empty, not even rumpled; her negligee lay in a heap on it. She was gone!

He raced back to his room and dressed swiftly, cursing.

At the cabstand outside the hotel, a black-mustached Mexican was standing by the telephone box. Did he have a driver named Salvador? Yes, indeed, *Señor,* but Salvador had gone off with a fare, a beautiful young *americana*.

"Where did they go?" demanded Reid.

The man tugged warily at one side of his mustachio. "You are perhaps the *señora's* husband, *Señor?*"

"She's a *señorita*, not a *señora*——"

"Her lover?"

"Look," Reid said. The pulse in his throat was going like a drum. "The *señorita* is a *turista*, and she is in my charge. I am responsible for her safety. How reliable is this fellow Salvador?"

He had switched to Spanish, and the man replied in his own tongue, shrugging.

"Who knows? He works much to make himself handsome and attractive, for the young tourist women often choose quick romance with a taxi driver rather than rely on chance meetings in the gardens. Salvador earns many large tips."

There was a roaring in Reid's ears. The man said, "*Señor*, you are ill?"

Reid jumped into the cab. "Start driving, *hombre*. We go to look for Salvador and my client."

For five hours they searched Guanajuato's romantic haunts: the reservoir, the monument, the narrow road leading to the mountaintop, the blind alleys and darkened plazas. At dawn he dismissed the driver and sat in his own car watching the *sitio* with unblinking eyes.

It was 9 A.M. before Salvador drove up and parked at the cabstand.

Leslie was not with him.

Reid was at the taxi window before the boy could turn off his motor.

"Where did you leave her?" he asked harshly; his throat was raw from chain-smoking.

"Who, *Señor*, who?"

Reid reached inside the cab and seized a fistful of corduroy jacket. He pulled, and the boy's head banged.

"La norteamericana. Adonde la dejaste?"

Salvador's eyes began to roll. *"Por favor, Señor . . . no sé nada de ella. . . ."*

Reid made a fist with his right hand and raised it. The boy's mouth opened with terror. At that moment, Reid caught sight of a policeman. He was standing on the sidewalk before the opera house.

Reid released the jacket. "We will see what lies you will tell the police." He turned away.

"Señor, no!" gasped Salvador. He was gesturing frantically toward the seat beside him. "Please. Get in. Let us talk. I will tell you the entire truth. . . ."

Reid got in. For the first time he noticed that Salvador's handsome dark face was haggard. Salvador told his story in an agitated voice, shrinking a little from the big Texan. He had thought the girl wanted amusement, but the moment they had begun driving she asked him to find her some *mota.* He had been afraid, but he had also been a fool. He had thought that if he found her some, then perhaps when she was happy with it. . . . He did not excuse himself; it he could he would gladly die for his stupidity. . . . He had driven her to León, some thirty miles to the west. There he had introduced her to a man he knew, who had taken her away in another taxi. He had waited and waited, growing more and more anxious; at last, the other driver had come back—alone—and handed him this message to send by telegram, which he had just done.

Salvador pulled a dirty piece of paper from his packet and gave it to Reid. He read the crude printing. Reid felt death rake his back.

MRS. MAY GIBSON
GREENGROVE, TEXAS

MOTHER, I AM ALL RIGHT BUT I NEED MONEY URGENTLY. PLEASE SEND FIVE THOUSAND DOLLARS TO

THE TELEGRAPH OFFICE HERE SIX O'CLOCK THIS
EVENING. I WILL BE OKAY IF YOU SEND THE MONEY.
LESLIE.

Reid folded the paper with numb fingers. It seemed impossible, but here it was.

Some Mexicans had found an obviously rich American girl wandering into those cold, empty spaces outside the law and had snatched her for a quick fortune. Maybe their time was running out anyway, or they were mixed up in other things beside pot, or they just didn't care. . . .

Reid snapped, "You say you know the man who gave this to you. Who is he?"

Salvador looked desperately unhappy. "I know only a little about him. He takes men to see the women. He takes others to buy *mota*. It is said that if you steal something he will take it away and bring back money. But I think he is only . . . in between. You understand, *Señor?* He does not have these things; he knows only where they can be obtained."

"You don't think he has the girl?"

"No, *Señor*, I do not think so."

"And you? All you were to do was to come back to Guanajuato and send this telegram?"

Salvador hesitated. The tip of his tongue just showed between his full red lips. Then he said miserably, "No, *Señor*. I was also to wait for the money when it should arrive——"

"And if you did not?"

"I do not even think of that! I would do it—for her——"

Reid hunched his shoulders a little, and Salvador wriggled as far back as he could in the driver's seat.

"How do I know you're not in this with them, Salvador? One of the gang? You approached her in the dining room last night—you were the one whose taxi she subsequently took. I think you're lying to me."

"No," whispered the boy. "On the breath of my mother —no, *Señor.* . . . I took her to the man in León only because she wished *mota.* . . ."

Reid looked at Salvador for a long time. Finally, he asked, "Why didn't you go to the police?"

The boy cried, "It would then be as if I killed her with my own hands! The man in León told me this. I believe him, *Señor.* You had better believe him also. I have heard of such things. At the first appearance of a policeman, they would cut her throat."

The kid was right, of course. The police were out.

Reid looked at the note again. He was quite calm now. He could not afford to get blind-mad or panicky. The thing was to get Leslie back in one piece. There was no room for anything else.

The first question was: Would May Gibson take the telegram seriously? He thought not. She would be certain it was a dodge on the part of Leslie and himself to chisel five grand out of her and take off for the South Seas or some other romantic place to have a ball for themselves at her expense.

Mama Gibson might send the money, but she'd be right behind it on a chartered plane loaded with cops. Didn't Leslie realize that? Of course, she did. The wire hadn't been written by Leslie—it was addressed to "Mother"—Leslie never called May anything but "Mama"— and the hand-printing was too crude to be the girl's work. No doubt they—whoever "they" were—had got Mrs. Gibson's address from some identification in Leslie's purse.

"Salvador, did the man give you anything belonging to the *señorita* to prove that they indeed had possession of her?"

Salvador looked startled. "I forgot! This." He reached into his shirt pocket and carefully took out a tuft of glowing chestnut hair. There was no mistaking it.

Hair can be taken from a corpse. . . . He pushed the thought away.

"Do they know of me?" Reid asked.

"I did not tell them."

"Let us assume they do not know of me. Tell them nothing. I shall try to get her back."

"And I, *Señor*," Salvador said, spreading his hands, "I shall pray."

"You do that."

Reid left a few moments later with a description of the León cabdriver and the information that Leslie had worn her beige skirt and cashmere sweater. As he drove through the fertile *bajío,* he planned his strategy. He would follow Leslie's route; he would be a man merely trying to score for pot, knowing nothing of Leslie. He would carry the transaction all the way through and keep his eyes open. If he didn't find Leslie at once, he might be able to spot the men who had her.

And if he were wrong about Salvador and the boy *was* in on it?——or if the snatchers had cased the job and knew all about his connection with Leslie?——or if Leslie had mentioned him inadvertently——?

Were they setting a trap for him?

It would serve me right, Reid Rance thought.

Four

It was 10:05 A.M. when Reid rolled into León. The city was twenty years more modern than Guanajuato, and it was stamped with the hallmarks of progress: clogged traffic, quivering neon, garish billboards, street banners proclaiming discount sales, and that special Mexican instrument of torture, the cruising sound truck.

He left his car with the attendant of an underground garage, saw it driven safely out of sight, and went out to the sidewalk and began to saunter along.

Reid could not ask directly for the taxi driver Salvador had mentioned; he would have to play the tourist down the line. He must get himself taken to the man in a natural way. The cabarets would make a good starting point, but not at this hour. The same objection applied to the bordellos.

He decided to approach a cabman. It was risky, but he had no choice. Time was racing by.

Reid made his way as if haphazardly to the palm-shaded plaza flanked by two hotels. At least twenty cabs were lined up. In some, the drivers slept, caps tipped over their eyes. Others were taking their siesta sprawled under the palms. Nothing moved in the plaza. This was the Sargasso Sea of León's taxi fleet where the drivers assembled to wait out the slow afternoon hours.

Reid strolled past several cabs. Which drivers could he trust not to turn him in? Which were in the pay of the police? Which would go on the take the moment they had something to sell?

He felt the vulture claw in his belly again; then a sudden

thirst. Mexicans were used to American tourists drinking in midmorning.

Reid turned away from the plaza and walked into the bar of the Hotel Mexico. There he ordered a straight Bacardi, drank it quickly; ordered a second. The second he drank slowly, chasing it with Tehuacan. Leaving, he fended off two lottery salesmen and a trio of *mariachis* who wanted to serenade him.

Squaring his shoulders, he returned to the plaza. He walked over to the oldest cab in sight and shook its driver awake.

The man had a swarthy face pocked like beaten brass and crowned by a cracked red leather cap. If I were casting a villainous Mexican cabdriver for a movie, Reid thought, I'd pick this man.

"I wish to see the city," he said in deliberately awkward Spanish. "Are you for hire?"

"*Si, Señor.*" The man grinned evilly.

Reid got into the front seat. For the next ten minutes the driver wheeled him past churches, the market, the hotels, giving him the *turista* spiel. Then they passed the bull ring, and he engaged the man in a discussion of bullfighting. They began to argue the relative merits of Spanish and Mexican *toreros*. It was the argument that decided Reid: the driver showed none of the subservience characteristic of stool pigeons.

"I have," he said, "a most delicate question to ask."

"No question is too delicate," said the man, glancing sidewise at him.

"I would like to buy some marijuana. I wish to see what it is like. I have been told it is easy to buy in your country."

From the corner of his eye, Reid saw the Mexican's face go blank. It remained that way for several seconds.

Then the man spoke in a totally neutral tone. "I know a man, *Señor*. I will take you to him."

There was no more conversation. They rolled back

through the center of town. The driver's face retained its blankness. He disapproves, thought Reid; probably he's mentally doubling the fare.

Near the edge of town they came to another taxi-stand. Half a dozen men were lying about on the ground. One jumped up as Reid's cab stopped, then lay back as if he recognized its driver.

"Wait here, *Señor*." Reid's driver got out.

Reid watched him walk onto the grass and gingerly toe the side of an immense man who lay on his back like a beached whale. The man heaved himself to his feet, fastened the suspenders of his bib overalls, and walked with Reid's driver away from the others. He looked too big to get behind a wheel, yet his walk was remarkably graceful. He fitted Salvador's description: the grease-blackened baseball cap on the back of his head, the larded neck overhanging the collar of a filthy T shirt. As the pocked driver talked, the big man turned in Reid's direction. His very small eyes were half shut. He smiled a languid smile. He was on the stuff high, high as an eagle.

Reid's driver came back quickly. "You go with El Gordo, *Señor*. For me, ten pesos."

Reid handed the man twenty and got out of the cab. The driver slithered behind the wheel, and steamed off.

El Gordo—the Fat One—had by some blubbery miracle managed to squeeze himself into the driver's seat of a rusty old Ford. Reid walked over and got in beside him. This was awfully easy. There was a tingle in the nape of his neck.

The fat Mexican twisted his bull's head to look at Reid, and grinned. The spread of his massive lips held an almost affectionate quality. He made no move to start the Ford.

"Where do you want to go?" El Gordo asked in Spanish.

"Did he not tell you?" Reid said, using the same *turista* accent he had used with the other cabman.

"You tell me."

"I wish to buy marijuana."

El Gordo's smile broadened. He seemed to be enjoying himself. "To buy what, *Señor?*"

"Marijuana." Reid kept his voice low. "I believe it is also called in your country *mota*. I wish to try some for excitement." He used the stiff word *estímulo*.

The fat man continued to stare. He was now moving his huge hands over the steering wheel as if it were a woman. Reid felt his skin crawl: He's way out, on his own time.

"If you do not know where to get it," Reid said with some petulance in his voice, "just say so. I will seek someone else."

El Gordo blinked and grunted; he fumbled for his key. As the engine caught, a thin little man jumped up from the grass and struck his knee with the edge of his hand. He was asking if the Fat One wanted help. El Gordo nodded. The little Mexican ran over, jerked open the door, and threw himself into the back seat.

As the Ford lurched off, Reid turned to look at the Fat One's pal. He was a sawed-off package of skin and bones, with a tangle of black hair over a knife-scarred, very dark face. A mustache hung from each corner of his mouth, making him look like a miniature Mexican Fu Manchu.

The cab began creeping up a side street. The little cadaver launched the conversation. "You want to buy *mota?*" He spoke in English.

"Yes," said Reid. His heart sank. El Gordo's friend was also floating on pot. He showed all the signs—the bright bloodshot eyes, the breathless rush of words, the way he squirmed in his seat and thumped his feet against the floor boards.

"Why you want it?" asked the newcomer.

"To smoke. *Por estímulo.*"

Little Skin-and-Bones trilled; the driver added a chuckle. Reid forced himself to smile back. Why were there two of them? He wanted desperately to watch where El Gordo was taking him, but he hated to turn his back on the little guy behind him.

"You know the man who brought you to me?" asked El Gordo, turning onto a wide, deserted thoroughfare.

"No," said Reid. "I found him in front of the Hotel Mexico."

"We think he is police."

"Police!" The fear in his voice was not altogether synthetic.

El Gordo nodded solemnly. Reid glanced at the other man; he was also nodding.

"He wants to put us in the *cárcel*," said the little man breathlessly. *"En el bote.* Have you been in the *bote?"*

"No!"

"There it is," said the little man, pointing.

It was a mustard-colored building decorated with Churrigueresque stonework. At each side of a studded door stood a soldier in light blue uniform and helmet with a rifle at slung-arms.

"You want to stop?" asked El Gordo, slowing the car.

"No!" said Reid, so frantically that the pair howled. El Gordo speeded up, and Reid decided that they had been testing him.

Apparently he had passed. He relaxed a little.

The man behind introduced himself. "Cara Prieta," he was called. Did the *señor* know what that meant?

Reid pretended to hesitate. "Black Face?" he asked doubtfully.

The little fellow seemed pleased; he grinned, showing stumps of blackish teeth. And the *señor,* how was he called? Reid knew that they did not expect him to give his real name. El Gordo and Cara Prieta—Fats and Blackie —were cover names; he was on the fringe of the Mexican underworld, the *abajomundo.*

"El Deporto," Reid said. The Sport. "That is my name."

It broke them up; El Gordo almost ran into a bus as he wheezed and choked over the joke.

A few moments later, the Ford wheeled into a slum street. The unpaved street, lined with shanties of gray adobe, was seething with ragged children, dogs and burros. El Gordo stopped his cab in the middle of the street, hit his horn twice, then lay back and yawned.

Reid asked, "Why do we wait?"

The fat man jerked his massive head. A tall slim boy was approaching the car with lithe strides. He was dressed in light beige trousers and shirt. His coloring was light. Curiously, he had patrician features.

Reid asked nervously, "Who is this one?"

"El Mono. He will take us to El Delgado."

El Mono, the Monkey. El Delgado, the Thin One. Reid's muscles tightened as the tall youth slid into the back seat beside Blackie. Three of them now . . . .

"Who is El Delgado?" Reid asked.

"El Hombre," said El Gordo, driving off.

Reid watched the car nose along the twisting street, plunging deeper into the adobe slum. He wanted very much to tear open the door and take off.

"How about a *tocacita?*" asked El Mono suddenly.

The boy had a high-pitched, insolent voice. *Tocacita* . . . "little touch"—in the patois of the *marijuanos* a few drags on a reefer.

El Gordo stopped the Ford beside a featureless mud wall. Reid could see nothing but adobe huts. He had no idea in which direction the central section of the city lay.

"I want much more than that," he said.

"But now," piped the Monkey. "Surely you would like a *tocacita?*"

Reid's head was going like a computer. He had not smoked marijuana for eight years. And he'd had those two Bacardis back at the hotel. Blowing pot on top of the rum, then walking into the Mexican underworld . . . not to mention the necessity of disguising his real purpose. . . .

"No," he said, "I never use it in the morning."

The instant freezing of the tall boy's face told him that he had pulled a boner. Even Fats peered at him suspiciously. To them, the weed was good any hour of the day or night. Reid thought profanity. Now he had to cover up.

"It is not good for me in the daytime. At night I can dance, sing——"

"Dance?" Blackie leaned forward, eyes bright. "You dance the Cha-cha-cha? Rock-and-roll? You know those dances?"

The little guy began to shuffle and sway, humming a tune. Sweat ran down his face. Suddenly he broke off and looked down at his hands; he studied his palms intently, a secretive smile on his face.

The other two were waiting for something. Reid felt the sun burning his back. Why hadn't Gordo parked in the shade? The others were sweating, too, but, of course, the pot kept them cool inside. . . . Reid's stomach began hurting.

"What are we waiting for?" Reid asked.

"For you," said El Mono, the boy. "You want a *tocacita*? Delgado will ask me."

"Why?"

"It is a thing of confidence. So that we know you are not of the police."

"A policeman could smoke it."

"Ah, but if he smoked with us, we would know him for what he is."

So that was it. Test Number Two. It was pretty tough to lie on pot; you become overconfident. Life was a game, and you had to play fair. *Will the real J. Edgar Hoover please stand up?*

Sweat trickled down Reid's back; he would have to do it. He would push Leslie so far back in his mind. . . .

"All right," he said with a shrug. "A *tocacita*."

The log-jam broke. Gordo laughed. Mono leaned forward and began explaining to Reid with great sincerity that the pot came in packets costing five pesos apiece. He would get one packet, they would have a smoke together, they would become friends, and then the *señor* would be sold more. How many packets did he want to buy?

"With seeds?" asked Reid knowingly.

"Yes. But you throw them out."

"It all depends on how well it cleans down—how good it is in the beginning. If it's good, I'll take two hundred packets." This time he left the awkwardness out of his Spanish.

Mono and Gorko blinked. Blackie came out of his lethargy. The three Mexicans looked curiously at Reid.

"A thousand pesos' worth?" shrilled young Mono. "How will you carry it?"

"If it's good, I'll go buy a valise."

The trio communicated silently, then began debating the merits of Reid's idea aloud. The valise idea evidently met with their approval. Their discussion centered on what size case he would need, and where he should buy it. They finally reached a decision. Mono asked for five pesos with which to buy the sample. Reid was digging his wallet out when Mono said, "I will not cheat you, *Señor*."

When a man says gratuitously that he will not cheat you, Reid thought, cheating you is what lies uppermost in his mind. He had been waiting for a signal of intention, and here it was. He considered his three Mexican friends as he feigned difficulty in getting the wallet out of his pocket. The boy Mono was tall and smoothly built; there was power in him. Blackie looked as if he could be blown away, but Reid had no illusions—he was undoubtedly a knife artist, and probably as quick as a snake. As for El Gordo . . . it would be like facing the bull without cape or sword.

"Why should you cheat me?" Reid asked. "We're going

to do good business together, aren't we?" He handed Mono
five pesos.

The boy was back in the car in ten minutes. He leaned
over Reid's shoulder. Something dropped into Reid's lap.
Fats made an ecstatic bass sound. The Ford jerked into
motion.

It was a piece of soiled newspaper rolled into a tube
and tucked in at the ends, like a surprise snapper at a
kids' birthday party. Reid undid the ends, unrolled the
newspaper and saw a compressed mass of twisted stems,
leaves and seeds. It was green, slightly musty. Second-
rate stuff.

"Here," Mono said, handing Reid a packet of rice
paper. "Roll it."

Reid acted nervous and unskilled; Mono said insolently
that he could do it faster and better. By the time Gordo
parked the car between the river and a crumbling wall,
the boy was setting fire to a thick, lumpy cigaret. Acrid
smoke rolled about the car; Gordo shut the windows.
Mono handed the cigaret to Blackie, who pursed his lips
eagerly and sucked. Blackie then turned his head away
and gasped; his eyes protruded as he held his breath. He
passed the joint to Gordo, who smoked the same way.
Gordo handed it over to Reid, saying in a croak:

"Si, es buena mota."

Reid drew the smoke into his mouth and expelled it
with his next breath. The three men groaned; he was
doing it wrong, they all protested.

"Like this," said Blackie. He snatched the cigaret and
sucked noisily a dozen times. His cheeks distended like a
chipmunk's, he handed the cigaret back. Reid tried again
clumsily; it was no problem to make his lungs rebel at the
fire blazing in them, and he doubled up, coughing. The
others laughed. Since he had lost the smoke, he must
smoke again. He held the smoke this time, and Fats took

the joint from him. He felt his head growing light, growing airy . . . .

His eyes watched the joint making another round. The pot was coming in, all right. El Mono looked handsome and more patrician than ever; Blackie was far less ugly; actually, a little on the cute side. Gordo, with his bloat and sausage skin, was a man he could love dearly, a pal to be trusted. How could good old Fats have had anything to do with——?

Forget her. Push her back back back . . . .

Reid felt the cigaret between his fingers. He wondered how it had got there. Didn't matter. He filled his lungs with acrid smoke, passed the stick and looked out the window.

The world was wonderfully bright. Details sharp as cat's teeth. A jumble of rocks in the river formed a beautiful pattern. As he studied it, pleasure surged up and threatened to choke him. He opened his mouth to release the pressure and a giggle came out. The sound was so incongruous that he burst out laughing. Laughing at the giggle made him laugh at the laughter. Then he tried to remember what was funny and could not. Suddenly a lumpy terror pervaded him. The flesh on his arms crawled; he could see his skin rippling like water, cool, but underneath burning. He was aware that his mighty friend El Gordo was pointing toward his feet and asking something. Reid moved closer, trying to hear, but Gordo's voice was mixed up with the sound of a truck that seemed to be in the car with them. Then he saw the truck a quarter of a mile away. Reid heard Gordo ask what he had paid for his shoes. Reid peered into his head and finally remembered that they had cost twelve dollars. He turned to tell Gordo, but Gordo was fingering a plastic doll that hung from the rear view mirror. Reid forgot about the shoes.

After a while he was looking out the window at the river. The water sparkled. It made him want to take off his shoes and go wading. He could already feel the water trickling over his feet, cool and pure and wet.

Wet. He was licking his lips. How long had he been licking them? It seemed like an hour. It couldn't be. The cigaret was still being passed around although it was nearly smoked out. Gordo was holding the butt.

Reid tried to remember why he was there. He struggled for a long time without success. But then he noticed the packet in his hand. Yes, he was going to buy some more of the stuff. Wasn't there something else . . .?

"You like the river?" asked Blackie.

He realized that he had been looking at the river again and thinking of the wet water. Blackie must have caught his brain wave. It happened sometimes on pot. Yes, this was good stuff. Great!

"We had a river back home," Reid said. "The Rio Grande. We used to swim in it. Sometimes we took off our shoes and waded."

Blackie applauded the idea. He and El Deporto would take off their shoes and wade in this river. "Hey, Sport?"

Gordo was still stroking his doll, growling endearments. It was the boy Mono who told Blackie to put his shoes back on.

"We have to get his valise," the Monkey said.

"We get it later," said Cara Prieta.

"But Delgado is waiting."

"But Sport wishes to wade in the river."

"He prefers to buy the valise."

"You stink," said Cara Prieta.

Reid had been trying to get their conversation straight. Deporto? The Sport? Who was he? They were looking at him but talking about a third party. *He* didn't want to wade in the river. There's something I have to do. Yes. What?

Suddenly he remembered and thought, But I'm so high. How am I going to get this job done?

"Let's get the valise," he said. The words were accompanied by gouts of perspiration.

Driving, oh so slowly, out of the slum.

Gordo was going the wrong way. Reid told him to turn around. Gordo stopped.

The three discussed the direction. It was Reid who was lost, not Gordo. The car proceeded. Reid wondered where they were taking him.

He looked at them. Blackie was a funny little guy out of a minstrel show. Mono was a young aristocrat who had squandered the family estate through gaming and wenching. Gordo, nostrils distended, was pawing the ground, the *banderillas* sagging from the hump on the back of his neck. Reid felt a great elevation of spirit. These were his friends. Only a fool distrusted his friends. Hadn't they smoked together? Hadn't they brought him the pot and not cheated? Weren't they on their way for more?

His elation drained away. They were driving along a narrow street. These Mexicans were taking him to jail. They were going to turn him over to the law because the law paid a reward for gringos who tried to buy *mota*. It meant three years in the *cárcel*. Three *years*.

"Where are we going?" Reid asked.

"To buy you a valise," said El Mono.

Of course. To buy a valise. That's why he had come with his friends, to buy a container for the pot. A pot for the container. A bag for the *mota*. A . . . .

Reid stopped singing. They were parked in the plaza. Fats had turned off his engine. The three were looking at him. Waiting.

Reid felt fear again. All those people out there. They would know all about him, and it took all his will to move just one finger. The sky looked dark. The people went too fast around the square. Everything was chaotic. Prattling people, honking cars, whirring bicycles. The noise roared in his ears. He would surely get hit crossing the street. He saw himself lying in the road like a sack of dirty laundry. The clock on the Woolworth store said twelve. Time to die.

With all his strength Reid opened the door and got out. Mono and Blackie got out, too, and they started across the steet. Reid tried to force one shoe ahead of the other. Funny. He could not feel his feet touch the pavement, so how could he be moving? A cold wind was blowing across the plaza. Two soldiers stood guard in front of the Presidencia Municipal. Reid thought: They're just waiting for me to reach the middle of the street, then they'll arrest me. When he reached the middle of the street, he thought: They're just waiting for me to reach the curb. When he reached the curb and followed Mono and Blackie into the luggage shop, he thought: They'll wait till I buy the valise, then they'll ask me why I want the valise.

"Forty-eight pesos," the shopkeeper said, holding out a bag. It was a good suitcase. Reid thought he should make a show of examining it; he tried to touch the leather. But his arm would not move.

He'll get suspicious, thought Reid. I must do something.

Carefully, he prepared the words in his mouth, then—quickly—he forced them out.

"I'll give you forty," The effort had exhausted Reid; he wanted to sit down and rest. He leaned against the counter.

"Forty-two," said the shopkeeper.

Reid got out his billfold and tried to count off forty-two pesos. It was damnably difficult. He could not get past three. Each time he got to three, he forgot and had to start over. Finally, he handed the man a hundred-peso note. He shoved the change in his pocket and followed Blackie and Mono out the door.

Mono carried the valise.

Five

Twice during the drive back to the slum Reid forgot where he was. But only twice. He seemed to be getting on top of the *moto* now. Those first thirty minutes had caught him off-balance. He suddenly realized that he had been humming a line from *Moñaquita Linda* over and over: *Dime si me quieres, como yo te quiero, dime si me quieres.* . . . He told himself to stop humming and he still hummed. He told himself to stop humming again; this time he did stop.

The old Ford dropped anchor by the same adobe wall. Reid said to himself you'd be a fool to let the money out of your possession till you get delivery. He stepped out of the car with dignity, carrying the valise, and walked away to wait. The trio in the car went into a quick huddle. Then Mono jumped out, followed by Blackie.

"This way, *Señor,*" the tall boy said courteously, leading the way up a precipitous lane that had once, long ago, been graveled. The clay of the lane was split down its length, making a gully, a real ankle-trap.

Mono was walking to the left of the gully, and Reid was a little behind him on the right. Putting one foot in front of the other was much easier now; also, separated from Mono by the gully, Reid felt more comfortable. The only trouble was, Blackie was walking right behind him, within knife range. But, for some reason, Reid was not afraid; the muscles of his back were quite indifferent.

He tried to think back to a time when at least two of them had not been with him. These boys were careful. If he had been a cop, he would never have stood a chance.

Reid's marijuana kick had entered a new stage. Gone was the spinning terror. His sight had never been so spectacular—objects seemed to fly up and stab him in the eyes; shapes flickered at the edge of his vision; he turned twice, sure he was being followed. But it was only Blackie. Reid chuckled. He was amazed to see that he had walked less than a hundred yards.

A moment later he heard a voice call out clearly in English: "Reid, come here a minute?"

He whirled toward the sound, but it was only a burro swatting flies. El Mono glanced at him and smiled, pointing to the valise. "They know what you're after with that."

The hell with the voice. The hell with Mono. The voice did not call him again.

He kept seeing movement from the corner of his eye. Each time he turned toward it, it was gone. He always forgot it between times, lost in comtemplation of the cracks in the walls. They formed pictures. He saw Old Faithful erupting. Salome wrapped in swirling veils. Leslie washing her hair in a porcelain basin. Leslie. The thought filled him with sadness. *So young to die.* . . . He began to wonder, Where are they taking me? How many corners have we turned now? Are they trying to get me lost?

They turned into an alley. The two Mexicans stopped and leaned against the wall.

"Now what?" asked Reid.

"Wait," said Mono. "El Delgado will come."

An apparition appeared at the end of the alley. It had a bald skull, empty sockets for eyes, cheekbones which threatened to knife through the leathery film of skin with deep hollows under them. The thing was dressed in a blue shirt and blue pants; the shirt flopped around on its shoulder bones; the trousers flapped about its meatless shanks.

It was, or once had been, a man. He looked like pictures Reid had seen of men in Büchenwald when they were liberated by American troops.

The Zombi. The Thin One. El Delgado, El Hombre, The Man.

The Man began to move toward Reid. He walked cautiously, as if he were afraid his paper-thin figure might be toppled by a breeze. He came to rest before Reid and held out the collection of bones that constituted his hand. Reid gave him the valise. Delgado held out the other bundle of bones.

Reid shook his head.

Señor," said El Mono, the boy. "El Hombre wants the money."

"When I get the stuff." There were eyes, Reid now saw, in those sockets, but they were not human eyes. They were only peepholes into darkness.

Nevertheless these non-eyes seemed to be taking Reid apart and laying the pieces out on a table. Reid thought: this man doesn't take pot.

A voice emerged from empty spaces in the sunken chest. "Let me see the money."

Reid pulled out his wallet. He knew immediately that he would have the same trouble counting out bills that he had had in the luggage store, so he merely opened his billfold and showed Delgado its contents. The man nodded, turned and walked off.

"Come," said El Mono. "We must wait for him in another place."

Reid wanted to protest; he felt secure here; he was too tired to move. But arguing took effort, too. So he walked back down the alley with Mono and Blackface.

"What's the matter with him?" he asked Mono.

"Delgado spent many years on a prison island."

"What for?"

Mono shrugged. "Who knows?"

"What if he has to go back?"

At the time Reid asked this question, it seemed terribly important to know how Delgado would react if he had to go back to prison. But Mono was slow in answering, and

Reid became engrossed in the shape of a rock. He picked it up, enjoying the way it felt in his hand.

"He says he will not go back," said Mono at last. "He will die, but first he will take some of the police with him."

Obviously Delgado—El Hombre—was insane. The hell with him.

After leaving the alley, they slid down a steep bank and began walking across the river on rocks. Reid knew it must be the same river he had seen before. He was also happy to discover that he no longer wanted to take his shoes off and go wading. What a childish idea. Maybe he was coming out of it. . . .

Then he was dismayed to find that he could not, for the life of him, remember where they were going or why. For a long time the struggle to remember occupied his mind. When he returned to awareness, he was stepping from a path that wound through a thicket of nopal cactus and thorny huizache into a small clearing. Reid was about to ask why they were there when it suddenly came back to him.

"Delgado will bring the stuff here, Mono, right?"

"Yes," said the tall boy.

The three stood waiting.

After a while, Blackie pulled a knife from his pocket. He exposed the blade with a flick of his wrist and began throwing the knife at a pad of nopal cactus. He seldom hit the mark; several times he failed to stick the point in the ground. Reid laughed to himself. Knife artist! I ought to be reported to the U.N. Committee on National Stereotypes. . . .

Abruptly, the laughter left him and the fear returned. He knew he would never be a user; the fear for Leslie's safety had been bad enough without marijuana. Now it was worse, lots worse.

He thought he caught a movement from the corner

of his eye and he whirled. He saw only cactus and trees, but he knew they were waiting, hiding in the bushes. They had lured him out here and planned to leave him stripped and robbed, maybe dead. He couldn't recall who "they" were, but he remembered riding in a cab with some men and he remembered that Leslie had run away from the hotel and that her mother was relying on him to take care of her.

Reid watched the boy Mono stoop for a rock. So Reid picked up a larger rock. Mono glanced at him, grinned, and threw the rock at a tree thirty feet away. He missed. He looked at Reid, as if waiting for him to throw, too. But Reid liked the heft of the missile in his hand. Mono picked up another rock, threw it, missed again. He tried over and over. Reid began grunting in sympathy each time Mono came close. How could he have distrusted the kid? They had blown a joint together, hadn't they? Friends to the end. Besides, Mono had a nice little game, even though he was lousy at it. Here, kid, let an expert show you.

Reid stepped up beside Mono, smiling. He made his windup, started his throw. A blurred movement at the edge of his vision made him turn: Mono was swinging a fist-sized rock in an arc that was monitored to land in his face. Reid watched it loom larger. At the last moment, he jerked his head back. The rock struck him on the collar-bone. Pain arrowed down his arm and shot out of his fingertips like static electricity.

But the pain was remote. It was as if he were standing off to one side while the gross part of him leaped into action, programmed by past struggles. With appreciation, Reid watched his arm streak forward, heard the crack as the rock in his fist met Mono's jaw. Mono spun around, fell on his face, and lay still. Some friend!

A weight landed on his back and clung there. Reid staggered, his reflexes took over, he reached back, and seized a head between his hands. He yanked the skull forward at the same instant that he doubled up and arched his back. A weight flew over his shoulder and Blackie thumped onto the ground at his feet. The ugly little face turned appropriately black as the man fought for air.

Reid straightened up. He felt tempered and fine, eager for more action. Then he saw El Gordo lumbering like a bull across the clearing toward him.

"Et tu, brute." Where the hell didst thou come from?

Sadly he sprang at the Fat One. His body smashed into a bone-jarring wall that felt more like stone than flesh, and Reid called on his brain, despite its condition, to take charge. His brain said: think before you leap. This man-mountain has muscles of rock under that greasy bloat. Once he gets those arms around you. . . .

Which was precisely what Fats was trying to do. Reid danced away from the menacing arms. He darted in, out, in, lashing at the beefy face. All the time, he was watching from one side. He knew part of him was landing blows because he could feel the jolt in his shoulders and he could see scarlet streams start from the flattish nose and spread over the mouth and chin. What was happening? Was he really in this clearing fighting for his life, or was he sitting somewhere over a beer and seeing all this on a TV screen? The actor on the screen moved in with a flurry of blows, sad to be hurting El Gordo because El Gordo had once been his dear friend. He also knew he had to get away before his three dear friends got smart enough to go for him at the same time.

Just as Gordo went down, the weight landed on his back again. Welcome, Blackie. Reid felt a sharp pain in his shoulder. The little bastard bit me. Again, he reached back, grabbed two handfuls of head, and heaved Blackie off his back. The Mexican Fu Manchu opened his mouth and screeched.

But the pain had not left Reid's shoulder. He felt for the hurt place and encountered the hilt of a knife. So they were starting to play dirty. He jerked the knife out and from the blood saw that less than an inch of the blade had gone in. He held it out low and straight before him, street-fight fashion, and swung it to include Blackie, who was scrambling to his feet, and Mono, who was on his knees silently groping for another rock.

"Don't move or I'll kill you."

Blackie and Mono froze. Gordo was crouched on one hand and both knees, a bright ruby swaying on his nose. The other hand pointed a gun at Reid.

Reid was horrified. This is real, I can die from it. A shadow fell over his mind. When it lifted, the world was again sharply clear. He heard the high, thin trumpet note split the air above the bull ring, felt the arena sand beneath his feet, the hilt of the sword in his palm. Gordo, blood dripping from his nose, was the beast. It was the moment of truth. Reid aimed for the sweat-gleaming hump at the back of the bull neck and thought: Over the horn! Make a good kill!

Gordo was squinting as he took aim. Reid felt no fear; he was matador, invincible.

"Uh, *toro*," Reid grunted; and he moved forward like a dancer with the knife held stiffly in front of him. It happened as though in a slow motion film. Reid saw that he was going in too far back; he delicately turned the knife downward at the last instant to a point just above the little knob of the topmost vertebra. He nodded as the blade sliced through the bull's flesh, felt the vibration in his palm as the point grated on cartilage, then slid neatly between the bones to sever the thick cluster of nerves connecting brain to body. The blade disappeared.

Reid let go of the hilt and stepped back.

Gordo's arms dropped. He looked stupidly surprised. His mouth opened and blood jetted out. He fell forward on his face, rested a moment with his buttocks in the air as if he were suddenly very tired, then tipped sideways with a sigh. A convulsion rolled him over, then another.

Finally he was quiet, sprawled on his back, sightless eyes open to the sun.

Blackie and Mono stared thoughtfully at their dead companion. All was silence.

To the left.

Reid whirled.

"Leslie!"

Her eyes—her face—looked strange. Her cheeks were swollen around the strip of adhesive tape over her mouth. Her arms were strained backwards. A man stood behind her, a Mexican Reid had not seen before. They seemed like the dragon's teeth. Springing up everywhere.

Reid saw the gun glinting on the ground beside Gordo's carcass and he was about to lunge for it when an H-bomb went softly off in his head and the ground rose like dreamland and then he was part of it.

Six

He opened his eyes and saw thorns, as in an etching. All sounds were distant. He sensed his aloneness. Pain filled his head and back, but it had a neutral quality; it was a mere pressure on the nerves, tolerable.

Reid sat up. Five o'clock by the sun. Out four hours. He tried to think, but his thoughts spun about without order or sequence, like a bottled emulsion that had been shaken.

Leslie will be killed they were waiting for me all ooooo yes good kill but shouldn't have Greengrove Mama police. . . .

Hold it, hold it!

Reid got to his feet. Yes, it had really happened. Gordo's blood-crusted face was busy with flies. A delegation of vultures sat hunched in a nearby *pirul* tree. He could hear dogs grumbling in the brush all around, waiting for him to go away. Death in Mexico brought plenty of company.

His valise lay on the ground. Reid picked it up. Inside he found a note printed in the same kind of rough capitals as in the first message:

NOW PRICE IS TEN THOUSAND. BRING IT IN SMALL OLD BILLS TO CHURCH IN SANGRE DE CRISTO TO GET YOUR WOMAN BACK. YOU HAVE SEVEN DAYS. ON THE EIGHTH DAY SHE DIES.

El Hombre wasted no words lamenting the death of his Fat One. Reid remembered Delgado's eyes; the man would care nothing for revenge; revenge was a human emotion.

Delgado had, nevertheless, made a human mistake: Leslie was not Reid's woman. But Delgado was right in a deeper sense. How could a man turn his back on a human being in distress? He would have to return to Green-grove, get the money, and come back for Leslie. And *without* telling Mama.

Reid walked in widening circles around the clearing, looking for the path. He could not find it. For a time his sanity deserted him. He did not remember leaving the cactus thicket or running among the thorns. The next thing he knew, he was standing on the riverbank watch-ing a woman wash clothes. His face and arms were bleed-ing from scratches; his clothes were in tatters. A burro train loaded with charcoal was moving placidly along the opposite bank. It seemed a very long time since he had crossed the river. How could the sun be indicating that it was not yet six?

He wondered if he should go back to hide Gordo's body to gain time. But suppose he got lost in the thorn thickets? He could feel his consciousness drifting away again. How much of that damn *mota* had he smoked any-way?

Then Reid found himself leaning against a wall, laugh-ing. The river was gone, the woman, the burro train. He was also out of breath. That made him remember. He had followed the river back into the 'dobe slum; he was thirst-ier than he had ever been in his life.

Then he evoked a sudden clear picture of himself in a *cantina,* gulping beer. Many Mexican eyes had been fixed on him—the domino players, the bartender, the old man with the newspaper. Their eyes glared hate. They were loyal friends of Gordo who had gathered to avenge his death. At that moment, a man rose from the domino game so Reid had run from the *cantina* tearing through the twisting streets.

Well, that brings me up to date, he thought; and he began to laugh again. Now he felt the wetness on his back; it sobered him. He stepped away, turned around and saw the red stain on the wall.

"Sure," he said aloud. "That's why they were staring."

The pain was worse; he had to hold his knifed shoulder still as he walked. He passed a hole in the adobe wall and heard a whining noise. He looked inside and saw a fat woman pedaling an ancient Singer machine. Beside her lay a pile of bright fabrics; behind her stood a rack of shirts and dresses.

He stepped through the doorway onto the dirt floor. "May I buy a shirt?" he asked.

The woman looked up. She was fat and greasy, but there was a deep sadness in her eyes that gave her beauty. She stood up heavily and turned to the rack.

"A red one," Reid said, thinking of the blood.

She handed him a short-sleeved red shirt embroidered with white arabesques. The material was heavy and coarse, the seams strong.

"Thirty pesos," she said.

He was surprised at first to find his wallet intact. But then he understood. Delgado was playing for high stakes. The kidnapper knew that Reid would have to go back to the States for the ten thousand dollars, and that he would need money to get there.

He paid the seamstress, and asked, "May I change here?"

She nodded and drew aside a curtain; he stepped past her into a packed earth courtyard. A pot of water was boiling on a charcoal burner. Reid stripped off his shirt gingerly, wincing as it came away from the wound. He heard the scrape of bare feet.

"I will fix that," said the woman's voice.

"Do not trouble yourself, *Señora*."

"And you, do not be stupid. Sit."

He sat down on the bench. She washed his back as if

all her patrons came to her with knife wounds, applied a rancid ointment with gentle fingers, and bandaged the wound with clean coarse linen.

"Did they take much money?" she asked as she tied the bandage.

"Pardon?"

"I have seen such wounds as yours before. Are you going to the police, *Señor?*"

"No."

The woman looked relieved. She helped him into the shirt and buttoned it for him. She smelled powerfully of garlic.

"Stay here for a time, *Señor*. They may be waiting."

"No," he said. "They could have killed me if they had wanted to. But I thank you, *Señora*, from my heart. May I pay you—?"

But she refused to take any more money from him. She told him how to reach the highway, and he left with a warm feeling.

He flagged a cab on the highway, rode uptown, retrieved his car without a hitch. His color sense was still unpredictable, but, as he drove out of town, it seemed to him the bad periods were growing shorter and further apart. Perhaps he was finally coming down off the *mota.*

During the drive back to Guanajuato, another memory came back, and he stopped to throw out the sample packet of marijuana he had bought from El Mono. Once he became aware of a car following him. He pulled off the road and let it pass; it was full of women. He drove on with relief, but the fear of being followed never left him. The marijuana daze waxed and waned like a flickering flame. His jaws ached from grinding his teeth, but he hardly felt it.

Go home.

Get the money.

Get Leslie back.

A knuckle-cracking Salvador was waiting for him.

"There is no need to worry now," Reid told the anxious cabdriver. "The *señorita* is flying home, and I am driving up to join her."

Salvador wiped his face dry. "That is good news, *Señor*," he said fervently. "I think I will go to Vera Cruz for a little change of scenery."

"You do that." Reid was glad Salvador would be out of the way.

The desk clerk told him that a Mrs. May Gibson had telephoned from Texas three times. She had said she would call again. If the *señor* was checking out, what could they tell her?

Reid slipped the clerk a five-dollar bill. "You tell Mrs. Gibson that her daughter and I are on our way to Oaxaca. Miss Gibson will phone her from there. Just that—no more, no less." He managed a wink, and the clerk grinned. Reid parked Leslie's luggage in the hotel checkroom and left.

He drove north without stopping, staying awake on pills and black coffee. At dawn two days later, Reid rolled into Greengrove.

Reid parked his dusty car in the alley behind the apartment building, and slipped up to his two-room flat over the barbershop by the backstairs. An accumulation of junk mail lay on the floor under his letter slot. The sofa was heaped with the clothes he had taken off to change for the trip with Leslie. The dirty dishes were still in the sink. The bed was still unmade.

Welcome home!

The bed looked very good. Enticing. Fatigue seeped from every joint in his body like sweat. But there was no time. He refueled on eggs, sausage, toast and coffee without tasting any of them; took a shower; examined his shoulder wound in the bathroom mirror. The inch-long cut had puckered; red streaks radiated from it. But the pain was only a dull, endurable throb; he decided it could wait for treatment. He doused it with methiolate and replaced the bulky bandage with a gauze pad. He got into clean underwear, socks, slacks and shirt.

Reid sat down at the kitchen table with a pencil and paper:

Cash in bank	$2000
Equity in car	1400
Travelers' checks	700
Cash on hand	50
TOTAL	$4150

With a margin for operating room, he needed $7000 more. It was 8:20 now; he might catch Jim Kilder before he left for the bank. The head cashier was a good friend of Reid's; an amateur archaeologist, he had made several trips with Reid to temple diggings in Yucatán and Guatemala.

He dialed; Jim answered.

"Jim. How much am I good for?"

Silence. Reid knew that Kilder's eidetic memory for numbers had spread an open account book out in his mind.

"Well, your note for a thousand comes due next month. We can refinance that and let you have . . . mmm, another thousand."

Reid said, "Jim. I need seven thousand dollars in cash—this morning."

A whistle came through the receiver. "Man, what are you biting off?"

"It's an old mansion on a cliff in Acapulco. A hotel owns it, the Mirador, but it's too isolated to pay its own way. They want to sell it to somebody who won't compete in the hotel business. I can unload it on a certain rich American writer and double my money in a month."

"Reid," said Jim in scolding tones, "you know the bank can't finance a real estate deal in Mexico."

"It's too good to pass up, I tell you."

Kilder was thinking. "Did you mean double your money, or was that the usual exaggeration?"

To make his answer sound sincere took great effort on Reid's part. "No exaggeration, Jim. One gets me two, period."

Jim Kilder thought again. "I'll tell you what, Reid. I'll cosign your note, and we'll go halves on the profit. That's the best I can do."

So now, Reid thought, she's turned me into a liar and a chiseler. It was bound to trip him up. However, that was tomorrow's headache. Today's was Leslie.

"It's a deal, Jim."

"Okay. Meet me at the bank and we'll sign the agreement."

"Why don't you come here?" Before Kilder could ask why, Reid added, "There's someone I'd rather not risk running into. If I see her, I'll lose a lot of time, and I'm in a hurry."

Kilder chuckled. "A single man and his troubles. Say no more, pal. Okay, I'll be about two hours——"

"Bring the money with you. And I'll need what I've got in the bank."

"You'll have to give me a check."

"And, Jim, I want small, used bills."

"Hey, are you pulling me into a shady deal?" The tone was only half jocular.

"Would I kick in my own money if it wasn't on the level? That's the way they want it; that's all I know. Who asks a Mexican why?"

Once more hesitation at the other end. Kilder was obviously weighing his misgivings against the chance to make several thousand dollars by merely signing his name. Reid waited, half hoping Kilder would back out. But cupidity won the battle.

"Okay, Reid. See you in a couple hours."

Reid gulped black coffee and concentrated. According to Delgado's note, Leslie had over five days of life remaining. But Delgado didn't know Mama. Long before the five days were up, May Gibson would have the police on both sides of the border hopping. Every minute counted. That meant he would have to charter a plane.

He called Paul Bowden at the airfield. Bowden was a free-lance pilot who flew a Bonanza; he was used to sudden departures. He promised to get flight clearance and have his plane ready in an hour.

Now for the rest of the stake. Reid stole out the back way, drove to the nearest used-car lot, and put his Dodge up for sale. Haste proved expensive. Instead of the $1400 he had figured on, he was offered $700 by a salesman who knew a desperate seller when he saw one.

"I'm sorry, brother, but that's my top."

Reid could not even try another lot; there was no time. He took the $700. With the travelers' checks and cash in his pocket, he now had $1450. Jim Kilder was bringing $9000—$7000 from the new loan, and the $2000 from Reid's account. Total: $10, 450. Just enough to pay Delgado his blood-money and get Leslie back home. After that. . . .

Still, he felt better as he climbed the stairs to his apartment. He was not surprised to find his door standing open; he had left it unlocked for Kilder. He walked in; there sat May Gibson like the Three Furies rolled into one.

"Mr. Rance, where did you leave my daughter?"

The shock tied up Reid's tongue. As his thoughts raced, he searched her face for clues to an acceptable explanation. What he saw made his belly act up again. Leslie's mother looked grim, very grim. There were deep lines around her aging mouth; her eyes were hot, tired and full of hate; she was quivering with malice. And no sign of hysteria. Bad, bad.

He grabbed for time. "Mrs. Gibson. How did you know I was back?"

"I'm a director of the bank. Jim Kilder had to call the board to get the loan approved."

"And the loan?" Reid knew the answer already.

"Disapproved, naturally." Mama was very pale. "Where is Leslie? Where did you plan to take her?"

He managed to shrug and smile. "May I offer you some coffee?"

"You may answer my question."

Reid stole a breath. *Here goes another lie, and no end in sight.*

"Leslie took off on her own. I couldn't talk her out of it; she met some kids who were going on a horseback tour around Oaxaca. Strictly her own age group, and they didn't want me. I came back here to clean up some odds and ends and leave the car. Now I'm going back to pick her up——"

"That's a clumsy story, Mr. Rance. What's all that money for?"

He was about to tell her the story he had told Kilder, when he remembered that she knew he had been nowhere near Acapulco.

"It's a personal matter, Mrs. Gibson."

She rose abruptly. "You leave me no choice. There are laws to keep men from carrying off underage girls. Since I can't get the truth out of you, perhaps the police——"

"Mrs. Gibson, I give you my word I'll have her back in twenty-four hours."

"I'd rather get her back myself. Just tell me where she is."

"Mrs. Gibson, would you like it better if I told you Leslie's been kidnaped? She's all right, I tell you."

She glared at him as if he had just climbed out of a septic tank. "You—wait—right—where you are!" she cried; and she ran out. He heard her clattering down the stairs.

The hell I will, Reid thought.

He flung some clothes into his bag. The $10,000 ransom was now out of the question; with the police of both countries casting their nets, Delgado would have to accept what he had. If he refused, he was a fool. Or a madman. Reid slammed his bag shut, shivering. A madman he might well be.

Reid opened the door and bounced off a wall of fat in a blue uniform. It was Tub Turner, the 270-pound chief of the Greengrove police department.

"Let's go inside and talk, Reid." He had a squeaky voice.

Turner had been chief when Reid was on the force. They had parted company on proper terms, neither too formal nor too friendly. Chief Turner had said: "You'd make a good cop, Reid, if the work was all bang-banging it out with holdup men. But it ain't; it's chalking cars and rousting bums out of the park and chasing prowlers that likely weren't there in the first place. You ain't got the patience for that. So I reckon I'll accept this resignation."

For a moment, Reid actually considered strong-arming his way past Turner; but then he remembered that one of his arms was *hors de combat* and that the chief had judo-trained his men personally. So he went meekly back into his apartment.

Chief Turner closed the door with his foot and began rolling a Bull Durham.

"I reckon you know, Reid, that May Gibson's got her bowels in an uproar. Are you fixing to run off with her kid?"

"Of course not. Chief. Leslie took off on her own, as I told Mrs. Gibson. I'm headed back now to pick her up."

The Chief struck a kitchen match on his thumb, lit his cigaret, and smiled at Reid through the smoke. "Kind of fails to explain why you wanted so much money, don't it?" His smile widened. "It ain't that I give a damn, Reid.

You want to make May Gibson mad at you, you want to kick over your business, you want to fix it so you can't live in Greengrove, it's okay with me. Maybe the kid's worth it to you." His grin disappeared. "But she ain't to me. May's got the law on her side, and I'm it. I ain't getting my tail burned so you can lay under a palm tree and play Romeo with Leslie Gibson. Where is she?"

"She's in Oaxaca, in the Hotel del Rey."

"That's better. Now, let's go down to the station and get Oaxaca on the phone."

"Sure, Chief." Reid walked casually to the door and opened it. The next instant he was sprinting toward the backstairs. He skidded to a stop. A figure in blue stood at the bottom, looking up. Reid dove through a side door and ran down into the storeroom attached to the barbershop. Another of Greengrove's finest was in the alley.

Reid went into the barbershop, forcing himself to slow to a walk. He nodded at Charley Holt and Harve Downs, who were getting their morning shaves, and stepped out on the sidewalk. Each arm was seized in a beefy hand, something twisted, and paralyzing pain shot through his wounded shoulder. The street began to whirl.

"Reid, that girl must really be something." Chief Turner's voice held no trace of friendliness. "Cuff him Ralphie."

On the ride to the station, Reid sat in the back seat squeezed between two policemen, hands manacled. The pain in his shoulder kept him fighting nausea. He said nothing about it.

At the station, Reid put his wallet, change and keys into a paper bag and pulled off his belt. He was removing his shoelaces when Chief Turner said affably: "Boy, I surely hate to lock up an ex-patrolman."

"You've got no case against me, Chief."

"I got a couple days to throw one together." Turner looked at Reid searchingly. "Reckon there's no use calling Oaxaca?"

"No," said Reid. He handed over his shoelaces.

"I figured not." The Chief sighed deeply. "Well, Reid, you don't have to be told your rights—phone call, anything you say can be used agin you, and so forth. You want to step into the office and make a statement?"

"No." Reid took his receipt. "Look, Chief, I can have that girl back here in twenty-four hours if you'll let me go."

"No deal, buddy-boy. I only got six years to go to retirement."

Turner took Reid's arm and propelled him toward the steel door that led to the cell block.

"Send a man with me, then," Reid said urgently. "Two men!"

"Nope." Turner gestured to the turnkey to remove the handcuffs. Reid watched the steel door open, saw the cold gray pattern of bars, and felt a mighty urge to cut and run. But the chief, the radioman, the desk sergeant, and the two patrolman who had brought him in were in the way.

So he let himself be marshaled into the cell; the door clanked, the key turned, and the law went away.

Five days left.

This time, when the trouble started in his belly, he was sick all over the floor of the cell.

Seven

By the time the noon whistle blew, Reid was desperate. He seized the bars and shouted, "Chief Turner! Chief! Hey, Tub! What's the matter with you—you deaf? TUB!"

The steel door opened. Turner moved massively down the walkway, looking annoyed. "You're making a hell of a racket, boy." *Whap!* A pacifier caught his knuckles where he was gripping the bars. Reid jerked back his hands, more surprised than hurt. "Prisoners don't call the chief like he was a goddam spic busboy. What you want?"

So May Gibson was really turning on the heat.

"Chief, listen to me. I'm just as leery of Mrs. Gibson as you are. That's why I didn't tell her my real reason for coming back here. She'd have gone off halfcocked and got Leslie killed. Leslie's been kidnaped, and I came back here to raise the ransom money. That's the God's truth, Turner. Will you please let me go?"

"Yeah?" asked Chief Turner. "Kidnaped, huh? Where?"

"It happened in——" Reid stopped. The police chief was grinning. "Turner, humor me and assume for a few minutes that I'm telling the truth. What would you do?"

The grin turned into a scowl. "You don't learn very fast, boy, do you? I don't answer questions around here, I ask 'em! " He glared at Reid. "But okay, I'll humor you. What would I do? I'd get down the details and I'd turn 'em over to the Mex *judicial,* that's what I'd do."

"Those trigger-happy commandos? Have you ever seen them operate? They'd surround the hide-out and start shooting and Leslie would be dead before their first bullet landed."

96

"That's Mexico for you. If you'd wanted first-rate police protection, Reid, you should of stuck to your own country. Now, has that kid been kidnaped or hasn't she?"

"No," said Reid wearily.

Turner guffawed. "You figgered we'd let you out so you could take us to her in person? And maybe give us the slip when we got across the border?"

"You're right, Chief. You're always right."

"When you're ready to tell me where you got her stashed away, boy, just sing out—politelike."

The chief trundled away whistling through his teeth.

Reid lay down on the steel latticework of the bunk. He had no thought of going to sleep, but someone dropped a sandbag on his head and the next thing he knew a dimly remembered perfume was tickling his nostrils. He opened his eyes.

Karen Frankel was standing over him, holding her purse before her like a shield. She was looking down at him with the absorption of an entomologist studying a strange bug.

Karen was wearing a dark blue suit which made her appear studious. She made him think of a young schoolmarm trying to look like an old one.

"Hi," Reid said. "Where's the rest of your sociology class?"

"Rance," Karen asked, "what happened to Leslie?"

"Now don't tell me they didn't fill you in."

"They told some stupid story about your coming back here to sell your car, raise some cash, and run away with her. It's ridiculous."

"Oh," said Reid. "How do you figure that, Miss Frankel?"

"Because it's so out of character."

"Well thanks," said Reid. "That sets me up, it really does."

"Not *your* character," May Gibson's older daughter said "my sister's. Leslie wouldn't dream of sneaking off. She'd phone Mama and tell her exactly what she planned to do. Then, if Mama didn't like it, she could go climb a tree."

"And me?" asked Reid. "What would I do?"

"Something foolish. Like coming back here and bankrupting yourself to bail Leslie out of some jam she got into while technically in your charge."

Reid sat up quickly, swallowed a gasp as pain arrowed through his back and swung his legs to the floor with caution. The girl watched him critically. He got off the bunk, went over to the bars and peered into the walk-around. There was no one in sight.

Karen seemed to understand his look. She explained, "Our fatboy thinks I can find out where you've got Leslie tucked away. What's the real story, Rance?" she asked quietly. "Tell me."

Reid felt an almost causeless relief. He motioned for her to sit beside him on the bunk and told her exactly what had happened. When he finished, Karen was silent. Then she got to her feet. She was pale.

"So the longer we wait," she said, "the worse it gets?"

"Yes." He watched her walk to the bars, her heels clicking on the concrete floor. Her face was a solemn cameo in the light from the cell window. "What time is it?"

"About eleven."

"I almost slept the clock around," he muttered. "We've got four days left."

Karen turned, her fingers tight on the strap of her purse. "Can you get her back safely if you're free?"

"It's the only chance we've got."

"I'll talk to Mama. Maybe I can get her to make Turner let you go."

"You'll tell her the truth?"

"No. You can be thankful she didn't believe your kidnap story. I hate to think what she'd do if she thought

Leslie were really in danger." She was walking around the cell now, biting her lip. "If I can't free you legitimately, I might be able to arrange an escape. Would you try?"

"Yes."

She looked at him. "You might get shot."

"Yes."

She hesitated. Then she nodded. "All right, Rance. Be ready."

Karen called out, and Chief Turner himself came at once to open the cell door for her. Reid watched her walk down the corridor with Turner waddling behind, a slim girl leading a hippopotamus.

He did not probe his feelings. He felt unaccountably better and let it go at that.

An hour later, the chief came in and handcuffed him. The fat man was grinning. "Couldn't sweet-talk her, hey, boy? You're sure going to feel sorry you tangled with the Gibsons. That Karen, she's even more set than her ma on you being formally charged." He yanked brutally on the cuffs. "Come on, you're going over to the court-house for arraignment." Reid thought: This is the chance Karen mentioned—the chance to escape.

They walked down the street; Reid, with his handcuffs hooked through his belt, looked like a man with stomach cramp. Turner huffed along beside him. Old acquaintances nodded at Reid, then saw the handcuffs and looked away. Hal Chesney yelled from the doorway of a restaurant: "Hey, Reid, come in and have lunch."

"Can't, Hal." Reid grinned. "I'm all tied up."

The insurance man gaped at Reid's hands. His jaw dropped.

At that instant, a woman's scream cut through the traffic noise. "He stole my purse! *Stop thief!*"

Reid tensed. Chief Turner's heavy face was a study in indecision; he was jerking his head about in search of one of his officers, but none of them seemed to be about.

He resolved the dilemma between his policeman's instinct to give chase and his fear of losing a prisoner by cursing, snatching out a whistle, and starting to blow furiously for help.

Reid peeled off the sidewalk into the road like a fighter plane going into its dive. In a deep crouch, he darted through the slow-moving traffic toward the disorderly parade of pedestrians on the other side of the street. He was not worried about Turner; the police chief could not shoot without hitting a car or a passer-by. Reid lunged and dodged, manacled hands tight against his belly, searching frantically for Karen Frankel.

Just as Reid reached the opposite sidewalk, an old black Cadillac pulled up beside him and honked; he turned and saw Karen behind the wheel. She pointed sharply to the corner. He made swiftly for the corner and rounded it and she came shooting around it with the car door open. Reid jumped in and dropped to the floor board. The car surged forward, flattening him. He lay there for a long time, catching up on his breathing and watching Karen's little foot work the accelerator and brake.

After awhile, he became aware that the sounds of the city had died out.

"Which way are we going?"

"North. They'd expect you to head south."

Karen did not look down; she concentrated on her driving.

Smart girl, Reid thought admiringly. He felt curiously at peace. It was a comforting sort of position to be in, lying on the floor looking up at her, the trim line of her leg and thigh and torso, the calm profile, the lovely head. She had changed to a white blouse and a turf-green skirt. He watched the play of her calf muscle as she slowed for a caution light.

"They'll be broadcasting my description," he said.

"Of course. So I went to your apartment and got your

bag. You'll be able to change your clothes. I also bought a bottle of peroxide for your hair. I wasn't sure whether that repulsive mammoth would handcuff you, but I brought a hacksaw just in case."

"You've been busy," Reid said softly. Her face showed no pleasure at his tone. After a moment, he asked, "Where are we going?"

"A place I know. You can sit up now."

Karen turned into a dirt road that threaded through a stretch of swampland. She followed it for two miles. Then she got onto a track that angled off into an abandoned oil field of crumbling derricks. She stopped beside the pumper's shack, turned off the motor, and jumped out.

Reid, made awkward by the handcuffs, got out, too. The shack was cracked and weather-blackened; half the roof was gone. He sat down on a wooden step. Karen reached into the car and came up with a hacksaw. He could feel the nervous reaction begin and he steeled himself against the shakes. She bent over him and got to work. She smelled good.

She sawed at the handcuffs with a skill and strength that surprised him. She was full of surprises.

She freed one of his hands and started on the other. "You've done a grand job, Karen——"

She looked up at him. "Will you please not say things like that in that tone of voice? I did it because it had to be done. If I did it well, compliment *me*, not my sex."

"Your sex!" he exclaimed, astonished.

"Didn't your tone imply, 'Thanks, that was pretty good for a woman'?" She brushed a strand of hair back and resumed her sawing.

Reid felt a certain amusement. She was right, he had been thinking that she was remarkably competent "for a woman." He had also been thinking that, as a woman, she was remarkably attractive. The severity of the bun at the back of the head bent before him could not conceal the thickness and luster of her black hair; if she'd display

it instead of trying to hide it, he thought, it would be as
beautiful as Leslie's. Her forehead and little nose were
dewy with perspiration as she labored with the hacksaw
in the hot sun; in her position on her knees before him the
blouse fell away and he could see that she was wearing a
bra which was too small for her. He felt a surge of warmth
for her, as much sympathetic as sexual. What kept driving her to deny her femininity?

"You're a lot of woman, Karen," he said, "and in my
dictionary that doesn't mean condescension."

"Thank you," she said tartly; but he noticed the instant
blush form above the bra. "I'll have this off in a minute."

Reid sighed. "Incidentally, all my identification papers
are in a manila envelope at the police station. I'll need
replacements to get across the border."

"What, for instance?" she murmured without looking
up.

"A birth certificate."

"I can get you a fake one."

He began to wonder if there were any end to her ver-
satility. "It would have to be a good fake, Karen——"

"It will be."

She was sawing in careful strokes now. He felt a short
sharp pain on his wrist; the metal parted. She laid aside
the hacksaw and pulled on the two sawed ends of the cuff
to widen the gap, frowning and biting down on her lip; it
made Reid feel very warm indeed. Then, with great gentle-
ness, Karen pulled the second handcuff down over his
hand. She got up, threw the manacles and hacksaw into
a patch of weeds and brushed her knees.

"What else do you need?"

"Registration certificate for the car." Reid massaged his
numb wrists. "And your written permission to take it
across the border."

"You won't need *that*. I'm driving it."

He stared at her. "You aren't going!"

"Of course I am. I packed a bag for myself, too."

"My God, Karen! I'm a fugitive, I won't be able to stop and sleep—there's considerable danger——"

"You think I'll be in the way?"

He groaned. "I don't mean that——"

"They'll be looking for a man alone. We'll have a better chance getting through as a married couple." She bit her lip. "I mean——"

"I know what you mean," Reid growled. "And I still say *no*. I'll manage better alone."

"Then you can go back to Turner's jail, Mr. Rance." Her hands were curled into fists. "Which will it be?"

Reid shrugged. "All right. Have the birth certificate give me blond hair. I'll bleach it while you're gone. You're a tough baby, you know that?"

That almost made her smile. She tossed her head and got into the old Cadillac.

"And don't forget the ten thousand dollars."

"The what?"

"The ten grand for Leslie's ransom. Remember? That's what this is all about. Can you lay your hands on that much?"

It seemed to him that she hesitated. But it was only for the flicker of an eyelash.

"I'll get it, Reid."

She raced off in a cloud of exhaust, leaving him with his mouth open. She had called him "Reid." Now, why in the world would she suddenly start doing that?

Shaking his head, he opened his suitcase, found the bottle of peroxide, and started rubbing it into his hair.

Karen drove swiftly north, her mind busy with calculations. She had only three hundred dollars in the bank and this ancient gas-thirsty Cadillac. Houston was murder on the wages of a reporter who insisted on paying her own way. Getting hold of ten thousand dollars would take some doing.

She set her jaw. *I'll show this Reid character I know the angles as well as any man. . . .*

The first angle took her to Bolton, fifty miles north of Greengrove, and a photostat-tattoo parlor. She had once done a series of articles on illegal documentation for her paper, and she knew that the tattoo artist could accommodate her with a forged birth certificate.

"A man?" The proprietor was a hunched, wrinkly old fellow who had to look up even to Karen; his position gave him an air of slyness. "How old? What color eyes and hair?"

"About thirty-five. Blue eyes. Blond hair." And, Karen added to herself, an insufferably masculinity. "How long will it take?"

"An hour."

Karen gave the old artist the other data and went over to the Bolton bank. Here, after a call was made to her bank in Houston, she was able to cash a check for three hundred dollars. An hour later, she picked up the birth certificate. It even looked old.

"How much?" Karen asked the tattoo man.

"Twenty dollars."

"Twenty? I thought it was only ten."

"That's when people want to be twenty-one. Why would anybody want to be thirty-five?" the old man asked, showing one brown tooth in a grin.

"Look, my bucko," Karen said. "I'll give you fifteen dollars for no trouble, ten if you want to argue, nothing if you're going to get nasty. Make up your mind fast."

He took the fifteen.

Karen headed back south to work out angle number two.

It was fast fading twilight when she reached the outskirts of Greengrove and dark when she got to the Gibson house. She hid the Cadillac behind some bushes and made her way softly to the rear of the big house. She sneaked up the outside backstairs and let herself into her mother's bedroom through a window. There were sounds of conversation from the dining room. Guests for dinner. Mama might be frantic with worry over Leslie, but the social charade played on. Karen opened her mother's wall safe and picked out a diamond necklace, an engagement ring with a three-carat stone, and a diamond bracelet—all gifts to her mother from Leslie's father—what could be fairer than that? Karen tossed the jewels into her purse, began to shut the safe, hesitated, opened it again, and appropriated the pearl-handled .32 May Gibson's lawyer had given her after Leslie's father's death. It was unloaded, but there was a box of shells in the safe, so Karen took that, too.

If Reid Rance thought that traveling with her as man and wife entitled him to marital privileges, she thought grimly, the little revolver should prove an effective dissuader.

She found Reid asleep in the pumper's shack with his head on his suitcase She flashed the light and he was on her like a cat.

"It's Karen!" she cried. "Reid, stop! You're hurting me."

"I'm sorry." He released her, and she backed off, heart pounding. "You shouldn't have come in like that. Are you all right?"

"Yes." She managed to keep the tremble out of her voice. Behind her back, she chafed the wrist he had seized.

"Did you get the certificate?"

She gave it to him, and he went out of the shack and sat down on the step to examine it by the light of the flash. He did not seem pleased. "I suppose it will have to do."

"I thought it looked pretty good," Karen said stiffly. Then she giggled.

"What's so funny?" Reid growled.

"Your hair. It's pink."

That made him grin. "That's as blond as Indian hair will get, apparently—with peroxide, anyway. Did you get the money, Karen?"

She showed him the jewels, and he scowled.

"You're a hard man to please," Karen snapped. "What's wrong with *them*? I assure you they're the real thing!"

"I don't doubt it. But our Mexican friends haven't my faith."

"For heaven's sake, Reid, these are worth I don't know how many times more than ten thousand dollars."

"What do you expect Delgado to do, send them out to an appraiser?" Reid asked dryly. "Why didn't you bring cash?"

"Because I don't have ten thousand dollars, Mr. Rance!"

He stared at her. "You really don't."

"Look, I stole these from my mother. If there'd been cash in her safe I'd have lifted that in preference, but there wasn't. Anyway, Leslie's father gave Mama these, so it's really not stealing—I'm sure he wouldn't mind seeing his gifts to Mama go to get Leslie back in one piece. We'll just have to turn these into cash, that's all. I'll go to some jeweler and pretend to be a rich man's wife who needs a bundle to run away with her boy friend."

Reid shrugged. "I'll be very happy if it works." He did not sound happy. "Let's go."

"Where?"

"Well, Reynosa's out because I just crossed there— they might recognize me. We'll cross at Laredo."

On the way to Laredo, Reid fell asleep, and as she made a turn his head flopped over and came to rest on her shoulder. Karen tried, unsuccessfully, to ignore it. Its weight was not unpleasant, and he did look kind of helpless asleep; but then she thought angrily how easy it was for a woman to lose her individuality when she got mixed up emotionally with a man. The Lord knew her mother was a shining example, trying to please first one man and then another and never being able to be herself . . . or a mother to her children, when it came to that.

Karen took one hand off the wheel and shook him. *"Reid."*

"Hunh?" He half woke with a start.

"Will you please stop sprawling all over me? It's hard to drive this way."

He mumbled an apology and leaned against the other side of the seat. In a moment, he was breathing heavily again. She felt a sense of loss.

It was still dark when they reached Laredo. Reid had her drive into a junkyard to wait until the jewelry stores opened. . . . The old Caddie, he said, was perfectly camouflaged among two acres of junk cars. At seven, Karen left the yard on foot and bought rolls and coffee and brought them back to the car.

"We'd better stay here," Reid said. "If I know Turner he's got everything out including dogs. And if your mother's discovered her jewelry's missing——"

At five minutes past nine Karen was in a fashionable jewelry store performing her runaway-wife routine. The jeweler examined the pieces, pushed up his loupe, and gave her a sharp look.

"The ring's not too bad. I'll give you six hundred for it."

"Six hundred!" Karen exclaimed. "That's a three-carat stone."

"It's also full of flaws," the man said. "Six hundred is the best I can do."

"Well, what about the necklace and the bracelet?"

"We don't handle imitation jewelry, madam."

"Imita——!" Karen's mouth stayed open. Then she asked furiously, "What do you mean?"

"Both these pieces are paste."

"Paste? They can't be! They were a gift from——"

The jeweler shrugged. "Try any jeweler in town. They'll all tell you the same thing."

Karen snatched the three pieces back and stalked out. But the man had been telling the truth. Three other jewelers declared the bracelet and necklace to be worthless paste, and the three-carat diamond flawed. In the end, she let the ring go for six hundred and fifty dollars.

Walking back to the junkyard, Karen boiled. All these years, her mother had cherished those jewels in tearful memory of her dear, departed Bradley Gibson. And he had simply cheated her, cynically aware that she was too ignorant to know the difference. Typical male trick, Karen thought bitterly. Well, it served Mama right. . . .

Suddenly it struck her. What were they going to do about ransoming Leslie from those cutthroats now?

Karen ran the rest of the way to the junkyard.

Reid listened to her tale of woe in grim silence.

"I'm sorry, Karen. We're in trouble, all right. More than money trouble. I bought a morning paper. Look."

A three-column photograph of him stretched across the front page. The accompanying story read:

GREENGROVE, TEX. (*Special to the* Times)—Reid Rance, Greengrove tourist guide suspected of seeking to elope with 17-year-old Leslie Gibson, yesterday made a daring daylight escape from the Greengrove police. Miss Gibson, heiress to the N.R. Gibson fortune, has been missing in Mexico for three days. Her whereabouts are still unknown.

In engineering his breakout from police custody, Rance is believed to have forced Karen Frankel, the missing heiress's half sister, to help him. Miss Frankel has not been seen since she went downtown yesterday to shop.

"There is no question in my mind that Rance overpowered Miss Frankel," Chief of Police Turner said. "He forced her to accompany him in her black 1947 Cadillac, Texas Plate Number MK-4 29213. It is my further belief that he forced Miss Frankel to open her mother's bedroom safe and take jewels valued at $40,000, also a .32 revolver.

The tourist guide and his alleged abduction victim are expected to head for Mexico, where Leslie Gibson is believed to be hiding. U.S. and Mexican border authorities have been alerted. Rance is now armed and presumed to be dangerous.

Karen sat staring through the windshield at the wasteland of twisted metal. Her eyelids burned and her throat ached. Something nudged her, and she saw that it was Reid offering her his handkerchief. She started to push his hand away, changed her mind, took the handkerchief and blew her nose.

"You think they'd let her go for six hundred and fifty dollars, Reid?" she snuffled. "That's what I got for the ring. Or wait, I've got three hundred more . . . though we need some money for expenses——"

"Not a chance," Reid said. "Delgado said ten thousand; he *meant* ten thousand. They'd just take the money, kill Leslie, and maybe you and me in the bargain. They might do it even if we *had* ten thousand. I'll have to get her back without money."

"How do we get across the border now?"

"We can't. I probably can, alone."

"No!"

"Listen, Karen, they're looking for two people now. And when those Laredo jewelers get around to reading the paper, they'll undoubtedly report your attempt to sell the jewelry. That would pin us down here. There might even be roadblocks."

"I'm in this up to my neck," Karen said quietly. "This was all my idea, remember? And there's Leslie to consider. Tell me what to do, Reid, and I'll do it."

He studied her for a moment. Then he said, "We'll have to steal a car and ditch this one. That's for openers."

She swallowed. "All right."

"Start driving. Keep your eyes open for a couple who resemble us, at least superficially."

She started the engine.

"And give me the gun, Karen. I'll need it."

Numbly, she took the gun from her purse and handed it to him. Her original reason for taking it seemed ludicrous now.

Eight

She drove south down Highway 83 while Reid scanned the road ahead through a small pair of field glasses Karen had had in her bag. They were south of Zapata, passing a Humble station, when he said: "Slow down. That couple in the two-tone Chevvy at the pumps . . . if he only has blue eyes——" He raised the glasses, nodded. "He has. Step on it."

Two miles out they set the stage. Reid worked the jack under the back bumper and Karen waved down the approaching Chevvy, feeling butterflies in her stomach. The Chevvy slowed and pulled onto the shoulder thirty feet ahead. She ran over to the driver's side and asked: "Do you happen to have a lug wrench? My husband——"

Reid's voice came like chipped ice from the other side: "Reach down and turn off your engine. Then hand me your keys and slide over."

He was pointing the gun at the woman. The man's face turned gray. He complied immediately.

"Get in the driver's seat," Reid told Karen.

Karen slid behind the wheel, smelling the sweat of fear from the man at her side. Reid opened the other door. He said to the woman: "You'll come with me."

The man stiffened. "Don't! Please——"

"Relax," said Reid. "We'll just get both cars off the road. Your wife rides with me and this young lady rides with you. Nobody gets hurt. Fair enough?"

The man slumped. "Go with him, Mary. Do what he says."

Karen started the Chevvy engine, waited until Reid and the other woman passed in the Cadillac and swung in behind. Reid turned onto a track that led through a cotton field, and Karen followed.

The man pulled out his handkerchief and mopped his face. "What . . . what's he going to do with us, miss?"

She felt sorry for the sweating man. "Nothing, if you don't make trouble."

"My God, he's welcome to whatever I've got. The car's insured. The money . . . I've got fifty-some dollars on me. I won't give him any argument. Will you tell him that?"

She nodded, and the man seemed to feel better. The Cadillac stopped behind the high bank of an irrigation canal and Karen pulled up behind it. Reid got out and motioned them forward. He had put the gun in his pocket.

"I need your car and your identification. I've explained the reason to your wife, and she's willing. You can say no and go free, but a girl may die if you do."

"A girl?" The man looked wide-eyed at Karen. "You——"

"My kid sister," said Karen. "They're holding her in Mexico. We've got to get her back without telling the police."

The man exclaimed, "Leslie Gibson! I heard about her, but I thought she was running away with some guy——" He looked quickly at Reid, then at Karen. "You're going on his word?"

"I believe him."

"I do, too, Bill," said the man's wife. "He's no criminal."

The man reached inside his coat and took out his wallet. "I guess the papers can be replaced. And the car. Anyway——" He gave Reid a lopsided smile——"you convinced my wife, Rance, so at least I won't catch hell from her."

Reid took the papers, glanced over them swiftly, stuffed them in his pocket.

"Can you wait twenty-four hours before reporting this? There's no reason why you should—but we need the time. I give you my word—it's all I can give you right now— that you won't lose a penny by any of this."

The man hesitated. Then he smiled and stuck out his hand. "Good luck! You have our address. I'd like to hear how it all comes out."

Reid shuffled through the papers as Karen drove the Chevvy down the palm-lined highway.

"We'll cross at Brownsville," he said. "We're from Dallas. Been married seven years. My name is William P. Streeter, I'm an engineer, and I'm thirty-four. You're Mary, maiden name Phillips—with two *l*'s—twenty-nine years old. Now run through it."

"We're from Dallas, married seven years. You're William P. Streeter, engineer, thirty-four. I'm Mary Streeter, nee Phillips, aged twenty-nine."

"You carry your age well."

Her lips tightened. "Reid, how can you be so flippant?"

"Bill. Keep calling me that. We're taking a second honeymoon in Mexico to recapture that old magic. Got it?"

"Yes . . . Bill."

"And try to look like a woman looking forward to it." He grinned.

Karen felt herself flush all over. I won't answer when he talks like that, she told herself. Second honeymoon. . . . Her nerves were screaming by the time they reached Brownsville.

Reid put the gun in her purse. "Keep that in your hands and don't get too far away from me. If I grab for it, that means we're in trouble, and you're to let go of it and run like hell. Do you understand?"

She nodded, not trusting her voice.

In the immigration office she found no difficulty obeying his warning to keep silent. She could only admire the

way Reid handled it; he was the most confused and ignorant tourist the Mexican officials had ever seen. He
spoke no Spanish and he could not understand their English. He went over to the wrong desks, produced the
wrong papers, and insisted on reading every word of the
documents he was asked to sign. Finally, when it became
apparent that this idiotic *norteamericano* was tying up international traffic, they were rushed through by a young
man who spoke perfect English and who looked relieved
as they drove away.

She felt better when they were rolling across the hot
brush-covered flatland south of Matamoros. She tightened
up again when Reid remarked thoughtfully that they
probably should switch cars again, since the Streeters might
change their minds about reporting the theft.

But Karen relaxed again when he said: "On second
thought, that's sure to pinpoint us. We'll hang on to the
car we have and trust the Streeters to keep their word."

He drove. Karen, tiring of the ugly unchanging view,
curled up beside him and dozed.

It was dark when they reached El Mante. Reid checked
into a second-class Mexican hotel where, he said, they
were not likely to meet gregarious fellow-tourists. In the
hotel room, she said accusingly, "There's only one bed!"

He nodded, yawned and began to unbutton his shirt.

"You'd better get used to this, Karen. We're stuck in
this husband-and-wife routine. I'll get twin beds where I
can. But we'll have to use the same room. I'm not going
to do anything to you you don't want me to do. Which
side of the bed do you prefer—the left or the right?"

"I'll sleep on the floor!"

He shrugged. "I hope you're immune to scorpion
stings."

She stood there biting her lip. After all, he hadn't
wanted her to come—she'd forced herself on him. . . .
She'd have to make the best of a bad deal.

She watched him peel the shirt off his bare chest. A

prickly heat was climbing her legs. Then he got up to go to the bureau, and she saw the discolored bandage on his back.

"When did you get hurt?" Karen cried.

He looked over his shoulder. "I was stabbed. I told you."

"Yes, but I had no idea. . . ." She tossed her purse on the bed. "Sit down and let me look at that!"

He gasped as she peeled off the tape. The wound was fiery red at the edge, purple at the center. She probed it gently with a forefinger and a yellow pus oozed out.

"It's infected. You'll have to see a doctor."

"No."

"Now listen, Reid, I can't have you getting sick on me and leaving me with all the responsibility——"

"Karen, I may be wanted for murder here in Mexico. I can't risk a doctor."

In the end, they compromised. She went with him to a drugstore, where the pharmacist gave him a shot of penicillin and sold him sixty-pesos' worth of antibiotic pills for a hundred pesos. The man asked no questions.

"He thinks I'm venereal." Reid laughed when they were outside. "You'd better be careful, *cara mia*."

She flushed only a little this time. Could it be that she was getting used to his suggestive remarks?

The shot had made him drowsy by the time they got back to the hotel room, and he fell asleep fully dressed on the bedcovers. Karen stole out and struggled through a Spanish menu; she found the food spicy but edible. When she returned to the room, Reid was twisting and turning, breathing noisily; his skin was doughy-looking and moist. She looked down at him. Should she undress him and put him under the covers? The thought brought another tide of warmth to her legs. She eased the blanket out from under him and covered him with it. She lay down beside him, but on top of the covers and without removing her clothes.

A groan awakened her. "Water . . . water?"

She rolled off the bed and fetched a glass of water from the bathroom. She had to lift his head to help him drink. His skin was now dry and burning.

"Can you see any ships?" he asked in a loud, belligerent voice.

"Ships?" He was delirious. "Yes, Reid, they're coming," Karen said softly. "Go back to sleep——"

He clutched her hand. "Leslie, don't go."

Karen froze. Leslie . . . who got everything she wanted. Was it possible that Leslie and Reid . . . ?

She could not sleep. She sank into the chair and watched the jump and fall of his chest, listened to his snuffly breathing. Even in sleep, and ill, he looked . . . what? trustworthy? strong? . . . manly, that was it. The way a man should look . . . ideally. What nonsense! she thought. I'm going on like a smitten teen-ager. And she wondered why her defenses were down. Perhaps it was because he was so helpless.

Karen went over to the bed and felt his forehead softly, and it seemed to her that it was not so feverish; it was getting damp—the fever was breaking. She brushed his hair back for a moment, that silly-looking strawberry blond hair with the Indian black roots, and caught herself smiling.

She went back to the chair.

No, Leslie would be too bold, too cocky, too callow for a man like Reid. He would prefer to take the initiative, even battle for what he wanted. . . .

The thought was peace-inducing, and Karen closed her eyes.

Karen opened her eyes to the sound of Reid's voice calling her name. To her astonishment, he was out of bed, in fresh clothes, haggard but clear-eyed. Gray daylight filled the gray room.

"Reid!" She sprang out of the chair. "How do you feel?"

"Better," he said. "Is it something I dreamed, or was I out of my head for a while last night?"

"You were a little delirious."

"Did I say anything stupid?" he asked quickly.

"You were talking to Leslie."

"Oh," he said, and turned to the bed.

Karen stretched her aching body. Then she noticed that the bed was littered with scraps of newspaper.

"What's all that, Reid?"

"I've been making a decoy." He picked up one of the five packages lying on the bed. It was about four inches thick and he had wrapped it in tough brown paper and tied it with strong cord. "Five packets of paper cut to U.S. bill size, with a genuine ten-dollar bill top and bottom of each packet. They'll find out they've been had if they cut the cords and unwrap the packages, of course, but I'm hoping their pickup man will simply grab and run. By the way, I had to dip into your fund of cash for the decoy bills."

She made an impatient gesture. "How will all this get Leslie back?"

"When the pickup man makes a beeline for their hide-out, I aim to be right on his tail."

At one P.M., Karen lay on her stomach behind a white-flowering bush and looked down on the ghost town of Sangre de Cristo—a hundred acres of crumbling stone walls; some, patched with rust-red adobe; others, over-grown with scrawny vines. Saguaros thrust up here and there like the remains of a stockade; magueys spread their huge fleshy leaves over the rubble. A goat blatted some-where in the distance, but there was no sign of human life.

"What happened to the people?" Karen asked Reid.

"Gold and silver played out a hundred years ago, a flood did the rest. The old church is there by the river."

He pointed to a flat plain which had been left by a bend in the river. Inside a walled rectangle stood the roofless church, larger than the railroad station in Greengrove. Karen raised the field glasses. The floor was littered with rubble from the fallen roof. Empty wall niches gaped back at her like empty eye sockets. The murals were grime-streaked and faded.

"When were you supposed to leave the ransom?"

"There was no time set. Delgado's probably had a man watching the church twenty-four hours a day." She felt his hand squeeze her shoulder. "I'll go down and leave the bait. If anyone goes in, try to spot which direction they come from. And don't move from here—that's an order."

He was gone, and Karen was very much alone. Ten minutes later, she saw Reid go slowly into the church with the shopping bag. A moment later, he reappeared empty-handed and ducked in among the willows that bordered the stream. Soon afterward, she heard the whine of the Chevrolet's starter. Karen knew he would drive away, hide the car, and come on foot to rejoin her.

A half hour went by.

Suddenly Karen remembered that somewhere nearby one of the murderous gang was watching the church, too. The thought rippled her flesh; she felt her hands grow slick on the glasses and perspiration dampen her armpits.

Karen jumped a foot. Someone or something had broken out in a raucous, triumphant cry practically in her ear. She looked wildly around, her heart hammering. *Reid, help me!* But then the cry came again, and she looked up and saw a Mexican crow scolding her from a branch of the eucalyptus tree overhead.

"*A-kaw! A-kaw!* yourself, damn you," Karen breathed fiercely . . . and jumped again at a scraping sound behind her. She whirled, and almost sobbed in relief. It was Reid.

"What's the matter?" he asked quickly.

"Nothing," Karen said. "Nobody's gone in yet." And damn *him* for having noticed!

He crawled up beside her and took the glasses. He scanned the ruins below for ten minutes.

"They're being too cagey to suit me. And if they check those bundles right away and learn they've been had——"

"What will you do, Reid?"

"Grab the man who comes and make him tell where they're hiding Leslie."

"*Make* him . . . tell?" Karen repeated faintly.

He lowered the glasses not looking at her. He looked sad and angry. "You won't have to watch."

Almost an hour passed before Reid said softly, "Blackie."

He handed Karen the glasses and pushed himself up. "You stay here, Karen."

She watched him half run, half slide down the hill. Suddenly she could not remain where she was. She scrambled to her feet and followed him. Halfway down the hill she caught her dress on something and ripped it. She pulled away from the obstruction frantically, ran, stumbled, fell, skinned her hand, got up . . . somehow, years later, she reached the roofless ruins of the church.

Reid was holding a skinny, very dark Mexican pinned against the wall. At their feet lay the shopping bag and the five packets. One of the bundles had been ripped apart; its contents of bill-sized pieces of newspaper lay strewn over the rubble.

"Reid!" Karen gasped. "Oh, Reid."

He did not turn, but she saw his jaw set angrily. "Didn't I tell you to wait up there? But as long as you're here— come here."

She came forward bravely, forcing herself to stare at the ugly mustached face of the Mexican. The man leered at her and said something in Spanish.

"Cállate!" Reid snarled. "Karen, take the gun from me and hold it on him while I work him over. It's your own fault if you have to watch."

She took the gun and backed away, pointing it at the cowering Mexican. To her horror, Reid deliberately pressed his thumb into the Mexican's right eye. She could see the eyeball begin to bulge under the lid. Her stomach flopped over.

"Reid!" she screamed.

Reid's thumb came away. "It's all right, Karen. I can't scare him, anyway. He's high on pot."

Relief washed over her. Reid began to walk the man toward the entrance.

"What are you going to do now, Reid?" she asked apprehensively.

"Give him the water treatment. Come on and keep him covered."

She followed, warning her knees not to give way. She had reported floods, fires, car wrecks, riots; she had seen people in pain, heard their screams. But . . .

When she got to the river, Reid was up to his knees in an eddy of clear water, holding the little man under, like a preacher baptizing a convert. The Mexican's face was quite visible under the surface; bubbles streamed from his nostrils. His back was arched and he was kicking frantically.

Reid lifted him out. *"Dónde está la güera?"*

The little man coughed, choked, and spat out a sulphurous word. Reid plunged him back into the water.

Two minutes passed. The Mexican was thrashing like a hooked fish. His mouth opened. . . .

Karen gave a cry of relief as Reid hauled him out. The little man coughed and choked; water streamed from his nose and mouth. When he could finally talk, he gasped out one word:

"Zihuatanejo!"

They were going back toward the bank when it happened. Reid slipped on the wet rocks and lost his grip on the man's arm. The Mexican tore free, leaped onto the bank, scrambled up the slope, and started running along the churchyard wall.

"Shoot, Karen!" Reid yelled.

She aimed the gun at the flapping legs. But something was wrong. She could not squeeze the trigger. She looked to see if the safety . . . yes; it was off. . . .

"Karen, *stop him!*"

She aimed again just as the man disappeared around the corner of the wall. The gun chose that moment to go off. There was a roar, and stone-dust flew six feet behind the spot where the man's head had been.

Reid raced up, snatched the gun from her, dashed along the wall, and disappeared around the corner. Karen waited for the shot, but it never came. Reid returned ten minutes later gushing sweat. His clothes were torn and his arms were bleeding from long scratches.

"Lost him," was all he said.

"I'm sorry," Karen was flushed. "I . . . just couldn't."

He looked at her and turned on his heel and went into the church. He came out with the shopping bag and made for the road, unwrapping the packages as he strode along, pulling off the ten-dollar bills, letting the scraps of newspaper flutter away. She had to trot to keep up with him, and after awhile it annoyed her.

"All right, so I couldn't kill the creature," Karen panted. *"Will* you slow down! Do I have to bring you a scalp before you'll talk to me? Anyway, you did find out where they're holding Leslie. That Zihuat-something."

Reid said nothing until they were in the car. When he did speak, it was with exasperating patience. "All we know is the name of the town. They'd hardly be holding

Leslie prisoner in the main plaza of Zihuatanejo, do you think?"

"I'm sorry," Karen said again, miserably. "How far away is it, Reid?"

"About a hundred and fifty miles north of Acapulco. It's wild country. Only one road leading in, and that was torn up by a flood not long ago. They've probably got her hidden in the bush. It may take us days to find out where, while Blackie will get there as the crow flies." He started the engine, glanced down at her. "You know what a Mexican kidnaper does when his ransom attempt fails?"

"Sometimes——" she licked her dry lips "——sometimes they turn them loose, don't they?"

He did not reply, and Karen shivered.

As he drove, she became conscious of the gun in her lap and she felt a helpless frustration curdle inside her.

He held out a hand. "Better let me have the gun, Karen. You aren't going to use it."

She gripped it tightly. "I will if they do anything to Leslie."

Nine

Leslie woke up and peered through the lattice of split palm that formed the walls of her hut. The banana leaves were a bright green in the morning sun; papayas hung in golden clumps at the top of the trees; coco palms rattled in the morning breeze. A *guacamayo* flapped its iridescent green and blue wings and scolded from a near-by mango. *Gu-wak-a! Gu-waaaak-a!* Its screech cut through the heavy silence of the clearing like a machete. The three net hammocks with their lumped sleeping men swayed gently between the palms like cocoons.

Leslie lay back on her straw *petate,* thankful that so far she had had the hut to herself. Soon Felipe would prepare her breakfast: beans and *tortillas,* an orange, perhaps, an egg if he could find one. Felipe treated her with old-fashioned chivalry. She would have enjoyed it if she had not felt like a valuable captive animal which must not be allowed to damage itself.

How long ago had it been when Reid was struck down in the thicket because of her stupidity? First, there was the long drive—all that night, and all the next day and half the night again. Then the boat ride up the river to the waterfall in the foothills of the mountains. Then the trek to this clearing. And six days here.

Eight in all.

Leslie had no idea where she was, only that it was near the sea because sometimes a breeze brought the scent of salt, and sea food was plentiful: red clams, oysters and some stunted relative of the abalone. Once Felipe brought her a live spiny lobster and dropped it into boiling water;

123

the tail was delicious. She could not say the same for
the chopped octopus he prepared with lime juice and
onions. And there were always coconuts, papayas,
bananas, mangoes, squash, plantain. Meat seemed re-
stricted to horrors like the baby iguana Felipe held up
for her with the air of offering a gourmet's *pièce de ré-
sistance,* or the little armadillo he captured alive which
tried pathetically to hide inside its useless armor.

Felipe was a dark, curly-headed boy only a few years
older than Leslie. His onyx eyes and broad arched nose
were pure Indian. He had made it clear to her that he
was not *flojo,* not a bum, like the others. This hut had
been his home, these trees, his source of livelihood. Every other day, Felipe would load his two burros with
bananas and plantains and then disappear down the path
to the river. In the afternoons, he would return with his
baskets empty, so she knew there must be a village not
too far away.

She was watched night and day.

Felipe was the only one of the gang with a proper
name. The others were all called by nicknames, like
Mexican versions of Damon Runyon characters. El
Mono, the monkey, fancied himself a girl-pleaser; he
had flirted with her the first two days and played his
guitar for her at the fire. On the third night, she had
awakened in her hut to the depredations of his hands,
busy at her clothing. Her nails had scored his face; her
screams had brought Felipe swiftly, his machete a red
glitter in the lantern light. He had backed Mono against
the center post and spoken in cold Spanish whispers while
the point of his blade dimpled the other's shrinking bare
belly. Since then, Mono had been sullen. He kept staring
at her and puffing his acrid cigarets.

The smell of pot sickened Leslie now; she wished she
had never heard of marijuana. She remembered the horror of that night in the thicket: the weird sensation of
being suddenly cut off from her own body, then the ter-

ror, the futile attempt to run, the brutal hands which told her eloquently that she was a prisoner. . . .

There was another man, a skinny little devil, whose name, Felipe had told her, meant Dirty Face. The name suited him. He had very dark skin, a tangle of sooty hair, and a straggling mustache. He had gone away three days ago; Leslie was glad to see the last of that sly, wrinkled face.

Then there was El Gato, the Cat; and this one, too, was well named. He walked with controlled violence, like a leopard. Sometimes the name El Gordo, the Fat One, would come up in conversation, and El Gato would curse, seize his machete, and bury its blade in the bole of the nearest palm. Leslie gathered that El Gordo was the cab-driver she had last seen lying dead at Reid Rance's feet; he had been El Gato's brother, and the Cat burned for revenge. He too was a *marijuano;* he would smoke in a smoldering silence, then suddenly break out in a volcano of curses, and, just as abruptly, fall silent again. Once he had glided toward her hut, and the others had promptly borne him to the ground. Only the mention of another name, Delgado, had caused him finally to turn away.

Delgado was mentioned often, with awe. She had only glimpsed the gang's chieftain when he had clubbed Reid from behind. Delgado had been in the thicket that first night, but the night had been dark and she had been blinded with fear. She remembered nothing about him but a hollow, inhuman voice.

The days would have been intolerable except for Felipe's passionate desire to learn English. He owned an ancient textbook—its ragged cover showed a Mexican and an American shaking hands across the Rio Grande. The American wore a straw hat with a string attached to his collar. From time to time Felipe would approach her, his face tortured with effort and wring from himself an English sentence. *Our automobile has a broken tire* or *I gets up very early this morning. Got,* Leslie would say, *I got up very early this morning.* He would practice until she conferred her approval, and then his white teeth would flash in an anguished smile. When he learned the English, he said, he would become rich. All rich people had the English.

On days when Felipe did not go to the village, he would escort Leslie to the waterfall, standing guard in the path until she had finished bathing. She had come to think of him as *simpático.* But even Felipe had his limits. When she tried to find out why they were holding her, he would say only that she would not be harmed, that she would be soon freed. Lately he had frowned when he said it, as though he were no longer certain.

Today she would bathe in the waterfall and get rid of this sticky feeling. And she would ask Felipe to help her escape.

There was an egg for breakfast, pale-yolked, with beans and a diced papaya. She found the food tasteless this morning.

When Felipe came to take away her plate, he asked: "You——" He made the tortured gurgle that meant he was searching for a word. "You . . . bath today?"

"*Bathe.* Yes, Felipe, whenever you're ready."

He returned leading a burro, a woven hemp riding pad over its back. She would have preferred to walk, but Felipe seemed to enjoy having her ride his beast. And that morning she wanted to please him.

At the waterfall she dismounted and Felipe backed off. She walked to the edge of the rocky pool, pulled off her now-gray cashmere sweater, unwrapped her faded skirt, stepped out of her panties, and laid the garments in shallow water, weighting them with a rock. She shivered as she waded into the waist-deep water; according to Felipe, it traveled a full mile down from the mountains. She stepped under the cascade that poured from a split in the rocks twenty-five feet over her head; she had to stand with her legs wide apart to keep from being knocked over. Her flesh quickly numbed. It was better than a massage; she could feel a quickening surge in her veins. She let the stream beat against her chest, stomach and thighs for a while, then waded into calm water and lathered herself with the gritty brown soap Felipe provided. Rinsing herself, she took her clothes from the water and spread them on a rock, then stretched herself out beside them in the sun.

Nice, she thought, to be able to lie naked like this and not have to worry. On her second trip to the waterfall, she had glimpsed movement behind the broad-leaved plants that lined the pool. Felipe had brandished his machete when she told him.

"Next time you call me. I drive them off," he told her. There was something overdone about his indignation.

"So you can look alone?"

His face had darkened in confusion.

"The burro wandered," he mumbled. "I could not help——"

"When a woman wishes to be seen naked she will show herself," Leslie had told him in a stern voice. "Only an animal peeps from hiding."

He had looked at her abjectly. "I will tie the burro better next time, *Señorita*. And I will keep the others away."

Since then he had stood watch on the path.

Leslie's clothes had dried. She dressed and called Felipe.

He appeared with the burro and asked eagerly, "You feel yourself better?"

"I feel better, yes." She made as if to get on the burro, then stopped. "You like to see me happy?"

He nodded. "I like for you to smile, *Señorita*."

"Then take me with you to the village. Now, Felipe."

He shook his head instantly. "I cannot do that."

"Then I cannot smile."

"But if I take you, I will get no money. And, without money, I cannot buy a car and become a taxi driver for the tourists in Acapulco. Cara Prieta—Blackie—brings the ransom tonight, and then you go free." Tonight, Leslie thought, climbing on the burro. Then there was no need to escape. She wondered how Reid had handled it with her mother.

Back at the camp, Leslie awaited the evening impatiently. Felipe prepared a filet of red snapper and sugared plantain for her supper, but she could not eat.

It was nearly dark when Blackie stumbled into the light of the campfire, looking like a casualty of some battlefield. He talked with great rapidity, making the palms-up gesture of failure several times. When he finished, El Mono and El Gato looked Leslie's way in a chilling manner. Felipe frowned at her and nodded his head very slightly in the direction of the hut. Leslie rose. Something had gone wrong. She might become a consolation prize.

She went to her hut and watched through the palm-leaf wall. The men sat talking in low, impassioned voices. Mono rolled a marijuana cigaret and passed it around. All smoked except Felipe. A strange silence fell over the group. Then Blackie said something which ended in a shrill giggle. El Mono got his guitar and began playing in an irregular rhythm, too fast or too slow. Leslie could see that they were high again. There was a dreadful joylessness in their gaiety.

Suddenly the guitar twanged a clashing chord and El Mono jumped up and started toward the hut. El Gato shouted something and El Mono whirled. The pair began to argue; Leslie heard Delgado's name mentioned several times. El Mono grinned evilly and returned to the fire. He began to strum again as though nothing had happened. El Gato rose and glided into the darkness.

A few minutes later Felipe crept up beside her hut. He

whispered that Blackie had met her tall *gringo* friend; there had been no money, only a trick; the tall one had tortured Blackie. The men had been furious. Felipe had feared they might kill her on the spot; but they decided not to touch her until they received new orders from Delgado. El Gato had gone to tell him the bad news. Felipe, meanwhile, was to go to the village to watch for the *gringos*. They were expected to appear, since Blackie had been forced to give the name of the town she was in while half-crazed from the water torture.

"They?" asked Leslie in a whisper. "He brought another man with him?"

"A woman," Felipe muttered. "A pretty girl with black hair. She held the gun for the man."

Karen! But why hadn't Karen brought the ransom money? Was it possible their mother had refused to pay? No, there must be some other explanation. . . . Leslie held her left breast in both hands. Her heart was hammering so hard she was shaken by each beat.

"Felipe! What will you do if you see my friends in the village?"

"Return here and tell Mono and the others." Felipe sighed. "I should run away to the mountains. There will be no money now for the car. I cannot become a taxi driver in Acapulco."

"You could, you could," whispered Leslie urgently, "if you take me to my friends. They will give you money!"

Felipe thought that over. "Delgado would kill me like a fly."

"My friend would kill Delgado first. You know how he killed El Gordo?"

"Yes." Felipe was silent. Then: "I will go to see if they have come."

"Then you'll help me, Felipe?"

"I will see."

Leslie tried to concentrate. As long as she was in this nightmare, she had to pretend that it was really happen-

ing. Should she try to escape, or should she rely on Felipe
and wait for him? Suppose Reid and Karen weren't in
the village? (And what would it be like when those
maniacs, El Mono, Blackie and El Gato, came for her?
But this possibility she froze out of her mind.)

Sleep was out of the question. She watched the two
men at the fire. El Mono played his guitar and sang
heavy, sad tunes, occasionally throwing his head back
and howling toward the treetops. Some time later, Blackie
staggered to a hammock and, after three attempts, managed to curl up in it. El Mono stared into the fire, cigaret
drooping from his lips, long dirty fingers brushing the
strings. He leaned gradually to the left and finally fell
on his side and stayed there. When Leslie rose from her
peephole, the boy was stretched out, caressing the guitar
and crooning to it as if it were a woman.

The next day was maddening. El Mono and Blackie
smoked and smoked. Their knowing smiles knotted Leslie's body. In the afternoon, a three-foot iguana blundered
into camp, looking like some prehistoric monster which
had wandered in out of its epoch. With casual skill, Mono
flipped a noose over its head and jerked the ugly creature onto its back. Blackie ran forward with another rope,
threw several loops around its legs, then tied the jaws
together. Laughing like children, the pair built a big fire
and boiled water in an old cutaway oil drum. When it
was steaming like the waters of hell they dumped the
iguana in alive. Leslie turned away gagging.

A half hour later El Mono ceremoniously offered her a
coconut shell filled with iguana meat. Leslie ran behind
her hut and retched. The smacking sounds of their feast
kept her doubled over and gasping. The two men laughed
so hard they fell on the ground.

Felipe returned in the late afternoon, looking grim and
shaking his head. No gringos. But to Leslie his eyes said,
Yes, they are here.

Leslie could have shrieked for joy. Instead, she rose and walked droopily out of the clearing, taking the path that led to the clump of bamboo which had been assigned to her for her private necessities. She waited a few minutes, then strolled back. Felipe was squatting beside the path, screened from the clearing by a stand of ferns.

She knelt beside him: "You saw them?"

Felipe looked over his shoulder. "I spoke with him."

"Did you tell him——"

"I said nothing of you. I told him only to meet me at a certain place tonight." He grimaced. *"Ay carai,* the man is strong. He grab me and try to make me tell more, but I free myself and run." He pulled up his sleeve and showed her the bruises on his right biceps. "When I meet him you must be with me. If not, I think maybe he kill me."

"I'm ready now," whispered Leslie. "Oh, let's go, Felipe, please!"

He shook his head negatively. "We go with the darkness. Say you are sick and would go early to bed. When you hear this song played on the guitar—" he hummed a tune "—leave the *jacal* and wait beside the path to the waterfall. I will come."

She had no trouble successfully playing sick. El Mono and Blackie laughed as she staggered toward the hut clutching her stomach; she heard them telling Felipe with many cackles about the iguana. From the hut, she watched as they smoked marijuana and played their offbeat music. A half hour passed. Then Felipe said something to El Mono, who nodded and began to play Felipe's tune. Leslie crawled through the slatted palms at the rear of the hut and circled the clearing. She had to wait ten interminable minutes before Felipe appeared with frantic gestures.

He kept hurrying her along during their flight to the waterfall. A hundred yards downstream, he waded swiftly into a cluster of canes and pulled out a small flat-bottomed boat with an outboard motor.

"We cannot use the motor," he whispered. "We must float downstream."

Leslie crouched in the bow while Felipe steered the boat with a short paddle from the stern. A dozen times they ran aground in the dark and she had to jump into the mud and push the boat off.

Hours later, it seemed, Felipe nosed the boat into the bank and said: "Here we can walk to the road."

She struggled up the bank and followed him as he sped silently along. Twice, he had to stop while she disentangled herself from mangrove roots. Another time, she fell in muck and when she got up she could no longer see him.

"Felipe," she whispered. There was no reply. She called in panic. "Felipe!"

She heard a grunt and started toward it. The water was knee-deep, and plants clutched at her legs with slimy fingers. She lost a shoe pulling free but decided there was no time to look for it. But she could not find Felipe.

It must be the wrong direction. Leslie turned back and then she saw the shadow waiting for her.

"Felipe!" She held out her hand gladly. "I'd better hang on to you——"

She saw then that it was not Felipe but El Gato. El Gato put his hand on her intimately and twisted her arm and propelled her up the path with derisive thrusts of his body, laughing all the while.

He yanked at her arm and she squealed with the pain. Then a bright light flashed in her face, blinding her. The light walked down her body like an animal and stopped at the ground before her feet. She could see now that the light was in the cadaverous hand of Delgado. In his left hand, for, in his right hand, he held a blackly glittering machete.

Leslie stared at the thing that lay on the ground between them and said, "Felipe," but Felipe gave no answer. He lay on his stomach with his arms out at his side like a swan-diver's; his head lay several feet away with the dark river of his blood between them. Leslie opened her mouth, but only a dry noise came out, like the cry of a beetle.

And then it seemed to her that a great many bees were humming far away.

The next sounds Leslie heard were the coughing of an outboard engine and a rush of water. She opened her eyes.

She was lying in the boat. El Gato was sitting in the bow making a hole of light in the darkness ahead with his flash. She turned her head. At the tiller sat the cadaver. Beside him squatted a woman in Mexican dress whose face was hidden by a dark shawl.

Delgado seemed to be looking at her. Leslie could not be sure because the sockets of his eyes seemed hollow. His lips moved and his hollow voice came out of his hollow chest.

"How much is your old lady worth, kid?"

Leslie looked around, but El Gato was intent on gouging holes in the night and the Mexican woman had not stirred. She turned back to gape at Delgado.

"You're an American!"

"That was a long time ago," said Delgado.

"An *American!*"

"A long time." He laughed.

Leslie watched him pull the machete from underneath the seat and lay it across his corpselike knees. The machete was patchy with Felipe's blood. The face above it was deader than Felipe's. Delgado hasn't been anything for a long time, Leslie thought mechanically.

"I asked you a question, kid."

"I don't know exactly," Leslie said.

"You got any idea why she wouldn't pay a lousy few grand to get you back alive?"

"No. It's not possible. There's something terribly wrong. She'll pay."

"You better hope she does. One other thing. Did Felipe spot your boy friend in the village?"

"No," Leslie said a little too quickly.

There was no time to prepare; yet she saw the action in minute detail as if this was all a film and she was watching it in slow motion. His hand came out. It was just bones covered with bloody skin. There were six fat hairs on the knuckle-to-first joint section of the middle finger. All his fingernails were torn. This was his left hand and it took hold of her hair and pulled up gently and she saw the machete come up in his right hand and come down, all very gently. That was all she saw because she fell back then in the boat.

Ten

Reid waited under the big banyan. The half-mile-long beach was deserted except for a few pigs rooting in the sand behind a sea-food restaurant. A silent juke box on a dance floor reflected the pale light of a gibbous moon.

He kept staring out over the long line of surf to the crawling waters of the bay. A light showed between two jutting ridges that all but pinched the bay off from the sea, but that was on a rock far out. Another light bobbed over the stubby charter boats clustered about the concrete jetty like the pigs behind the restaurant. And there were lights in the resort hotels along the eastern shore of the bay. But that was it.

Reid did not expect Felipe to come at all now. It was three in the morning; the Mex had said before midnight. But what else was there to do?

A foot scraped on the terrace of the Bel Mar Hotel. But it was Karen, wearing a beachcoat over the shorts and halter she had worn since her arrival. He stepped out from under the tree.

"He's not coming, Karen."

"Is there any chance he really knew where Leslie is?"

Reid nodded, studying her drawn face in the dead light. Karen had certainly changed. She had shrugged the chip off her shoulder, dropped her false-face of masculinity. She no longer opposed him for opposition's sake; there was the inkling of a partnership, even a touch of tenderness when she changed the dressings on his healing wound.

135

They had hardly slept since leaving the ruined church in Sangre de Cristo. It had been a thirty-hour drive down to the Pacific Coast village of Zihuatanejo, whose only connection with the world was a landing strip and a hundred and fifty miles of hurricane-devastated highway which passed through villages still buried in sand. The last fifty miles were unpaved, gullied by the rains and rutted by banana trucks.

How to begin looking for Leslie had been a question still unresolved on their arrival in Zihuatanejo. Then Reid worked something out. El Mono and Blackie were *marijuanos;* if they had contacts here, the contacts might also be smokers.

Cautious inquiries had turned up the information that all *mota* connections in the area led to soldiers. It was said that many of the *soldados* smoked. Reid had lounged across the street from the barracks and after watching the men drowsing on the steps and plodding sleepy-eyed along the beach, he knew it was true.

The only thing was, he could not approach them. Their lieutenant was a clear-eyed young officer with a .45 on his hip. And Reid had overheard him speaking excellent English to the Americans who flew in from Acapulco and Mexico City. The lieutenant was the only law there was in this back country, and his eyes and his .45 made a forbidding combination. Reid kept out of his way.

So he had had no recourse but to begin a search of houses in and about the village. He and Karen strolled the streets hand in hand like lovers, tense with the knowledge that they were walking targets. And then they had been accosted by the little Mexican, Felipe . . . .

Reid slipped his arm about Karen's waist. She went iron-hard for only a moment. Then she became all softness again, and he began to walk her back to the hotel. He was very conscious of her hip against his thigh.

"He knew, all right. It's possible he couldn't make it

tonight. In which case, he may try again tomorrow. If he does, we'll set a trap for him."

Karen came to the slightest pause as they reached the door of their room, looking up at him. But when he smiled, she nodded and went into the room. He heard the key turn over.

Reid slung a hammock before the door. He had borrowed it from the hotel manager with the explanation that he liked to sleep in the open. The manager had naturally looked incredulous; they were registered as man and wife. But then he had shrugged and gone for the hammock. Who could say what went on in the head of a crazy American?

The hammock had been a security measure as well. But it was chiefly because of Karen's embarrassment each time they had had to share a room in their man-wife masquerade.

Reid got into the hammock, arranged the netting around his head, and fell asleep with his hand on the .32 in his belt.

The following morning Reid rented a house. It was a beach house on a narrow strip of sand a quarter of a mile from the village proper, separated from the main beach by a shallow river and a rocky headland thrusting into the sea.

The house had blackened walls, a tile roof, and two tiny rooms containing a table, two stools, a two-burner kerosene stove, and two canvas Mexican beds swathed in mosquito netting. Conch shells lay in a line before the house; bleached, half-covered by sand, they looked like the bones of the long-dead.

He went over the plan with Karen and then climbed the cliff behind the house. He crept out on an overhanging rock covered with brush and hexagon cactus, searched the ground for scorpions, lay down on his stomach.

He could see the entire bay through the field glasses.

Their own beach was a yellow ribbon of sand dotted with black rocks that looked like seals in the sun. To the east, a barrier of rock isolated them from the crescent beach that served the Hotel Irma. Further east, a pebble beach ended in a sheer cliff, the height of a five-story building. Then came the two-mile-long ribbon of Las Moscas Beach, anchored at one end by the Hotel Catalina and at the other by more cliffs. It was early; only a few fishermen were out, casting their nets in shallow water.

Reid saw Karen come out of the house with a blanket and a bottle of lotion and stroll down the narrow beach a bit. She threw the blanket on the sand, smoothed it out, sat down, daubed herself with the lotion, then set the lotion aside, stretched out on her stomach and unfastened her halter. Her golden back lay exposed to the coccyx.

That ought to do it, Reid thought. In Mexico or anywhere else, for that matter. It was a mighty pleasant sight, mighty pleasant.

He laid the .32 on the rock. He could not hope for accuracy at this distance, but it beat throwing stones.

Not a soul showed up until nine o'clock, when half a dozen boys romped onto the beach and began playing soccer. Karen adjusted her halter, got up, and went into the house. When the boys left, some schoolgirls appeared and dashed into the water with their clothes on. Reid watched them for a while. The sun climbed. Perspiration soaked his shirt.

The schoolgirls left, and Karen reappeared. She was still in shorts and halter, but she had put on the enormous floppy hat he had bought her in Acapulco. She began strolling up and down the beach, stooping idly now and then to pick up a shall.

At noon, Reid ate the canned beef and biscuit he had brought with him.

For the next three hours, the beach was deserted except for Karen, who had borrowed a book from the hotel and lain down under a palm-leaf shelter to read. Her body looked relaxed, but he noticed that she was chain-smoking. He found himself wishing she would stop.

Suddenly, a figure appeared on the rocks at the western end of the beach and climbed down. Reid's stomach tightened. It was the lieutenant of the soldiers.

The officer strode briskly along the hard-packed sand, his .45 slapping against his hip. Reid watched him with welling anxiety. He stopped before Karen, saluted impeccably, and through the glass Reid saw his lips move. After a moment Karen laid aside her book and got to her feet, saying something. The lieutenant saluted again with great courtesy and began to follow her. Karen walked rather quickly back to the beach house and the soldier went inside with her.

Reid waited nervously.

Five minutes later the lieutenant came out and strode off toward the village. A moment later Karen appeared in the doorway. Without looking toward the cliff she held her hand close to her stomach, and with her thumb and forefinger formed a circle. *All okay.*

Reid relaxed. He watched her stroll to the rocks at the end of the beach, climb them, and disappear from view.

Five minutes later, her voice said behind him: "The lieutenant wanted to see our papers." She was standing on the path looking out to sea.

"That's all we need," he said, without turning. "To have the army on our backs! What did you do?"

"I showed him mine and said you were out exploring. He was very polite. Said there was no hurry, you could bring them in any time this afternoon."

Reid chewed this over; he looked eighty years old. "Maybe he'll forget. You'd better get back. No, wait." He knuckled his eyes. "Our man may be afraid to show himself in daylight. When it gets dark, light the kerosene lamp and turn it down for just a second every ten minutes. That way I'll know he hasn't sneaked in the back way."

"All right," Karen said. He heard the retreating scrape of her sandals.

Toward sunset, the beach came alive. A pair of skin divers swam past, snorkels whooshing, vanishing from time to time with a flash of swimfins. Charter boats returned from the sea; people collected on the jetty to examine the catch. Full darkness saw the arrival of strolling lovers; trolling fishermen began to spread out over the bay; their lanterns bobbed on the swell. Reid watched the lamplit patch of sand before the house, feeling relief each time the light dimmed and brightened. The moon climbed in the east, casting black shadows on the sand. Reid tried to loosen up. If something didn't happen soon . . . .

He braced himself. One of the beach strollers had stopped five yards from the house. A flash of white, a tinkle of glass and the man started running away. Reid jumped up, stumbled, cursed his stiffened joints, and scrambled down the cliff. He reached the beach just as the man was pushing a boat out through the surf. Reid heard the sputter of an outboard, fired the .32 and missed. He ran into the surf and fired again, but the boat was almost out of range. And there were only three cartridges left in the gun. Raging, Reid watched the craft scud between the rocks and head south in the open sea at full speed.

A boat, a boat, he thought. He raced for the house. Karen . . . .

Karen stood, dazed in the lamplight. She tried to speak, failed, and pointed to a sheet of crumpled newspaper on the floor, evidently the wrapping for a group of objects lying on and near it that the fleeing man had thrown through the window. Reid knelt to examine them.

The objects were: a small rock, a swatch of rich chestnut hair—Leslie's, unmistakably, a note . . . and a human finger.

It was a female finger, a little finger, which had been severed neatly at the second joint. The flesh had retracted from the bone and was lightly spattered with dried bloodstains. Circling it, was the birthstone ring Reid had seen last on Leslie's little finger.

Blindly, Reid picked up the note and smoothed out the dirty piece of paper:

Get the dough from her old lady. Every day it goes higher. Now it's $15,000. Two days from now it's $20,000. And every day, I will send you another finger.

Reid got to his feet. His voice sounded very strange. "I'm going after him."

Karen was in shock; he had to take her arm and haul her along the sand, over the rocks, onto the main beach. Halfway to the jetty Karen fell to her knees, sobbing.

"It's too much, Reid. I can't take any more."

He leaned over her. "All right. You wait in the hotel."

"Reid, please. Let's wire Mama—have her send the money. What good are we doing? Let's put this in the hands of the Mexican authorities. We've got enough proof —this note, the finger——"

Karen shuddered and hugged herself as if she were cold. Reid pulled her to her feet. She was limp; he had to half carry her.

"Karen, you've got to believe me. I know these people. If we invite the Mexican law in, it will only get Leslie killed before she can be rescued."

"How can you be so sure they'd kill her?"

"These men are *marijuanos*. They're in a constant state of detachment from reality. Killing means nothing to them —no more than cutting off the finger. It would be like acting in a movie. All but Delgado—he's something else again. But he wouldn't hesitate, either, if he's threatened."

She shook him off suddenly. "All right. I'm coming with you."

He looked at her tearstained face. It was set hard.

"Then come on. Run!"

At the end of the jetty sat a group of Mexicans, smoking. Reid pointed to a fast-looking diesel launch named *Margarita*.

"De quién es?"

A small man got to his feet, tossed a cigaret into the water, and sauntered to the edge of the jetty. He peered at the boat as though he had never seen it before.

"I am the owner," he said in Spanish. "Where do you wish to go?"

"Out to sea," said Reid, waving.

"Sí, mañana."

"Right now!"

The man shook his head. Reid pulled out a wad of U.S. currency. It came to about a hundred dollars. The man shuffled through it, shoved it into his pants pocket, and untied the line.

Reid shoved Karen aboard, leaped to the wheel and pulled on the starter. The engine sputtered and caught and the owner gave an angry yell as the *Margarita* roared off without him.

They were only a few yards out when a spotlight stabbed Reid from shore. He glanced over his shoulder and saw the silhouette of a jeep, alive with helmeted men, parked at the end of the jetty. A splinter of wood flew from the cabin and he heard the crack of a .45.

"Get down!" he shouted to Karen.

She seemed frozen. More wood spattered, accompanied by the bark of rifle fire. Reid tripped her roughly to the deck and crouched as low as he could at the wheel. More bullets struck the boat. A splinter of wood gouged his forearm. Reid jerked it out and looked back. The *soldados* had stopped shooting and were piling into a launch.

He slipped the boat between the rocks and headed for the sea. To starboard, black water stretched emptily to Japan. He felt the old grip of fear and fought to shake it off.

Two miles down the rocky coast Reid caught sight of the outboard. It looked like a little dark chip, floating on the choppy sea—bobbing, disappearing, then bobbing up again. It hugged the coast just outside the breaker line. Reid estimated that he would need five miles more to overtake it.

Reid shook his head and turned to Karen, who was standing beside him, her black hair tumbling in the wind. "Go into the bow and watch him through the glasses. Sing out the moment he heads in to shore."

Karen scrambled for the bow. He glanced back. The launchful of soldiers was four hundred yards behind, riding low in the water and not gaining. A Mexican standoff, Reid thought with a sour grin. Rifles were going off in the other launch; they sounded like faint firecrackers and twinkled like fireflies. A bullet thunked somewhere in the *Margarita*'s hull, close by, and his back began to itch. He was glad that the cabin was between the pursuing launch and Karen.

"He's pulling in!" Karen cried.

Reid peered ahead and indulged in some fancy Texas profanity. The outboard he was chasing had darted into what appeared to be an inaccessible lagoon. It was cut off from the sea by toothy rocks that chewed the surf into pulpy fragments. The shallow-draft outboard had managed to get over, but the *Margarita* drew at least three feet of water . . . .

"Come here, Karen!" Reid shouted. "Show me exactly where and how he went in. And keep down!"

She came running back in a crouch and jabbed toward

a low point in the rocky wall. Three waves crashed and
broke there, but the fourth went over in a sheet. He eased
up to the gap, and fought with engines reversed to keep
from smashing the hull, praying for a wave big enough
to carry him over and into the lagoon. The soldiers'
launch drew nearer; a bullet splintered a spoke of the
steering wheel. Karen hit the deck without being told.
Reid, wishing he could join her there, gripped the wheel
and looked around. The sea was mounding up behind
him; a giant was coming. Behind it the sea stretched flat.
It was now or never.

He aimed the keel carefully to pass through the lowest
point of the barrier. The boat began to lift, and he gunned
his engine to stay precisely with the crest of the wave. As
they went through he heard a monstrous scraping sound.
The *Margarita* shuddered under his feet and careened almost onto its side. And then they were in the lagoon.

"You made it!" Karen screamed.

Reid grinned, not sourly this time, and steered straight
for the black hole in the jungle that marked the river's
mouth.

Then Karen was shrieking, "Reid, they're coming over!
They're coming over, too!"

Reid glanced back quickly. He saw the cruiser heave
up, smash down with a thundering thump, then lift again.
After it smashed down the second time, it stayed down,
stuck. Helmeted figures began splashing into the lagoon.

They were a mere hundred yards upriver when the *Margarita* stopped with an impact that slammed him against
the wheel. Reid reversed the engines with no effect. The
launch began to settle fast. He took a look into the cabin
and caught the sheen of water on the floor.

"Got holed crossing the reef." He killed the engine.
"We'll have to make it on shoe leather, Karen."

They waded to the bank and Reid found a burro trail
winding alongside the river. He began to slosh along in

the pearly moonlight with Karen trotting in his wake. He stopped abruptly, and she bumped into him.

"Don't look, Karen," he said swiftly; but she had already seen it. She grabbed his arm and held on, shuddering.

It was a savagely scattered collection of human bones picked nearly clean by buzzards, wild dogs and ants. The clothing had been ripped to shreds. What was left of the head lay some distance from the rest of the body.

"Turn your back," Reid muttered.

She obeyed, gulping. Fighting his own battle with nausea, Reid poked around in the remains of the clothing, took a close look at the neck and the distant head.

"Close your eyes, Karen."

She closed her eyes, and he steered her around the remains and back onto the burro trail.

After awhile he said, "It's all right now."

She opened her eyes; she was still gulping.

"That was Felipe," he said.

"Who?" Karen asked feebly.

"The Mexican boy who didn't show up. And that's why he didn't. I recognized what was left of the clothes."

"But how——?"

"He had his head sliced off with a machete."

She shuddered again. "You mean because——?"

He gave her his indifferent Mexican shrug. When Reid realized what he was doing, he deliberately put his hands into his pockets.

"You'd better sit down on this stump for a while, Karen," he said gently. "You're panting like a puma."

"But that outboard we were following——"

"Listen." The sputter of the outboard upriver was almost inaudible by now. "We'll never catch him on foot. Sit down. You'll need your strength."

She sat down on the stump. He squatted against it, breathing deeply. You'll need more than strength if Delgado catches us, he thought; and kept breathing deeply.

"All right, Karen, let's go," Reid said.

"Didn't you hear that voice?" Karen asked.

"Yes." He had been listening for some time to the faint sounds of the Mexican lieutenant's voice giving commands. The soldiers were not too far away.

"The soldiers, Reid?"

"That lieutenant will go far if Mexico ever fights a war. Now we'd better make tracks."

She nodded and jumped up. He hurried her up the path.

It wound up and down the bank, crossed gullies, wandered through stretches of overgrown muck. Every few minutes he made Karen stop for a breather. She had long since been reduced to moaning misery by the mosquitoes. The sounds of the pursuing *soldados* were faint, but it seemed to Reid that he and Karen were losing ground.

"We can't afford to stop any more," he said. "We've got to step up the pace."

"I can't, Reid——"

"Then I'll have to carry you."

He carried her piggy-back until she protested that she could walk again.

As he set her down, she said, "What's that roaring up ahead?"

"A waterfall. He'll have to leave his outboard there. From here on in, it's walking on eggs, Karen. I was out of my mind to bring you."

"I was out of my mind to come."

They found the outboard drawn up on the bank of a rock-walled pool fed by a twenty-five foot waterfall. Reid hid Karen under an overhang and circled the area. When he found another path he came back for her and the way she clutched him told him a long story.

Stealthily, they followed the path. They had not gone more than a few hundred yards when Reid put a warning hand on Karen's arm. He left her crouched in a bush and crawled forward. He was gone five minutes.

When Reid came back he whispered, "There's a camp up ahead. We've found them. Can you move like a ghost?"

"I can try." Her whisper gurgled.

They lay in the brush at the edge of the clearing. In the moon's eerie shine, the clearing looked dead. But Reid silently pointed out hammocks hanging between the trees; from the ashes of a campfire, a trickle of smoke arose. He watched the hut concentratedly for several minutes. Finally, he put his mouth to Karen's ear.

"Stay here."

She nodded. Her mosquito-bitten face was swollen up like a balloon; she had to squint to see clearly.

Reid disappeared. Minutes later, Karen heard a very slight sound to her left and saw his hand appear from behind a big palm tree and work a machete loose that had been stuck in the bole. He waited and watched again. Then he stepped noiselessly into the clearing and signaled to her.

She came to him then, gladly, and he handed her the .32 and took a good grip on the machete. They tiptoed to the hut. There was somebody in there, a dark and shapeless figure curled up on a straw *petate*, a woman.

Karen's heart jumped. Leslie!

Reid read her thought and shook his head. He sprang into the hut and was on the woman in a moment, knees pinning her arms to the pallet, left hand over her mouth. She struggled for a moment, then went limp.

"Light a match, Karen."

In the flare of the match they saw that it was a Mexican woman, her dark skin bearing the telltale reddish undertint of the *mestizo*. She appeared middle-aged.

"Dónde está la güera?" Reid asked harshly.

She stared back at him with feverish black eyes. Her left hand was wrapped in a bloody cloth. He seized her wrist and unwrapped the cloth. Karen uttered a faint cry. The woman's little finger was missing at the first joint. The wound was festering.

"The finger wasn't Leslie's after all," Reid said. *"Quién lo hizo?"* he asked the woman. "Delgado?"

She nodded sullenly.

"Do you work for him?"

She looked at him with contempt and drew her shawl together. "Does not a wife always work for her husband?"

"Delgado is your husband?"

"Since he took me from the prison island, we have lived together. That makes me a wife, no?"

"Where did he take the American girl?"

She pinched her lips together and pulled the shawl over them. Reid controlled himself—he was wasting irre- trievable time, the soldiers were hot on their necks, but this *mestizo* woman could not be forced.

"I don't want Delgado. I just want the girl." He put his hand on Karen's shoulder. "This is her sister, *Señora.* Look at her and say to her, *Señora,* that you are willing to let her sister die."

The status symbol of the title did it. Delgado's woman stared at Karen, then slipped off the pallet and shuffled out of the hut. They followed her to the edge of the clearing.

She pointed to a path leading off through tall grass. "Follow this path for four kilometers, *Señor.* You will come to the place where they grow the *mota.* That is where my husband took her."

Reid took a fresh grip on the machete and started up the path, Karen at his heels.

It happened with great rapidity when they were only a short distance from the clearing: Reid's consciousness of a different sound behind him, Karen's cry, the weight land- ing on his back and bearing him to the ground.

His attacker was all speed and power. A steel forearm had Reid's nose crushed against his face and his breath cut off; a knife blade caressed his throat. This is it, this is curtains, Reid thought—no preparation, no warning, the stupid end of a stupid enterprise, without meaning or purpose. He felt the man's muscles bunching for the slash and then there was a dull *crack!* and the man collapsed on him, a dead weight.

Reid pushed him off and got to his feet. Karen's swollen face was rigid with accomplishment. Smoke curled from the gun in her hand.

He touched his throat; it came away bloody. "That, Miss Frankel," he said huskily, "was as close as I ever want to come. Thanks. You learned how to shoot at a very good time."

Karen's lips moved. "I couldn't let him kill you, Reid."

He examined the dead man in the false dawn. Karen's bullet had left a small hole below the left ear; it had lodged in the skull. Most of the blood had come out through the mouth. He recognized the man as the Mexican who had been holding Leslie in the thicket. Judging by the streaks of black grease and dried salt on his shirt sleeves, the dead man had probably been Delgado's messenger, the one who had hurled the note through the beach cottage window and escaped in the outboard.

Reid got up. "We'd better hurry," he said to Karen. "Maybe they didn't hear the shot. If they didn't—and if the lieutenant and his men don't catch up with us first—we may be able to take them by surprise."

They topped the ridge at sunrise. At their feet, stretched a long narrow valley; beyond, rose a high cliff. Smoke swirled upward from the matted jungle at the foot of the cliff. The smoke was the only sign of human life.

They worked their way cautiously around until they were on the opposite cliff. From there, they could see down to the clearing in the valley. Through the field glasses, Reid made out a lean-to of palm leaves and Leslie lying inside, her hands tied behind her. Her clothes were in rags, she was scratched and dirty, but, otherwise, she appeared unharmed. Blackie was walking restlessly about the clearing playing a game of throw-the-machete with a coconut tree as his target. El Mono sat astride a fallen palm trunk strumming his guitar. And Delgado . . . Delgado was there, too, squatting on the ground, his caricature of a face totally without expression. Occasionally, his death mask squinted over at the jungle.

"He's waiting for his messenger to report delivery of the note," Reid muttered to Karen. "Looks as if they didn't hear the shot after all."

"What do we do now?" Karen whispered. "There are three of them."

"I'll have to cut down the odds."

"Kill them?"

"Well, if I go in blasting, one of them is almost sure to get Leslie. I'm afraid I can't risk it."

"No," she said fiercely. "Kill them one at a time."

Reid waited until he saw Blackie give up the game and leave the clearing. As the little man disappeared into the jungle, Reid tapped Karen's arm reassuringly, crawled to some undergrowth which encroached on the cliff, and made his way silently down the slope, slipping from bush to bush until he reached the valley floor some distance from the clearing but on a line with the point at which Blackie had entered the jungle. Here he stopped to listen. He heard a rustling and some muttered Spanish and followed the sounds . . . .

Blackie was squatting in the bushes in a primitive fashion, knees hugged to his chest. His back was to Reid.

Reid stood up and threw the machete. It turned in the air and the hilt struck the back of Blackie's head with a solid thud. The little man fell forward on his face and lay still.

Reid worked in swift silence. He bound and gagged Blackie with the man's shirt and jeans, rolled him under a giant fern, then listened intently. He made his way back to the top of the cliff. "I got Blackie. That leaves two," he informed Karen.

She nodded. "You'll have to hurry. Look!"

Reid looked at the ridge across the valley through which they had come and to which she was pointing. Bobbing along the path which Reid and Karen had climbed were numerous dully gleaming helmets.

"The lieutenant must have got Delgado's woman to talk," Reid said. "We may have just enough time. Listen, Karen."

He told her his plan quickly. They would slip down to the clearing together. El Mono and Delgado were too far apart to be covered by the same gun. He would have to attack from the far end of the clearing with the machete and jump El Mono. The trouble was, El Mono's log was twenty feet from the jungle's edge, and there was a machete leaning against the log at El Mono's feet. So her confrontation with Delgado at the other side of the clearing must not only immobilize Delgado, but, at least momentarily, hold El Mono's attention, too. To this end, Karen must step out of the jungle near Delgado before Reid showed himself and say something sharply. Could she do it?

Karen licked her lips and nodded.

"Are you sure? You'll be covering Delgado with the .32. He may respect it or he may not. You're to shoot him without hesitation if you have to. Can you do that?"

She nodded again.

"Good girl. Here we go."

They separated at the bottom of the slope under cover of the jungle. Reid made his way around to where El Mono was sitting. He peered through the foliage of a banana tree, saw Karen step out of the jungle across the clearing with the gun before her, heard her begin to say, "Put your hands——" and waited to see and hear no more. He hurled himself across the twenty feet of clearing toward El Mono.

Something went wrong; what it was, Reid had no time to analyze. All he knew was that, before he could reach

El Mono, the boy was on his feet, machete in hand, ready to parry Reid's slash. Their machetes clanged together, striking sparks. Then Reid was fighting for his life.

El Mono was quick, quick. His long arms moved like whips; his machete was like a tongue of flame. For an eternity Reid parried death. Then he sensed a sudden slackening in his opponent. El Mono was puffing, sweating. It was the marijuana. The boy's lungs were burned out . . .

Reid called on the coiled fury—against Delgado, Mexico, May Gibson, his own stupidity—in his body. He sprang to the attack; El Mono dodged too late. With a soft *tic!* Reid's machete sliced through the slim throat just below the bulge of the Adam's apple. A geyser of red shot up and El Mono was falling. Before the blade completed its arc, Reid whirled to see what was happening at the other side of the clearing . . . and groaned.

Delgado was clutching Leslie Gibson to him, knife point pressed to her throat; the girl's eyes were glassy—Reid doubted that she was conscious. Karen stood facing them with the most stricken look he had ever seen. Her gun was pointed at the ground.

He heard Delgado's surprising American voice say, "Throw the gun towards me," to Karen, and to Reid, "And you, Sport. Drop the blade. Or the kid gets stuck like a pig."

Reid dropped the machete.

In a voice brittle with horror Karen said, "I tripped, Reid, I tripped, I tripped. What am I going to do?"

"Do what he says." The words tasted very bitter.

Karen tossed the .32 at Delgado's feet, sank to the ground staring at her half sister.

Delgado did not let go of Leslie until he had picked up the gun. Then he went about the clearing gathering up the other weapons. At no time did he turn his back on Reid. Leslie simply sat on the ground, glassy-eyed; if she recognized Karen or Reid, she gave no sign of it. She had apparently gone through more than even her ebullient spirit could fight off.

The cadaverous man pointed the gun at Reid. "Where is the dough?"

"There isn't any, Delgado. We came to tell you that. Give us the girl. You can still go free."

Delgado cocked his head like a listening bird. He was staring at a point several feet above Reid's head. "You got the note, right? So you know it's twenty grand now. You get it and you bring it here."

He stooped, circled Leslie's waist with one arm, straightened up and, half dragging her, backed into the jungle.

Reid did not move. Where were the *soldados?*

Karen made a sound.

"What?" Reid asked.

"Doesn't he understand that there's no point in any of this?"

"He doesn't understand anything, Karen. The record is going around and around in the same groove. The only voices he hears are the ones in his head."

"He's . . . crazy?"

"Quiet." He listened. "He's taking her up the cliff. *Karen.*"

"What?"

"Do you hear me?"

"I heard you."

"I'm going to try to draw his fire. Maybe I can get him to empty the gun. Meanwhile, you start climbing up the other slope and see if you can delay those soldiers. Keep them from firing on Delgado till you don't hear any more shots."

Karen asked stifly, "What about Leslie?"

"She's the only protection Delgado has. She's no good to him dead. We've got to hope he's rational enough to realize it."

Harry Schmidt, alias Delgado, crouched behind a boulder and watched the tall man's darting, erratic progress up the cliff. Across the valley, on the far slope, he could see the soldiers coming down toward the clearing with the other girl, this one's sister, waving her arms, clinging to some of then, trying to hold them back. It interested him in a mild sort of way. There were other things to think about. Harry Schmidt, alias Delgado, was run to earth. He knew it; there was no escape from this one. It was the end. Of a full life. Not a good life, but certainly full.

He laughed, talking to himself. When were you ever such a tough guy, Harry? They didn't know how you hated fights, how scared you were. And they also didn't know—till it was too late—that when they pushed you into a brawl something inside of you took charge, a little red beast that never knew when to stop. That time you were beached in Tampico and the drunken soldier went for you and the little beast saw its own bright blood and made you smash the bottle and go for the throat—lunge —slash—twist. They gave you ten years on the Island for that, but the little beast didn't mind, he lived on that soldier's blood for a long time. On the Island, men died from *paludismo,* from bushmasters, from amebic dysentery, from God knew what. But the little beast saw that you survived.

He glanced at the American girl trussed up beside him. He had ripped off her sweater and tied her feet as well as her hands, and he had used a piece of the wool to stuff in her mouth. She had a big mouth, this kid, with her talk of *why-don't-you-give-yourself-up-you're-an-American-they-wouldn't-kill-anyone-in-your-condition,* as if he were some sort of nut or something. She was bad news, all right. It was all Fatty's fault for snatching her in the first place.

He stared at her flesh and the torn brassière and tried to remember the last time he had had an American woman and could not. They were no good, anyway. She was still talking to him with her eyes. He didn't like her eyes.

"Stop talking to me!" Along with the shout, he clouted her across the face. Under the gag she screamed; it came out more like a whinny, and Harry laughed again.

Helen's eyes had been something like that. Especially when she had begged him not to go off to sea, to stay and take a job in the mill and get hitched. And again, but worse, that time he came back and found out she'd got married and the little red beast climbed to the back of his neck and sank its lobster claws into the base of his brain and made him leave her for her husband with her face black and her tongue sticking out under the pillow, and her eyes . . . .

He struck Leslie again. She fell back and lay quiet. That would teach her to talk to him with her eyes.

Not that she was a bad kid, this kid. She had guts. Well, it was too bad. Life was tough and he had seen a lot of people die. On the Island, each death had meant more life for Harry Schmidt—fewer mouths to feed. More for old Harry. And, of course, for the beast.

Delgado raised the gun, took aim, and fired. The man fell down behind a rock about twenty yards away.

"Got you," said Delgado.

"Guess again," yelled the man, showing himself. "You're a lousy shot, Delgado!"

He shot again and again. And then the gun would shoot no more. The man rose and began to walk up the escarpment in a leisurely way.

"Give up, Delgado," the man said, very friendly. "The gun is empty."

"The hell it is, Sport, I got one more," said Harry Schmidt, alias Delgado. "You take another step and I shoot it right in the kid's eye. She talks too damn much with that eye."

"Don't, don't!" the man cried, and got down behind

a rock again. He began to wave frantically to the soldiers, who were on their way up the cliff. "Back, stay back!"

Harry laughed and picked up a stick and began to sharpen it with his knife. It was good hard wood and it made a good spear.

"Leslie! You all right?" yelled the man.

The kid was game, all right, she tried to get to her feet; she couldn't make it, but she was game. The best she could so was get to her knees and her head must have showed or something because the guy gave another yell and began to assure Delgado that, as long as he hadn't hurt the girl, he could give himself up and no one would hurt *him*. That was a funny thing to say because all the time he was yelling about giving up, the guy was trying to claw his way the last few yards to the top of the cliff.

Delgado got to his feet. The girl was watching him from her knees, her eyes stiff with horror. Speechless, at last.

"Better shut your eyes, kid," Harry Schmidt, alias Delgado, said to her kindly; and he planted the tip of the stake between two of the ribs over his heart, and, gripping the stake firmly with both hands, he fell over on it just as a bullet tore into his brain from halfway down the cliff. Over the lip of the cliff came the Sport, clawing at him like the little red beast who would claw at him no more.

"You were taking a hell of a chance, Lieutenant," said Reid angrily, "snapping off that uphill shot. You might have hit the girl."

"I thought he was going to stab her," the lieutenant said. "My apology, Mr. Rance."

"I'm sorry," said Reid. "Of course, you couldn't know. That was a most delicate shot."

The lieutenant nodded, pleased, and offered Reid a cigaret. They puffed in amity. "And yet I should have known," the lieutenant admitted.

"That he would kill himself?"

The officer shrugged and toed Harry Schmidt's body, rolling it half over. "I have been studying this man's face on the posters for many years, *Señor*. I should have known he would kill himself in the end. He would surely have been executed. He was a wolf, a tiger, a madman." He added with a smile, "A countryman of yours."

They went down the cliff to the clearing while some soldiers followed with Schmidt's body. Leslie and Karen sat on El Mono's log with their arms about each other. Leslie had her head cradled between Karen's breasts. Karen was murmuring to her. A few yards away, the flies were busy on El Mono. The lieutenant said something in Spanish and two of his soldiers took machetes and ran into the jungle to cut palm branches for stretchers to transport the corpses.

"Lieutenant," said Reid. He was very tired, but at peace. "Why did you follow us from the jetty?"

"The men there said you shot at a man who was going off in an outboard. One man complained to me that you had stolen his launch. I could not avoid the conclusion that you were a desperate criminal. Otherwise, would you not have asked me for assistance?"

"That, Lieutenant, does not necessarily follow," said Reid. "Anyway, it's a very long and probably incomprehensible story."

"On the contrary," the Mexican lieutenant said. "I understand very well about the kidnaping and what led up to it. Your wife has explained everything." He glanced admiringly over at Karen.

"Well, not everything," Reid said dryly. "For instance, the lady isn't my wife."

"Not your wife?" The lieutenant's brows arched. "But you occupied the same house, Mr. Rance . . . Ah, I see. I beg your pardon." He gave Reid a little bow. "It is the same with us, *Señor*. Perhaps the formalities come later?"

Reid looked at Karen. She was still crooning over Leslie, rocking on the log like a little girl with her doll, or a young mother with her infant. She looked nothing like the Karen who had started out for Mexico with him, nothing at all. She seemed to feel his glance, because she looked up suddenly, and smiled.

Reid smiled back, and said to the lieutenant, "Perhaps. *Quién sabe?*"

Beware the
Young Stranger

Cast of Characters

1.

Vallancourt was the last of the foursome to reach the locker room. Coming off the eighteenth green, he had been hailed by a gushing, well-padded matron he barely knew.

She had three out-of-town guests at a cocktail table on the clubhouse terrace, and she insisted on introducing John Vallancourt to them as "our own *distinguished* diplomat, the man who knows all the secrets of those nasty foreign countries."

Lanky and trim, a silver-and-tan man of fifty-odd years, Vallancourt exchanged small talk, managed a tactful escape, and immediately forgot the incident. He had more important things to think about. Nancy, for instance, his daughter.

In the deserted locker room, he stripped, showered, toweled briskly, and put on the dark gray Italian silk suit he had worn to the club this morning.

He made an admission to himself: he was disturbed. Playing around sixty-five hundred yards of golf course with Keith Rollins today hadn't quieted his sense of caution. Vallancourt had experienced similar emotional radar in foreign capitals when United States prestige and best interests were at stake; and in the solitude of big-game country, when the hunter was cut down to size.

His wariness over Rollins was not because the time had inevitably arrived when there must be a change in his relationship with Nancy. He was preparing for the change. The emergence of his daughter into womanhood was welcome and good. He looked forward to seeing his bloodline extended in Nancy's children . . .

Vallancourt thought he was alone. But then he turned and saw Keith Rollins at the far end of the row of lockers. The diplomat's usually warm brown eyes chilled slightly. He wondered how long the man had been standing there watching him.

Keith was smiling as he came forward—a good-looking young man of twenty-two, heavy-shouldered. His face was cut in firm, rather angular lines. He had restless eyes of dark blue, almost purple, under brows as heavily black as his curly hair.

He lit a cigarette. "Afraid we all ducked when we saw the old biddy making for you. Mr. Conway and Mr. Hibbs are in the cocktail lounge."

"I'm used to old biddies," Vallancourt said, also smiling.

Keith squinted through a wreath of smoke. "You play a bang-up game of golf, Mr. Vallancourt. Nancy warned me."

"You don't play so badly yourself. You had me scrambling right down to that wild second-shot gamble on seventeen."

"Maybe next time," Keith said.

In spite of Keith's casual friendliness, the words came out with an I'll-get-you-yet undertone. It stuck Vallancourt, coming after a whole day of observation, as being prompted by something more than a mere desire to win. The older man wondered suddenly how often before Keith's need had carried him almost to victory, then turned on him in the final moment, as it had today on the course.

Keith moved ahead, holding the locker room door open for Vallancourt.

"Anyway," Keith said, "today meant a little more to us than a golf game, didn't it?"

"In what way?"

"You wanted to look me over, didn't you?"

There was a flicker of resentment in the nightshade eyes.

"I suppose I did," replied Vallancourt.

They started down the rubber-tiled corridor in the direction of the dining room and cocktail lounge.

"At least," Keith laughed, "I'm glad you didn't suggest a weekend hunting trip in the mountains. I show up better with golf clubs than a rifle." They walked on a few steps, and he went on without a pause. "From what I hear you're pretty good at assessing people. I'd value your opinion of me, Mr. Vallancourt."

"Do you think I've had a proper chance to form one, Keith?"

"Some men in your spot would have formed one right off—even before they met the poor guy."

"And what do *you* think of *me?*" asked Vallancourt.

"You're Nancy's father. That's good enough for me."

Clever, Vallancourt thought. Designed to put the opponent on the defensive. Does he see opposition in all people? They reached the end of the vaulted corridor. Wide doors ahead swung into the dining room and bar; an archway to their left, fringed with ivy, led onto the terrace. Faint sounds of people drifted to them.

Keith paused, looking through the arch at the sun outside. "I get the message, Mr. Vallancourt. In your silence."

"Keith," Vallancourt said quietly, "aren't you jumping to conclusions?"

"How come?"

"Aren't you actually anticipating that I'm set on forming a negative opinion of you? The contrary is true."

"I know Nancy is all you have, Mr. Vallancourt, how close you two have been."

"It was my job to bring her up, Keith. Her mother died when Nancy was very young."

"More than just a job. Lots of men would have parked her in a school and let it go at that. But all those years in Cairo, Rome, Athens, you kept her with you."

"They were wonderful years." Vallancourt sighed.

"If the Secretary of State or the President need you, you'll go again. You always have. Only this time without Nancy. That must be a grim prospect."

"You're a perceptive young man, Keith, but you're wrong about that."

"I see," Keith said, slowly. "You're glad to see her grown up."

Vallancourt smiled again.

"I've known it was coming, of course."

"You just want to make sure she doesn't fly out of the nest with the wrong pigeon."

Vallancourt felt a prickle of the nape of his neck. This boy, he told himself, carried himself in an eggshell.

"Keith, why don't we give each other a little time?"

Keith's glance slid away. "Maybe you're right, Mr. Vallancourt. I get the feeling we've started off like two tomcats rounding a dark corner from opposite directions." He hesitated. "I don't want it that way, Mr. Vallancourt."

The quick shift in the boy's mood was ingratiating. Vallancourt said warmly, "Neither do I."

"Nancy and I wish it could be perfect for us," Keith said. "But, perfect or not, I know how we feel about each other. Nothing can change that, nothing."

"Then we'll have to try to put a light on that corner, won't we, Keith?"

"Yes, sir. Well, I'll cut out now. I know you want to have a drink with Mr. Conway and Mr. Hibbs."

"You're more than welcome to join us, Keith."

"Thanks. I'll take a raincheck."

"Are you seeing Nancy this evening?"

"Yes, Mr. Vallancourt."

John Vallancourt watched the boy move through the archway to the terrace. Then he slowly turned toward the cocktail lounge.

Howard Conway and Ralph Hibbs were at a table near the floor-to-ceiling windows. Vallancourt had little trouble spotting them. Few people were in the lounge; most had sought the terrace in the perfect weather. A promise of summer was in the air.

With gestures, Conway was talking golf. Hibbs nodded morosely; he had had a miserable time of it, from the first tee.

They glanced up as Vallancourt approached the table. Conway lifted his drink. "The old girl inveigle you into addressing the Thursday Literary Society?"

"Not quite."

"Buffoon like that, calling you across the terrace. It would bug me." A robust man whose awkward appearance was misleading, Conway finished his drink and eyed his glass thoughtfully.

"Oh, she probably has her points," Ralph Hibbs said. "If it was a feather in her cap to introduce John to her friends, I'm sure John didn't mind."

"For you, Ralph, everybody's got points," Conway said with a sigh. "What are you drinking, John?"

"A short Scotch will do it."

"I owe you five bucks," Hibbs said. "Let me add a drink for interest." He turned to order from the trim waitress who had come to the table. He was a big, placid, very likable man, in Vallancourt's opinion. He golfed as he did everything else, with sweating, honest effort.

"I might as well shell out, too," Conway said. "You trimmed us today, John."

"Playing over my head," Vallancourt smiled. "Keith was pressuring me. The boy is good."

"If he'd let himself be." For the benefit of the waitress, Conway jiggled his glass. He and Hibbs had a common heartiness of physique, bone and flesh. But otherwise the two men differed. There was a kind of fagged-out quality in Ralph Hibbs, a softening at the edges, a sagging of the jowls, an under-pallor in the full cheeks. His hair had grayed, thinned, and all but vanished. An ophthalmologist had put bifocals on him; an internist had prescribed pills, which Hibbs carried about with him and took faithfully.

Howard Conway's large, firm face, thick hair, quietly clear eyes made Ralph Hibbs seem bumbling by contrast. Vallancourt wasn't at all sure.

"By the way," Hibbs said, "where'd Keith get to? I thought he was waiting for you, John."

"He was. He had to leave."

"Burned off in that sport car, I bet," Conway said.

"Oh, I don't know," Hibbs said. "He's conservative behind the wheel, considering his age. Good with cars. If I add a European make at the agency, I may ask Keith to go to work for me. I think he could sell cars."

"What do you know about the boy, Howard?" Vallancourt asked Conway.

"Not much."

"You're married to one of his aunts."

"But it wasn't Ivy who brought him here to live, John."

"Then he didn't arrive at Dorcas Ferguson's on a casual visit?" Dorcas Ferguson was Ivy Conway's sister.

"No," Conway said, "he's here for good, from what I understand."

"Early today, Keith made a casual reference about his father's being in town."

"Yes, Sam Rollins got rid of that two-bit business of his downstate. Maggie—Keith's mother, the sister between Dorcas and Ivy—died last fall. The Rollinses have no more ties or connections in their old home town."

"Is Sam Rollins staying with Dorcas, too?"

"No," Howard Conway said, "he's living in a small apartment on the north side."

"I'd like to meet him." Vallancourt nodded to the waitress and tasted the mellow Scotch.

Light glinted on Hibbs's glasses as he leaned forward. "You think Nancy is really serious about Keith Rollins, John?"

"Knowing my daughter, I wouldn't be surprised if she decided to marry him. And it's happened quickly, you know. Very quickly."

"I'm sure he's a fine boy. If there's a . . . well, a hint of strain in his personality . . ."

"You noticed it, too?" Vallancourt said slowly.

Ralph Hibbs shrugged. "It hasn't been long since he lost his mother, you know."

"I was in Europe," Vallancourt said. "I'd never met Maggie Rollins or her husband or son. But I was sorry I could do nothing more than cable a word of sympathy to Dorcas."

"Dorcas managed," Conway grunted.

"Doesn't she always?" Hibbs laughed.

2.

John Vallancourt's Continental whispered its way up the elm-shaded driveway the next day, stopping in the Normandy shadow of Dorcas Ferguson's castle-like home.

Vallancourt was acquainted with the history of the mansion. Dorcas Ferguson's grandfather had built it. Her parents, social gadflies on the fringes of the international set, had lost the estate to mortgage holders in the process of squandering the modest fortune handed down to them. Years later, Dorcas had returned to native soil, paid cash for the place, and restored the house to its original condition.

The heavy oaken door swung open and Dorcas's matronly housekeeper, Mildred Morgan, smiled out at him. "Good morning, Mr. Vallancourt. Miss Ferguson is expecting you."

The housekeeper ushered him into the spacious entry hall and took his hat.

Vallancourt liked this house, for all its size. It was sound and solid, qualities which Dorcas, like

her grandfather, esteemed. She had put a great deal
of herself into the house, Vallancourt thought, in
the décor and furnishings. The lack of pretentious-
ness appealed to him. It was the home of a woman
of character.

"Miss Ferguson will be right down," Miss Morgan
said. "Mrs. Conway is waiting, too. Would you care
to join her?"

Vallancourt nodded.

"May I get you something, Mr. Vallancourt? A
cup of coffee?"

"Thanks, no."

He stepped into a long, friendly living room. Ivy
Ferguson Conway was at the grand piano, playing a
sentimental melody badly.

"Morning, John." Ivy swung herself around on
the bench. Vallancourt detected a nervousness in
her manner. "Do you have a cigarette?"

He offered her the thin, engraved gold case Nancy
had given him on his last birthday, and held a light
for her, thinking that if Dorcas was a throwback to
her grandfather, Ivy, her younger sister, was the
orthodox product of her parents.

Ivy's life was a continuity of cocktail and bridge
parties, fashion shows, country club gossip, and
shallow squabbles with Howard, her husband. Occasionally, she and Howard went abroad, and when
Ivy referred to these trips it was always with an
accent of condescension for foreign places and
foreigners.

She gave a first impression of prettiness, being
delicately made, with a fragility of feature. She had
small eyes and mousy hair worn in a casual trim.

Although she was in her thirties, girlishness clung to her.

"Oh, damn!" She coughed, her hand fluttering to her throat. "John, must you smoke these unfiltered weeds?"

"Don't inhale," Vallancourt suggested.

"Then what's the use of smoking?" Her glance kept going beyond him, to the living room entryway.

"Are you expecting someone, Ivy?"

"No," she said quickly. "You're Dorcas's only caller. I dropped in while she was phoning you this morning."

Vallancourt waited.

Her eyes pinched at the corners. "Aren't you going to ask me what she has on her mind?"

"I assume Dorcas will explain the call."

"Sure. The way she wants it explained." Ivy's nervousness was suddenly gone. She snubbed out her cigarette as if she were pressing the hot coal against something more animate than an ashtray.

"John, you're right in suspecting him," Ivy said.

He made no pretense of not understanding to whom she was referring.

"Howard told me," she said, "how you were sizing him up yesterday, during and after the round of golf."

Vallancourt lit a cigarette.

"I see," she said icily. "You don't care to discuss it."

"Is there a reason I should, Ivy?"

"Oh, most naturally not!" Her gaze was haughtily fixed on a point over his head. "Nancy, of course, is merely your daughter, and Dorcas will come in here with a whitewash brush in hand."

"Without a sense of fair play? Dorcas?" John said gently.

"Better drop the rules in the trashcan, John. I know you would value Dorcas's opinion over mine. But any human personality has its foolish zone. Including Dorcas's. No matter what she tells you, remember this: Keith Rollins is a bastard, John!"

She picked up a small handbag from the piano bench, rose, and started stiffly from the living room. But before she reached the foyer she stopped and turned.

"John . . ."

"Yes?"

She was worrying the handbag. "Do make allowances for me." The rosebud mouth pleaded; she was very much the little girl now. "Having Keith brought into this house after what happened . . . It upsets me to think about it." Then she hurried out, leaving Vallancourt frowning.

He was standing at the windows overlooking the long terraced lawn when Dorcas Ferguson appeared.

"I'm sorry to have kept you waiting, John. I had a call from Baltimore."

"I didn't mind. This house is a pleasant place in which to wait." The statement was a half-truth. Today, some of the pleasantness was gone from the house.

She glanced about the room. "Did Ivy leave?"

Vallancourt nodded.

Dorcas was paler than when he had last seen her.

He had met her five years ago, when he and Nancy had returned home for the summer. He had formed a strong feeling for her almost at once.

She was not a beautiful woman, although she was lithely attractive, wide-shouldered and tall, in contrast to Ivy. Dorcas's almost Indian face was dominated by a firm and generous mouth, high cheekbones, and large dark eyes. Her glistening black hair, stranded with silver, swept in a high widow's peak from her wide forehead.

She took his hand in both of hers. "It's so good to see you again, John."

"Could I say less?" Vallancourt smiled.

She gestured him to a deep chair. He sat down, and she began to pace in a fretful manner that was uncharacteristic of her.

"Dorcas . . . if you have something difficult to say, please remember how I feel about you."

She gave him a grateful look. "It's about Keith, John."

"I suspected as much."

"I want you to like him."

"I've the same wish," he said.

"But you don't."

"That's not quite true, Dorcas. After all, I haven't had a chance to get to know the boy."

She eased herself to the edge of a chair. "But you do have reservations."

"I honestly don't know. I like some things about Keith. He has a good mind, quick, above average. In his off-guard moments, he's very personable."

"Off-guard?"

"It's what I sense inside the boy that disturbs me, Dorcas. There is a turmoil, a kind of watchfulness, in his eyes."

"The cub, backing up, prepared to growl defiance," she said in a faint, bitter voice. "Many people would look at him and never see. But not you. Not when he moved in on someone dear to you."

"Would you rather I were less candid with you, Dorcas?"

"You know I wouldn't. There's always been honesty between us, John. I've found little enough of it in the world." She drew a deep breath, seemed to derive strength from it. "That's why I called you here this morning. I want you to know . . . what you should know . . . about Keith.

"You never knew his mother. Maggie was the middle sister, John. Somehow she got lost between me and Ivy. She was the gentle one. She lacked Ivy's brittle selfishness and my energy. The very act of living was bewildering to Maggie. When her final illness came, she didn't know how to put up a real fight. She simply died, helplessly, one morning before dawn.

"I wonder whether it would have made a difference to Keith if Maggie had lived a little longer. I think not. He would have made the trip anyway."

Dorcas had spoken with composure, in a soft, even voice. But she had aged before Vallancourt's eyes. She raised her slender hand and brushed the corners of her eyes.

"John, you know the latest spring vacation custom adopted by college students. It's become a stupid tradition. They pile in cars and drive non-stop as much as two thousand miles to converge on coastal resort towns. A sleepless weekend on a main diet of hamburgers follows.

"Individually, they're everyday, normal kids. They go, some of them, because it's the thing to do. Parents permit it because they're too busy to think it through, because everybody's doing it, and because such jaunts by the youngsters have taken on the earmarks of status symbols. The results are not always pretty."

Vallancourt waited patiently for Dorcas to go on.

"This past spring, a lovely girl from Keith's home town—Cheryl Pemberton was her name—talked her parents into letting her go with a group of girls to Port Palmetto, Florida. She put up the usual arguments. The girls had reserved a cottage, quite apart from the boys, she assured them; girls from the best families in town were going; she simply had to fit in with the crowd; she could take care of herself; and, finally, didn't they trust her?"

Vallancourt watcher her shiver.

"Cheryl Pemberton's parents never saw her alive again."

"Dorcas . . ."

She looked resolutely away from him, spine stiff, hands locked in her lap.

"Don't, John. Please. I have to get this out quickly.

"When darkness came to the beaches at Port Palmetto that Saturday night, the ferment began to work. No one knows just why or how these things

get started, but before midnight, in the light of
bonfires dotting the beaches, hundreds of young
people were snake-dancing and chanting a pagan
praise to beer, sand, and sex.

"The local police came out in force. Their appearance on the beach touched off a riot. Several officers
were hurt. Squad cars were overturned. The jail was
literally packed with youngsters.

"Early the next morning, a city sanitation crew
was put on emergency duty to clean the beaches of
débris.

"The nude and battered body of Cheryl Pemberton was found under an old wooden fishing pier.
Indications were that some boy, inflamed by liquor
and mob pyschosis, had lost control of himself and
momentarily become a fiend.

"Keith . . . it was Keith whom the police suspected. He and Cheryl were classmates, completing
their senior year. There'd been a tacit agreement
that they would be dating each other in Port Palmetto. Keith was the last boy to have been seen with
her. He was picked up as he was leaving town."

Vallancourt mercifully looked out the window.

"Keith withstood nearly sixty continuous hours of
interrogation, John. He was able to do this because
he was telling the truth. I know he was telling the
truth!

"The truth was that he had got separated from
Cheryl Pemberton, knew nothing of her death until
the police took him in custody. The scenes on the
beach had sickened him, and he had decided to
leave.

"He was released because there wasn't a shred of evidence against him, just suspicion. John, that suspicion mustn't destroy the only living soul close to me I care anything about!"

3.

Vallancourt turned back to Dorcas with sympathy. But he lacked her subjective entanglement. He had already sensed the tension and hostility in Keith Rollins. He reserved judgment. But then, he could afford to. Dorcas must be prey to her uncertainties and their clash with her loyalty and attachment to the boy.

Vallancourt caught a swift mental glimpse of the girl's beginning to struggle as panic overcame her, and of a drink-crazed boy losing control. It was conceivable that Keith had acted during a black-out, without later recollection of the event. He would then feel only revulsion and a desire to get away.

"I think," Dorcas was saying slowly, "I've been working all these years for Keith's sake. They haven't been altogether pleasant years, John. When my parents died and left three young daughters in a world of bankruptcy and creditors, the responsibility fell on my shoulders. Poor Maggie would have survived on charity. Ivy might have drunk herself to a bitter, self-pitying end. I picked up the scanty remains, John. I planned, I badgered loans from creditors and bankers who saw the chance of recouping their losses to my parents, I worked eighteen hours a day. And I rebuilt it, John, I rebuilt it.

"Now—I know what drove me to do it. Given the chance, Keith will mature. He'll pick up where I leave off."

As Dorcas spoke, cold purpose came into her eyes. Without knowing it, Vallancourt thought, in declaring herself she has warned me. The shadow of this boy Keith has fallen across us.

He felt a touch of sadness; he knew the shadow had already darkened the relationship between him and this admirable woman. She would struggle in Keith's behalf. And Vallancourt would fight for his daughter.

"As always, Dorcas, I'm glad things are open and aboveboard between us."

"I knew you would make inquiries about Keith. After all, she's your only child. I wanted you to hear the truth about Keith."

He rose. She remained on the edge of her chair, looking up at him.

"I wish I could read your face, John," she said quietly.

"I'm not given to snap judgments."

"Will you take Nancy away?"

"And lend the enticement of forbidding the fruit?" he asked wryly. "I don't think that would be the answer."

"John, if she finds her only satisfactory answer in Keith . . ."

"She's twenty-one years old, Dorcas."

"Then you won't stand in their way?"

"Did you expect me to?"

"Frankly, yes."

"I could think of no better way to defeat my own purposes."

"You're not yielding so easily." She moistened her lips. "Right now, you frighten me. You've always awed me a little. Many men born to wealth and an old name are plagued with uncertainty about their identities and personal worth. Not you. You've never needed ego-satisfactions; you've taken full advantage of your heritage. But if you were marooned naked in the world's worst jungle, you'd walk out alive—and probably bring a valuable assessment of the area with you."

"I hope none of us has to yield, Dorcas."

"What can I do, John? What must Keith do?"

"What all of us must do. Be patient. Take time to be sure about the answers, all the answers."

"Thank you for coming, John."

"Goodbye."

He heard the faint sound of weeping from the living room as Mildred Morgan showed him out the front door.

Vallancourt had lunch at an inexpensive place on the south side of town where he was not likely to run into anyone he knew.

He needed some time to himself.

Rape-murder . . .

He ate without much notice of the food. The boy had defenders—Dorcas, Ralph Hibbs. Even Howard Conway had exhibited yesterday the tolerant friendliness of an older man unbending for a companion from the next generation. Howard's grouchy remark about Keith's driving habits had been on a plane of general prejudice, words Howard would have spoken about any male driver of Keith's age.

So far, Ivy was the boy's only detractor. But Vallancourt didn't believe she really sensed Keith's potential. Ivy would feel the same way if there was illness in the house requiring her to put a halt to a gay party.

Ivy, Vallancourt thought, resents the boy for personal reasons—for the care and attention Dorcas lavishes on him, care and attention of which Ivy had always been the beneficiary.

A brief recollection came to Vallancourt of the desperate time when there had been guerrilla warfare in Greece. In all Athens, it had seemed, only he, an American diplomat, had suspected the treachery of Koutsourais—until the night Koutsourais had arranged, impeccably, the details of a regrettable accident. Everything had gone beautifully for Koutsourais, up to the final detail when he had discovered that his intended prey, too, had shark's teeth.

Vallancourt left the restaurant and drove without haste past the country club where he had golfed with Keith the day before.

As the Continental swept into the privacy of Canterbury Boulevard, the uniformed guard in the gatehouse waved a brief greeting. The first of the meticulously landscaped estates flowed past. The greenery gave the air a heady freshness; it was

cooler here, the giant shade trees throwing a mantel
of shadows over the boulevard.

Vallancourt turned in between the ivy-grown
stone columns that marked his own driveway.

When the Continental purred around the sweep-
ing curve of the driveway, the house came in view.
It was a multi-storied mansion of antique brick and
leaded windows. The house reposed quietly in its
bed of lawns and gardens.

Vallancourt entered the house, his steps quick and
restless on the parquet. He rang for Charles, and
when the lean, grave houseman appeared, Vallancourt left word that he wanted to see his daughter
when she got home. Then he went into his study.

Vallancourt relaxed a little as he stood at the tall
windows and lit a cigarette. He moved noiselessly
to the mammoth desk that had been created for this
large, wood-paneled room with its high arched ceiling and hand-rubbed beams. Beyond the desk was
a solid wall of books, for each of which Vallancourt
felt a particular regard. Not all the volumes personally inscribed to him, memoirs of world leaders
and works of famous writers, were included here.

Seated at the desk, he forced himself to go
through the morning mail. But his thoughts kept
circling around to his forthcoming talk with Nancy.
He thought of Keith Rollins embracing Nancy, kiss-
ing her, caressing her. And the hellish phrase wrote
itself again in burning letters across his brain: *Rape-
murder* . . .

He attacked the mail. He knew it had already
been weeded out by Mrs. Ledbetter, Charles's wife.

The couple had been in Vallancourt's employ for many years as secretary and houseman.

He sorted the mail quickly into two piles. The letters in franked envelopes he dropped on the further pile.

He attacked the nearer pile. In several minutes he had created a third pile, for which he would dictate on tape the earliest replies. Mrs. Ledbetter would transcribe from tape and clear the decks before nightfall.

The whispered sigh and click of the door caused him to raise his head.

Nancy had slipped in quietly. She gave him a smile, and it brought light to the room.

"Hi, daddy."

She hasn't had time to step out of the sun yet, Vallancourt thought, his heart wrenched. She would soon enough find the ugliness lurking at the boundaries of her world.

He got up, went around his desk grinning at her. She was lovely—rather tall, well made, full of spring. So much like her mother. Just a trace of angularity about her, but no awkwardness. A wide, barely lopsided mouth that smiled even in sleep. A slightly pugged nose given to peeling from sunburn. Wide-spaced, clear eyes with an oriental slant. Hair to match the sunlight streaming through the windows.

He opened his cigarette case and offered it to her. She hesitated. He knew she had started smoking a very short time ago; she was still not completely at ease about it.

Nancy chose a cigarette almost carefully. Vallan-

court struck a light for each of them, eased himself
to a half-sitting position on the edge of the desk.

"Well, are you going to be a senior next fall?"

"You know me, dad. Lit, anthropology, ancient
history, the art courses I have as an appetizer before
breakfast. But get me in the realm of math and
science . . . She crossed her eyes as she looked at
him and shuddered. Then she grinned. "Anyhow,
I'm in there plugging away."

"Fine. Then we can make plans for the summer."

He watched the smile begin its death. "Is that why
you wanted to see me, dad?"

"I usually like to know what you have in mind,
Nancy."

She stood in a hesitant attitude; then the tension
went from her shoulders.

"I think," she said, "the time has come for a pow-
wow."

He matched her effort to keep it light. "Big chief
all ears."

"I'm in love, dad."

"With Keith Rollins?"

"Yes."

He studied her through the smoke. "How does he
feel?"

"The same way."

"Are you sure, princess?"

"Completely. It's one of those once-in-a-lifetime
things for both of us."

"I've had a hunch about it," he said lightly.

"I know, dad. Keith told me of your inspection
yesterday."

"Do you resent it? Or does Keith?"

"Don't be silly! Wouldn't it be goopy to have a father who wasn't interested in me? Only . . ." Her lips quivered.

He touched her chin with his forefinger. "What is this?"

She caught his hand and pressed the back of it to her cheek fiercely. "Growing up is just plain *hell*."

"Not always, Nancy."

"When you find that relationships change?"

And Vallancourt thought: She's trying to tell me she will always love me, but that I'm no longer the center of her universe.

"Change is the natural order of things, darling. All we can do is try to make sure it's chiefly for the better."

She dropped his hand and half turned toward the window, no longer facing him directly. "I've wanted to talk to you, daddy."

"Why haven't you?"

"I've been afraid. Not of you. Of my botching it. You see, Keith was in Port Palhetto, Florida, this spring when a dreadful thing happened."

"I know all about Port Palmetto, Nancy," he said gently. When she flashed him a startled look, he added: "I haven't been keeping it from you. Dorcas Ferguson called me this morning and she's told me all about it."

"I see," she said slowly. "Then you know Keith is innocent."

"I know the police released him."

"He told me everything, dad, when we began to get serious. Told me—and offered to go away."

He would, Vallancourt thought. He felt a tightening inside. The boy had played it cool and smart. His admission had actually increased his stock with Nancy. He had known what his self-sacrificial offer would do to her.

Vallancourt realized that Nancy was studying him in a covert way. She glanced aside when his eyes met hers.

"If he asks me," she said, "I'm going to marry him."

Vallancourt knew the importance of the next moment, his words, every inflection and nuance.

"When a woman prepares an answer," he said with a smile, "she's usually pretty sure of the question. But don't be disappointed, Nancy, if he doesn't ask you right away. I'll hazard the guess that Keith will withhold the question until the Port Palmetto thing is settled. Feeling about you as he must, he wouldn't want to begin with an ugly thing like that hanging over him."

She turned to him then, and he gave her the shelter of his arms.

A subtle change had taken place in his position, Vallancourt knew. He felt no qualms. Let the boy show the depth—or shallowness—of his feeling for Nancy. After all, if he measured up, he *would* want to wait until the Port Palmetto police had announced a solution to the rape-murder of the Pemberton girl.

Nancy slipped away from him, moving with her angular grace. "Pardon, please," she said in a slightly damp voice, "while a lady seeks privacy to blow her nose."

She hurried from the room, leaving her father to stand very still for a long time.

4.

Sam Rollins, Keith's father, called at four o'clock that afternoon. Charles showed him into the library and carried news of the caller to the study, where Vallancourt was working with Mrs. Ledbetter.

Entering the library, Vallancourt saw a tall, thin, intense man whose clothing, while of good cut, was rumpled as if from chronic lack of attention. Rollins's lips were thin, his nose a high-bridged blade of bone, his eyes small and restless under salty brows that matched his hair. The aroma of alcohol surrounded him.

"Good afternoon," Vallancourt said. Rollins's feverish eyes were going over him in a quick, envious appraisal. "Won't you sit down, Mr. Rollins?"

"Call me Sam. The mister is too damn formal for me." Rollins dropped into a chair, gripping the arms with his long, predatory fingers. "So you are John Vallancourt." The shifty eyes darted about the library. "Nice place you got here. But I don't guess you have time, with all you have to do, to really read all these books."

33

"There's time for everything, if you make it," said
Vallancourt. "Incidentally, I'm glad you dropped in,
Mr. Rollins. I've wanted us to get acquainted. As a
matter of fact, I'd intended to phone you this evening."

"I figured as much," Rollins said. Vallancourt
wondered if the man realized his own insolence.
Apparently it had been many years in cultivation,
becoming an automatic response. Briefly, he felt
compassion for Rollins, and for the son who had
been exposed to this seething belligerence during his
formative years.

"I played a round of golf with your son yesterday."

"I heard. He tried to win, too, didn't he?"

"Is there any reason why he shouldn't?"

"Hell, no." Rollins's bony shoulders twitched. "It's
just that it's so pathetic. He failed. Naturally. Keith
always does, you know."

"Did he tell you about the game?"

"Keith? Confide in me?" Rollins uttered a thin
sour laugh. "He didn't have to tell me. I guess I
know my own son."

"I see."

"But I don't blame you." A hint of obsequious-
ness crept into Rollins's manner. "If I had a knock-
out daughter, I'd want to know something about the
stud, too."

"I'm glad you understand," Vallancourt said
dryly.

"Does Port Palmetto mean anything to you?"

He sat down in a chair only partially facing

Rollins's. The man had to turn his head to look at him.

"Yes, it does, Mr. Rollins."

"Keith tell you about it?"

"No, someone else."

"I didn't think he'd have the guts." Rollins waited; and when Vallancourt remained silent, Keith's father said, "Okay, okay, I guess you claim diplomatic immunity in protecting your source of information. The only thing is, not all stories are the same."

"Would you care to give me your version, Mr. Rollins?"

"The girl was raped, killed. They picked Keith up, then let him go. He says he's innocent."

Vallancourt began to feel as if the room needed airing. "You've nothing to add?"

"Maybe you think I should get sentimental?"

"A young girl has been killed—and Keith is your son."

"A son should be a comfort to his father, Mr. Vallancourt. You haven't had to worry about that boy for twenty-odd years, or you'd know what I'm talking about."

"I'm sure there are a great many things about Keith that I don't know."

"I was hoping you might know the inside," Rollins said. "You've got connections. You've made inquiries. You may know more about Keith in one respect than I do."

"In respect to what?"

"His innocence—or guilt," Rollins said.

"I'm sorry, but I can't help you." Vallancourt rose, and Rollins took the hint with a flattening of his lips and a glitter in his restless eyes. He rose, too.

"It was kind of you to give me so much of your valuable time, Mr. Vallancourt." The insolence again. Or frustration. Perhaps a little of both, Vallancourt thought.

After Rollins was gone, he found it hard to return to work. His thoughts kept returning to Keith. Having met the father, he felt a sympathy for the son. But he was not reassured. Knowing why the young lion was hungry did not make his appetite less dangerous.

Vallancourt was on the point of driving off the next morning when Mrs. Ledbetter called to him with unaccustomed shrillness.

He stopped the car and hurried back into the house.

"It's Miss Ferguson, Mr. Vallancourt. I've never heard her so upset. She says it's very urgent."

He crossed the high, vaulted entry hall. Charles was plugging in a phone, extending it.

"Dorcas?"

"Thank God! John . . ." Her voice was gurgly, as if she had been sobbing. "I must see you."

Keith . . . rape-murder . . . The words sprang into his head.

"Dorcas, what's the matter? What's happened?"

"I can't tell you . . . not over the phone. Can you . . . I hate to break in on you this way—"

"I'll be right over," he said.

She made a choked sound of gratitude and the line went dead.

Vallancourt swung into the Ferguson driveway twenty minutes later. The Norman lines of the house wheeled into view.

Two cars were parked at one side of the driveway ahead of him—a small open sports car, and behind it a blue sedan.

The door of the sedan on the driver's side was open. Howard Conway had apparently just got out and gone forward to look into the sports car. He turned toward the Continental as Vallancourt brought it to a nose-dipping stop.

Vallancourt got out quickly and moved to the fleshy younger man.

"I just got a call from Dorcas, Howard—"

"So did I. Just minutes ago. What's up, John?"

"I don't know." He glanced at the sports car. "Keith's?"

Conway nodded.

They hurried across the strip of lawn between the driveway and the house.

"Dorcas?" Conway called when they were inside. He glanced at Vallancourt, moved a few steps further. And then a tremendous shock rippled over Conway's frame. All the color left his face.

"God Almighty!"

Vallancourt rushed into the living room where Dorcas lay, and dropped beside her. His heart seemed to dissolve, leaving a cold cavity in his chest.

He knew instantly that Dorcas Ferguson was dead. The black, silver-stranded hair was fanned across her Indian face, wisps of it sticking to her unseeing eyeballs. Her lower jaw hung to the limits

of its hinges, making an ugly red and black hole of
the once-warm, generous mouth.

From the odd, twisted position of her head, Vallancourt raised his eyes slowly. Up the leg of the
heavy table. To the edge of the table where the
finish was marred by a smear of blood and a few
hairs. He guessed what the table's edge had done
to the base of her skull. He did not care for a closer
look.

He was aware of Howard Conway standing
nearby, grasping the back of a chair. He rose, started
toward Conway . . . and out of the corner of his eyes
saw a drapery move.

Vallancourt lunged, ripping the drapery aside.

It was Keith Rollins.

Vallancourt saw the blow coming and rolled with
the punch, taking it high on his cheek. His brain
jarred, his left knee buckled slightly. Then he was
all right. With his right foot he thrust himself forward, ducking under Keith's next frantic blow. His
fingers touched the boy's arm. Keith screamed softly
and lashed out with his foot. Vallancourt slid to one
side, and Keith had an instant in which to turn. He
covered his face and head with his arms and plunged
through the tall window in a shower of glass.

"Look at him! Look at him!" Conway shouted
senselessly.

Keith struck grass, tripped, rolled, bounced to his
feet, tore his way through shrubbery. He did not
pause to look back, but darted toward his sports
car.

Nearer to the front door, Conway was outside
before Vallancourt. The sports car was fishtailing

around the bend in the driveway. The breeze carried the pungency of scorched rubber back to them.

"Call the police, John," Conway shouted as he ran. "Tell 'em to head him off!"

Conway threw himself in his car, fumbled with the ignition, shouted a four-letter word, and got the car started. The sedan shot away in pursuit.

Vallancourt phoned the police.

Dorcas Ferguson is dead. The most important woman in this end of the state has been murdered.

He could see the headlines, the editorials. The short-wave police band would soon be chanting the old litany that was always new:

All cars . . . Wanted on suspicion of murder, Keith Rollins . . . age twenty-two. Husky build. Black hair. Dark blue eyes. Driving MG, late model, license BF-3850. Fleeing estate of Dorcas Ferguson, victim. Approach with caution. Suspect was recently questioned in connection with a Florida rape-murder . . .

Vallancourt returned to the front door, watching the driveway. He made a pad of his handkerchief and applied it to the bruise Keith had left, only partially aware of the throb in his cheekbone. In these scant remaining moments of quiet, the fact of Dorcas's death was a vaster pain. Dorcas dead. Dorcas dead.

Grief was acid in his throat.

He heard the sound of an approaching car, and looked up. It was Ivy Conway's compact sedan.

She parked sloppily, leaving the driveway barely passable.

"Hi," she said wanly. She looked tired. She manu-
factured a grin, touching her temple. "Long evening
at the country club bar," she confessed. "Why do I
always say never again?"

She started toward the front steps, the breeze
feathering the gossamer brown hair about her small
face. "What's wrong with you, John? Don't tell me
you tied one on, too! This I would have to see."
She laughed.

Vallancourt touched her arm. "Before you go
inside, Ivy . . ."

"Whatever is the matter with you?"

"A dreadful thing has happened."

"Happened?" Then she said quickly, "Not to
Dorcas!"

"I'm afraid so."

They had stopped midway up the front steps. She
jerked her head toward the house.

From the distance came the approaching wail of a
police siren.

Very slowly and carefully, Ivy turned.

"An ambulance, John?"

"No," he said gently.

"Then—police?"

"Yes."

"Dorcas . . . the *police?*"

She darted into the house. She was at the edge of
the living room when Vallencourt caught her. She
looked into the room, struck herself in the temple,
and began to scream.

5.

During the police preliminaries Ivy Ferguson Conway crouched in a chair and refused to move, like a child waking in the dark after a nightmare.

Her husband's voice mingled finally with that of the uniformed policeman on duty in the foyer. Conway came in, shaking his head. "Lost him, John. He must have slipped the MG through that parking area at the shopping center. When I tumbled to it and backtracked, there was no sign of him."

Vallancourt tilted his head in Ivy's direction. Conway looked startled. He crossed the room, stooped over her, spoke quietly. Some of the blankness left her eyes. She moaned suddenly, grabbed her husband about the neck, and began to sob. He picked her up, glanced at a policeman, got a nod, and carried Ivy out of the room.

A lanky, sweating detective in a rumpled gray suit followed the Conways out. Vallancourt knew him; his name was Woody Britt.

Britt was in charge at least for the moment. He had questioned Vallancourt in a halting fashion, unsure of himself. The man was obviously dreading the important investigation that had fallen to him.

Vallancourt needed to get out of that room. He walked to the front door and lit a cigarette. An ambulance with Dorcas Ferguson's body inside was vanishing around the curve in the driveway. He looked away from the heavy vehicle.

In one respect, he thought, Britt had shown tact, barring TV and newspaper reporters. Dorcas would not be subjected to the horror of having pictures of her battered corpse frontpaged all over the state.

A station wagon eased to a stop at the end of the string of parked cars. Ralph Hibbs backed out and came puffing up the driveway.

Behind his glasses, Hibbs's gentle eyes were bewildered. His large, soft body was shaking.

"It's true, John?" he said. "It's true?"

"I'm afraid so, Ralph."

"Those policemen guarding the driveway . . . I had a time convincing them I was a friend, not a reporter. Have they taken her away, John?"

Vallancourt nodded.

"I can't *believe* it! How could it have happened?"

Easily, he thought. In a moment of violence, she was shoved, went over backward, and the edge of the table was waiting for the base of her skull. Very easily.

"The news is flying around town," Hibbs babbled. "There was a special bulletin on TV. Said that she'd been murdered and her nephew was being sought. Have they caught him yet?"

"Not to my knowledge, Ralph."

"Just think of it! A couple days ago we were playing golf with him, and Dorcas was full of plans for his future . . ."

There was movement behind Vallancourt. He glanced over his shoulder, saw the detective.

"Hello, Woody," Ralph Hibbs said. "Terrible thing! Have they assigned you to the case?"

"I'd rather be chasing down a nameless punk," said Britt gloomily. "Well, at least I can wrap it up quick and get it off my back."

"It's so damn unbelievable," Hibbs said. "Dorcas had taken Keith in, was giving him the chance for a new start."

"And got her head stove in for her trouble." Britt added a bitter note: "Too bad you and Mr. Conway let him get away, Mr. Vallancourt."

Vallancourt let it pass. He had been the victim of surprise, in a moment of shock. If Britt didn't understand that, no explanation would suffice.

"What do you think happened, Britt? he asked.

"It's a cinch it goes back to that Florida murder," the lanky detective said. "They almost had a case against him, you know, and Dorcas Ferguson was nobody's fool. Something the boy said or did must have told her he was that girl's killer, all right. The way she called her brother-in-law and you, Mr. Vallancourt, shows how upset she was. She wanted help and advice. I figure she wasn't quite ready to pull the string on the murdering louse."

The two men said nothing as Britt paused to light a cigar. "Miss Ferguson was alone, remember. It was the maid's day off, and Mildred Morgan had taken the chauffeur-handyman to the center for the week's shopping. We've just finished talking to them.

"Miss Ferguson was in her study when the servants went grocery buying. She must have been there when Keith Rollins showed, suspecting a chill wind was about to blow his way. A few words with his aunt convinced him of it.

"I don't think the boy wanted or intended to kill her," Britt frowned. "He got panicky, is all. Wanted to make tracks. He needed dough and had a fat chance of getting it from his aunt right then. But she always kept a metal cashbox in her desk. And, friends, that box is now missing."

"But she wasn't killed in her study," Hibbs protested.

Woody Britt gave him a sour look. "He threatened her, see? And took the box. Started out of the house, coming through the doorway connecting the living room and study. You expect her just to sit there? Not Miss Dorcas Ferguson.

"In the living room, she catches up with him. She's plenty put out after all she tried to do for him. She gets in his way, and Keith . . ." Britt made a shoving motion with his hands. "So she falls backwards and her head . . ." Britt snapped his bony fingers.

The man's teeth were yellowish clamps on his cigar. "Only he ain't out of the woods, not by a long shot. He's in the living room with her dead body, and two men are walking in on him, Mr. Conway and you, Mr. Vallancourt. He ducks behind the drapery, hoping you'll take one look and run like hell to get help, giving him a chance for a getaway."

"That's all pretty much guesswork, Britt," said Vallancourt.

"Sure, but how the hell else could it have happened? You figure another way, Mr. Vallancourt?"

Vallancourt shrugged. "Do you mind if I leave now? I've given you all the help I can, and I'm anxious to get back to my daughter."

"Sure. Go on. If I need you, I'll give you a ring. But I don't think I'll have to. We'll have him behind bars by nightfall. The state patrol's been alerted, roadblocks set up. We got this Rollins kid bottled up in this section of the state. If he gets out, it won't be alive."

Charles and Mrs. Ledbetter had heard the news. Vallancourt called them into his study and briefed them on the details, concluding with the thought uppermost in his mind: "It's possible, perhaps probable, that Keith Rollins will try to contact Nancy."

The Ledbetters, he suspected, had already considered the possibility. Charles said, "We'll bear it in mind, Mr. Vallancourt."

They left and he placed a call to the dean's office at the college. When Dean Hansbury was on the line, he said, "This is John Vallancourt. I'm reluctant to disrupt her schedule, but can you have someone contact my daughter in class and have her call home? It's urgent."

As he hung up, the sound of a voice drifted in. He went out quickly. Charles was at the front door, firmly insisting that he would have to determine if Mr. Vallancourt was home.

The caller was Sam Rollins. Vallancourt said, "It's all right, Charles."

Rollins's clothing flapped about his scarecrow frame. Beads of sweat glistened on the sharp planes of his face.

"We can talk in the study," Vallancourt said. Rollins preceded him, and he closed the door behind them.

Rollins pulled a handkerchief from his hip pocket and massaged his palms. Then he teetered on the balls of his feet. "What are you and Howard Conway up to, Vallancourt?"

"I don't believe I follow you."

"The hell you don't! Accusing my boy of murder!"

Vallancourt's eyes went cold. It was rather late for the man to be putting on the conscientious father act.

"I've accused no one of anything, Mr. Rollins. I simply told the police what happened."

"You didn't *see* Keith do anything, did you?" Rollins punctuated his words with a soiled finger. "You bet you didn't! Even that lunkhead Keith wouldn't hang around after a killing. You scared him, he lost his head and ran. If he'd killed her, he wouldn't have panicked. Maybe later, but not then. He's cold as a snake when he's in a corner. I've seen him . . ." Rollins suddenly broke off, as if he had said too much.

"Yes, Mr. Rollins?" Vallancourt prompted.

"I mean, I've seen him as a kid when he had to take a licking. Go cold as turkey. Not a nerve. Afraid of nothing. Couldn't reach him if you used a razor strap. Him being in Dorcas Ferguson's house today don't prove a thing."

He was pretty damned cold and nerveless behind the drapery, Vallancourt thought, primed for anything.

"I'm not trying to prove or disprove anything, Mr. Rollins."

"A stinking, lousy break," Rollins said. He dropped into a leather chair and his face drooped. "A square shake for my kid, that's all I'm after."

"He'll get one."

"Like hell. It's stacked against him. All the Ferguson heirs, the Ferguson interests. They'll throw him to the wolves. Fat chance my boy'll have of saving his skin, much less collecting a dime of his inheritance."

So that was it!

Vallancourt's teeth acquired an edge. He reminded himself that he was a civilized man.

"What is it that brings you to me, Mr. Rollins?"

"Your girl, of course. I'll lay you six to one Keith tries to contact her. If we play it right, she'll lead us straight to him."

The study door sighed open. Charles said, "A call for you, Mr. Vallancourt."

Vallancourt reached for the phone on the desk. "Yes?"

He listened.

His face went bloodless.

He said, "Thank you," and hung up.

Rollins came sliding up from the chair, looking interested.

"You'll have to excuse me, Mr. Rollins."

"Now listen here! You can't dismiss me like I was some kind of—"

"Get out of here, Rollins."

When the door clicked, Vallancourt reached for the phone. He would start the search here and now, calling everyone she knew.

But his hunter's instinct told him he already had the answer.

His caller had been Dean Hansbury. Nancy had attended none of her classes today. She had not arrived at the college this morning.

She must have gone to a rendezvous with Keith. Innocently, in the manner of that other girl in Port Palmetto, Florida.

6.

As the MG growled deeper into the hills on the winding country road, Keith tried to keep out of his thoughts the picture of his aunt's lifeless body.

The strange slow-motion quality was fading from his surroundings. A bird flitted normally across the path of the MG, and the details of the creature were not agonizingly clear.

The acuity of his senses in times of crisis was frightening. It was as if the phenomenon did not really belong to the dweller in his flesh. He had heard or read somewhere that soldiers under fire often experienced the same sharp appreciation of danger. He could not remember when he had experienced the feeling for the first time. He was nagged by a dark suggestion, that his father was somehow mixed up in it. The experience went a long way back, to the beginning of memory. As if he had been under fire since the birth of consciousness.

He braked the MG and took a steep curve under light acceleration. The car was a friendly tool in his hands. Below, the shallow valley rolled blue-green. Only the throaty tones of the car broke the silence.

The MG nosed up, framing the cloudless sky in the windshield. The crest of the hill swept past and the car began to drop.

She had felt so loose, so boneless . . . He bit his lip. Like a bundle of rags . . .

And when he had jerked his hands away, there had been a smear of red jelly on his fingertip.

The memory needled his face with a sweat which the rush of wind over the MG could not evaporate.

It was an out-of-kilter, Dali-like grotesquerie, this portrait held in memory. He could identify the wavering outlines of a crouching figure as his own. He had looked at her stillness and the smear of red on his finger, and he knew she was dead.

Then a scratchy needle on an invisible turntable brought forth sound. Voices belonging to Howard Conway and Jonathan Vallancourt.

He felt again the flowing movement of his muscles, the touch of drapery fabric against his cheek. He had stood behind that frail armor, not breathing, hearing Howard and Vallancourt come into the room.

If they would only leave the room for a moment, he had thought, he could slip out of the window, re-enter the Ferguson living room from the rear of the house, pretend he had been looking for his aunt.

Oh, God, let them go away. Please make them go out for just a few seconds . . .

Instead, Vallancourt had jerked the drapery aside.

He shivered, remembering. And not remembering. For there was no real recollection of the next few minutes, merely a sense of motion. And an echo of Howard Conway's astounded voice: "Police, John . . . Head him off!" The voice had been swallowed in the roar of the MG's engine.

Keith lifted his hand from the wheel and wiped the sleeve of his checkered sports shirt across his face.

At least they hadn't yet headed him off. He had been able to reach this lonely, little-used road. They didn't know his destination, his reason for being here . . . unless Nancy had let it slip.

No, he thought. She wouldn't. She couldn't have. They won't suspect I'm here.

He dared to think he might get away for good. It had happened. Men disappeared, changed their names.

The System was the thing you had to beat, not individuals. The System digested a man's habits, appearance. It was electronic devices, test tubes, cameras, micro-filmed files; it never rested, never slept. It picked up a man in one place and through simple routine discovered that his fingerprints matched those left a thousand miles away.

With the name-change, therefore, had to come a change in personality, habits. He had to find a steady job, live quietly in the endless shadow of the System, never let it touch him, never draw its attention.

A dense woodland threw a heavy blanket of shadow over the MG. The air was cooler. It felt good on his face.

"I can. I will," he said to himself. "This won't be

like the other times when I've almost made the grade, only to see everything go sour."

His stomach muscles quivered at the thought of failure, of letting the System net him. Failure now meant total destruction. They had that Cheryl Pemberton thing in Florida, and now the death of Aunt Dorcas . . .

The road coiled with the contour of the land, dropping gradually. Through a break in the timber he glimpsed the sapphire lake. A boarded-up summer cottage shot past, then another. Several such cottages were about the lake, but not in sufficient quantity to spoil its natural beauty.

The MG rushed past the timber line, and the splendor of the cold, silent, miles-long lake, embraced by the green hills, monopolized Keith's view. He began to feel better.

My *querencia*, he thought with a bitter smile. He wondered if it was the right Spanish word. *Querencia*, the place where the bull feels strongest. The spot on the sand to which *el toro*, tortured by the blood-lusting *olé* from twenty thousand throats, returns time after time. The brave bull, Keith recalled, with the matador's sword finally piercing his heart, will strive blindly to reach his *querencia*, his dying place.

Always the bull dies, he thought, alone on the bloody sand. Always.

He tried to shake the thought from his mind. A bull was a dumb animal, with no gift or chance for making a choice. He was born to die, his end planned before he dropped from the cow's womb.

But a man was different.

Wasn't he?

Opposite a flimsy pier and boathouse, a graveled driveway lay tangent to the road. Keith braked the MG, nosing into the drive. With a brief spurt of crushed stone, the car rounded the curve; and there was Dorcas Ferguson's lodge, a rambling, rustic building with a railed-in gallery across the front.

Parked near the house was a small sedan.

Keith stopped the MG behind the other car. He got out quickly. As he did so, he heard Nancy Vallancourt's quick footsteps crossing the porch.

His throat tightened as he looked at her.

She ran to him, laughing in relief. And she took his hand, and leaned toward him, and kissed him lightly.

"I was wondering if you'd changed your mind," she said.

He drew her over to the split-log steps, sat down on one of them, pulled her down beside him.

She looked away, staring across the mirror of the lake at the distant blue mist of the hills. "Have you, Keith?"

"I haven't changed my mind," Keith said.

"Then why that look in your eyes?" She touched his chin. He jerked away.

"I beg your pardon," Nancy murmured. She let her hands drop to her lap.

He turned to her then. "You don't understand, Nancy."

"I think I do." She jumped up. "We went over all

this last night. It wasn't easy for me to come here, you know."

"Nancy, please . . ."

"I suppose it's better this way. For a while there you almost made a believer of me, bud."

She ran toward her car. Keith rose. Let her go, he thought. Don't say anything. Just let her go, back to the safe and normal world.

He stood slack-mouthed, sweating. She had reached her car. She was touching the door handle.

"Nancy!"

She paused then, but she did not turn to look at him. "Save it, Keith. At least you haven't tried to postpone the elopement and substitute sex by the lakeside."

"Listen!" he said. "You listen to me! What do you think I am?"

"I thought I knew, Keith."

"Okay," he said. "Remember it, will you?"

She ventured a look over her shoulder. "Do you really want me to go?"

"Why not?"

"What's the matter with you, Keith?"

"Nothing."

"You're lying to me. What happened in town? Did my father get across to you?"

"No."

"Tell me if he did, Keith. He means well. He may even be right."

"He is, Nancy. He's a smart man. Go back."

"Come with me. We'll tell him what we planned, and why. We'll make him understand that nothing can come between us."

He said nothing.

She was facing him now, trying to grin. "All right, let's follow the original plan and find a justice of the peace. I prefer it to returning to town, anyway."

He said nothing. How could he tell her?

"Lately, Keith, my bed feels cold. It isn't a place to sleep, just to think of you. How can I be so shameless?"

"Nancy, I can't take . . ." It burst out of him.

"But it's got to be legal, Keith. The way we planned."

"Nancy . . ."

"No. I can't talk myself again into treating dad this way. It's now or not at all, Keith. If you let me get into this car and drive away, that's it."

He stood with dangling arms. The wind off the lake was cold. The day began to take on the old slow-motion clarity.

"All right," he said through stiff lips. "Here it is. They're looking for me. They're saying I killed Aunt Dorcas."

She stared at him as if she were about to giggle.

He ran over and caught her arms and shook her hard. "Did you hear me, Nancy?"

She continued to stare at nothing. Holding on to her arm, he guided her toward the cottage. When they reached the porch steps, she sank down.

Then something snapped in her. With a clawing motion, she put her hands to her face and started to sob.

Keith wanted to clap his palms over his ears. The sight of her, the sounds coming from her, added to everything else, were too much to bear.

7.

When she stopped sobbing, he lit two cigarettes and offered her one. He was standing on ground level, one foot on the bottom step, his shadow enveloping her.

"Please sit down, Keith."

He eased down on the step.

"Don't you want to tell me?"

"Would it help?"

"You owe it to me."

"It's really simple, Nancy. Aunt Dorcas phoned the apartment where I'm staying with the old man. She asked me to hurry over. She sounded so upset that I went right over. I knew it wouldn't be long until you'd arrive at the lake here, but I didn't think the few minutes would matter."

"Of course not, Keith. I didn't mind waiting."

"When I got there, the place looked deserted. No sign of the servants, so I figured she'd sent them out. I called her name a couple of times, looked in her study. Even went through the kitchen and had a look out back from the windows."

He broke off, sat looking at the ground. "You know, a funny thing happened then. I'll remember it a long time. I got sore at her, Nancy, really miffed. I was anxious to get up here. I thought to myself, she has one hell of a nerve, jerking strings any time she feels like it, making people jump."

"She wasn't like that, Keith. Not at all."

"Don't I know it? All my life she did for me, for my mother, for that louse of a father of mine. If it hadn't been for Aunt Dorcas, we'd have gone hungry plenty of times. My old man with his rotten liquor and his big deals that never paid off . . . Always Aunt Dorcas was a kind of fairy godmother to us.

"The old man . . . Being married to Dorcas Ferguson's sister gave him a leg up on a pretty soft life. He could be a country club bum instead of a saloon rummy."

"Keith."

"No, I've got to say it, Nancy. The way I got so put out with her this morning, just because she wasn't there. As if she'd ever failed me! The way she came to my rescue after that Florida nightmare, and afterward, in my home town. God, I hope she forgives me, wherever she is.

"All the time I was swearing at her, she was lying in the living room dead."

"Keith. Don't. No more, darling."

He raised his head slowly. "I decided to go into the living room and wait for her. That's when I found her."

She took his hand and held it protectively.

"Then I heard them coming, Nancy, Aunt Ivy's husband and your father. All of a sudden I realized the spot I was in. So I really corned the whole deal off. I hid."

"Oh, Keith!"

He ground the cigarette under his heel, savagely. "Your father found me, skulking behind the drapes. All I could think of was making a break for it. I lost my head—what there is of it."

An early jay berated them from a nearby sapling. Water whispered against the pier and boathouse.

"I'm in real trouble this time, Nancy."

"Yes," she said. "Yes, we are."

"Not we!"

"Why not?"

'Nancy, I can't involve you in this. You've got to go back."

"Did you do it, Keith? Look at me and tell me. Did you?"

"As God is my witness, I loved Aunt Dorcas. I didn't lay a finger on her."

"Then how can I turn my back on you?"

"You've got to."

"You don't understand," she said softly. "You're everything that has meaning for me. Keith?"

"You're crazy, Nancy," he said in a hoarse voice. But a part of him was wildly rejoicing. He sat struggling with himself.

"I'm not being altogether unselfish," he heard Nancy say. He wished she would get up and leave now, while he could still let her go. "If I turned my back on you at the first sign of trouble, Keith, what would I think of myself? Keith, this is so new to you, isn't it? Having someone . . . You don't know how to react, do you?"

"I should have passed up the lake and kept going," he muttered.

Her hand slipped from his arm. She uttered a shaky laugh. "If I were swimming naked, you'd hesitate to get your feet wet. Jump in, bud, there's water enough for two."

Without moving any other part of his body, he thrust out his hand. "Keys," he said.

"Keys?"

"To your car. We'll leave the MG. They'll be looking for it."

The keys clashed. His hand closed over them. He got to his feet and brushed off the seat of his pants.

They walked over to Nancy's little compact without looking at each other.

"I'd better drive," he said.

She nodded and walked around the front of the car to get into the suicide seat.

"With you in a sec," he said.

The gravel of the driveway crunched beneath his feet as he went to his sports car. He had no luggage. He had planned, upon his aunt's sudden call this morning, to stop back at the apartment and pick up a few things after he met Nancy.

He kept a lightweight London fog in the MG. The coat lay on the front seat. He leaned across the door of the car and picked the coat up.

There was a small metal box lying on the seat. Frowning, he triggered the catch and opened the box.

He didn't lift the money out right away, merely stood there touching it. Then with a jerk, his fingers closed over the sheaf of bills, scooped it out of the box, slipped it into the side pocket of his trousers.

He went back to Nancy's sedan and slid under the wheel. He turned the key and started the car.

They dropped out of the driveway, wheeled around the edge of the lake. He felt a need to talk. But he did not say anything. Neither did Nancy, until the car turned away from the lake and burrowed into the woods.

"Got a cigarette?" she asked lightly. But there was a tautness in her voice.

He handed her the pack.

"Want one?"

"Please."

She lit a cigarette for him, one for herself.

"What's the agenda?"

She was resting her head against the seat back, smoking calmly, blowing the smoke in a cool stream.

His stomach writhed. This was not the Nancy he had known. There was now a cold-bloodedness about her, as if she had deliberately shut out of her mind all the guilty questions, doubts, and fears. The change alarmed him. It wasn't like Nancy. And he shared it. A sort of hardening process had set in. In both of them.

"I won't go back, Nancy."

"The police usually dig out the truth."

"I had a round with those small-town cops in Florida," he said. "They had no evidence, but it was rough. The police here . . . they've got a lot more on me. The minute I'm jailed they'll throw away the key."

"I don't know, Keith, you may be right. Whoever

killed your aunt may get careless. The longer you're missing, the greater the possibility the real murderer's tipping his hand."

"Sure," Keith said.

She hadn't, he realized, quite understood that they weren't going back, period. The implications of vanishing, of never again seeing familiar faces or surroundings, were unreal to her. Maybe when the chips were down she'd regret her decision back there at the lake house. Probably would. He would have to watch, be prepared. Wait and see, he told himself. Take one thing at a time. Act as if there weren't a screaming nerve in your body. Improvise. Regard everything and everybody as a potential enemy.

Even Nancy.

The dark sadness reached deeper inside of him.

Like a beetle, the little sedan stretched the distance between itself and the lake. The timberland fell behind. They met no traffic as they moved across the hills on the secondary road.

Finally the stop sign at the intersection with the primary road came into view.

Keith braked, quietly waiting for a heavy car and house trailer to trundle past. Then he gunned the engine and swung onto the highway.

Nancy was again lighting cigarettes.

"Don't burn yourself," she cautioned him. "Here."

Without taking his eyes from the road, Keith took one hand from the wheel and let her put the cigarette between his fingers.

The highway was not of the best. A two-lane road

a generation ago, it had been widened, patched, repaired until it was a crazy conglomerate of tar, asphalt, concrete.

Keith checked the dashboard. Plenty of gas; nearly a full tank. Temperature gauge showed the engine running cool. Generator operating properly. He held the car to an even fifty miles an hour. He could make more than two hundred miles before having to stop for gas. The countryside lay quiet. Traffic was light, and the day was perfect for driving.

He began to feel easier in his mind than at any time since he had walked into his aunt's home this morning.

A big diesel rig chuffing from the opposite direction caught his attention. It might have been the glint of sun on glass, but it was not. Its headlights were on.

Keith touched his switch, blinked his lights. The truck blinked in reply.

The two vehicles drew abreast, and Keith gave the trucker a brief wave of his hand. The trucker perched in his cab, a grin on his face, returned the wave and was gone.

Nancy sat up. "What is it, Keith?"

He did not answer immediately. His eyes were searching, his body drawing itself up over the wheel.

A filling-station-garage-and-country-store appeared a quarter of a mile ahead. The weathered buildings lay well back from the highway. There was a hard-packed apron that offered ample room for a U-turn.

Keith toed the brake, steered off the highway, turned in a tight half circle.

He sat nerveless, waiting for a chance to fire the sedan into the farther highway lanes.

"Why are we turning around, Keith?" Nancy asked.

"You see that truck?"

"The one you waved to?"

"He was tipping off oncoming truck drivers and any other hep characters to trouble ahead."

"Trouble? What kind of trouble?"

"A weight or license check. Or a state cruiser hiding behind a billboard with a radar whammy and a fresh book of speeding tickets. Or a roadblock. We'll have to go back—until nightfall."

"To the lake cottage?"

"Can you suggest a better place?"

8.

Vallancourt got home from police headquarters late in the afternoon. Charles had the front door open before he reached it, and Mrs. Ledbetter had made it her business to be hovering nearby. As he handed Charles his hat, Vallancourt shook his head.

"Mr. Hibbs is in the study, Mr. Vallancourt," Charles said.

"How long has he been here?"

"Five minutes or so. When he arrived, I called the police station. You were on your way here. Mr. Hibbs said he would wait."

He went quickly to his study. Ralph Hibbs was thumbing through a travel magazine. He let the heavy periodical fall to the desk.

"Anything at all, John?"

The question and the anxious eyes behind the glasses killed his faint hope that Hibbs might have heard something.

"Not yet."

"Surely Nancy is too level-headed to get herself in trouble."

"Nancy is in love. At least she thinks she is, which amounts to the same thing."

"Are you sure she's with Keith Rollins?"

"Every other possibility has been eliminated."

"Maybe she'll talk some sense into him."

"Don't remind me which of the runaways will influence the other, Ralph."

"I didn't mean . . ."

"Of course not." Vallancourt walked to the window, looked out. darkness was falling dismally. "There's a breed of woman, Ralph, who can't attach conditions to loyalty."

"I can't believe she would deliberately . . ."

"How about you, Ralph? You'll have to make plans of your own, won't you?"

"You mean about the agency?"

"Yes."

"With so many other things on my mind, John, I hadn't given it much thought. But you're right, of course. I'm still running the biggest auto agency in this end of the state, and Dorcas Ferguson was a major stockholder. But right now the business doesn't seem important. What about you, John?"

"I'm not sure. I haven't had time to talk to Howard since this morning. I left word for him to come over when he felt he could leave Ivy."

Howard Conway arrived a few minutes later. A look of gauntness had managed to attach itself to his robust frame today.

"How is Ivy, Howard?"

"You can imagine."

"Anything I can do?" Hibbs asked.

"No, thanks, Ralph. She'll live through the

ordeal." Conway lit a cigarette with jerky motions. "I don't need to ask you if you've heard anything, John. It's all over your face."

"She's with him somewhere. We're sure of that. We've had the day to check the college, her friends —to turn the town over and shake it out."

Howard's face tightened. "Too bad we didn't nail him this morning."

"Now we have to be very careful," Vallancourt said. "He won't back into a corner pleasantly."

"He's hardly more than a boy . . ." Hibbs mumbled.

Conway regarded him coldly. "The trouble with you, Ralph, is that you view every situation with the same preconception."

"But he wouldn't . . ."

"He'll run himself right into a stone wall if he's pushed to it. And when his own destruction is inevitable, he'll wreck everything he can lay his hands on. Do you agree, John? Isn't that what's sticking in your craw?"

"I'm afraid so," Vallancourt admitted. There was a helpless silence. Then he said, "The roadblocks haven't stopped him. It means he stole a car and got through. Or else he's still in this area."

"Stealing a car would be risky," Hibbs argued.

"A poor swimmer won't regard a river as much of a risk with a forest fire behind him," Vallancourt said grimly. "Anyway, a switch of cars wouldn't be difficult. Take your own used-car division, Ralph. Stalwart, clean-cut young man comes in, looks around. Would any of your salesmen refuse to let him try out a car?"

"No, but we'd report it stolen."

"Sure," Conway said, "in an hour or so. When it became clear he wasn't coming back. After you'd inherited one secondhand MG."

"Which puts the search on a nationwide basis," Vallancourt said. "Let's take the smaller bite first."

"You think he's still in the area?" Hibbs asked.

"Yes."

"One chance in two," Howard said.

"On the surface, yes. Actually, the odds are in our favor."

"I don't dig," Conway said.

"I don't believe he'd realize at first that a whole section of the state had been cut off by roadblocks. He's under tremendous pressure. He wouldn't start sorting out details right away."

"So he spots a string of cars at a roadblock." Conway ran his fingers through his untidy hair. "He sneaks a turn-around on a sideroad and slips back to town."

"No," Vallancourt said. "He wouldn't do that."

"Why not?" demanded Hibbs.

"Because, Ralph, the roadblock turns his pressures inside out. Now his brain starts exploding with details, real and fancied. Every pair of eyes that looks at the MG is filled with recognition, or suspicion. Everybody in sight is running for a phone to report his location. He wouldn't dare venture back into town."

"Stealing a car in the country wouldn't be like going into a car lot."

"Or walking city streets until he finds a car with the keys in it," Conway said.

"But he can still pull a switch." Vallancourt read the question in their eyes, and he gave them the painful answer: "Nancy's car."

Hibbs blinked. "Sure!"

"The sonofabitch," Conway cried. "He may be three hundred miles from here by now!"

But Vallancourt shook his silvered head. "A switch occurred to me immediately. A description of Nancy's car was sent out by the police. The only thing is, neither car has been spotted, in use or abandoned. The odds are that Nancy and Keith are still in the net."

"In an area covering about four counties," Conway said.

"Parked on a side road waiting for night?" Hibbs suggested.

"Waiting for night," Vallancourt nodded. "But not on a side road, tavern, even a motel. No public place. A private place where he would feel safer."

"His father's apartment?"

"The police put Sam Rollins's place under surveillance the first thing," Vallancourt said, "along with the homes of Nancy's friends."

"He needs his attic room," Conway said.

"His what?"

"Something Dorcas mentioned when she was planning to bring him here to live. One night at dinner she got pretty emotional about the poor darling's lot in life."

"Let's get to this attic room, Howard."

"It seems that Keith had a favorite spot back home, an attic room, where he would hide when his father decided to enforce his orders with a club, or life got too tough some other way."

"We all occasionally need to close a door," Ralph Hibbs said.

"Sure. Even a woman with the self-possession of a Dorcas Ferguson."

Vallancourt came to quick attention. "She had such a place?"

"A cottage on the lake," Conway said. "She never advertised the location. Would have defeated her purpose. It's a kind of lodge. Now and then she'd take a day there to dig in the garden, or lie in the sun, or get drunk. Depended on her mood."

"Did Keith know about the lodge?"

Conway paused with a cigarette lighter half raised. "Come to think of it, yes."

Vallancourt's eyes caught fire. "His *querencia!*"

Hibbs said blankly, "His what?"

"The other Sunday Nancy was talking to Keith on the phone. She laughed and said they'd picnic at 'the *querencia.*' I dismissed it at the time as some sort of new catch-phrase among the college set."

Conway remembered his cigarette and lit it with a triumphant drag. "You've got it, John! We'll corner the sonofabitch and make him sorry he ever walked through his aunt's front door!"

"We'll do nothing of the kind, Howard."

Conway stared, and Hibbs sluiced moisture from his pale forehead with his finger. "We'd better call the police."

Vallancourt caught him by the wrist. "We'll not do that, either, Ralph. With Nancy there, the last thing I want is a posse of armed men and a battery of searchlights. Anyway, we're not sure yet we've pinpointed the location."

"All right," Conway said on an unwilling note, "we'll play it your way. Approach him nice and friendly. Talk Nancy away. Then let him look out." He glanced at Tibbs. "You in?"

"Certainly, if I can be of help."

"On my terms and conditions," Vallancourt said in an iron voice. "Otherwise I go alone."

The other two men nodded.

They rode in silence, Vallancourt holding the Continental to a fast, steady clip. Howard Conway had shucked his boredom; there was a pleasurable excitement working up in the man. An occasional uneasy rustling in the back seat reminded Vallancourt of Hibbs's presence.

"Turn here," Conway said intently.

The heavy car slued a trifle as it entered the right fork of the narrow county road. The countryside lay in a twilight hush through which the car's rushing passage was a whisper.

The twilight was instantly transformed to black night as the Continental swooped down through the timber.

A graveled driveway flicked into view. Vallancourt touched the brakes.

"Not this one," said Conway. "It belongs to the Harkleroads. They never get up from Florida until midsummer. We're going to the upper end of the lake . . . Watch the curve when the road reaches the lake, John."

The big car rocked. The lake was a limitless glass,

unsilvered, mysterious. The hills made a broken black horizon against the deepening purple of the sky.

"The next driveway, John."

"We'll park on the road." He stopped the car, leaving the headlights burning. His glance made a rapid orientation, marking the boathouse and dock to his left, the driveway toward his right, the outlines of the lodge with its long open gallery crouching on the hillside.

The three got out. Vallancourt and Hibbs carried flashlights.

"We're making a social call," the diplomat reminded them.

He was first up the driveway, keeping to its center. He held the flashlight steady.

"Keith," he called in a clear, calm tone. "If you're here, we came alone. We'd like to talk to you. You may show yourself safely. We're not armed and we'll keep our distance."

A breeze, surly with the last chill of spring, snapped through the pines. Gravel crunched beneath the footsteps of the three men.

"Nobody's here," Hibbs whispered.

Vallancourt continued to climb toward the cottage. He raised his light to play the beam across the front of the building. The windows shone blackly. A hoseful of wind swept a shower of pine needles from the porch.

Vallancourt spoke over his shoulder. "Got a key, Howard?"

"Nope."

"Does Keith?"

"I don't know."

"Listen," Ralph Hibbs said.

"What is it?"

"I heard something."

They stood listening.

"You're hearing things," Conway decided.

"No," Hibbs insisted. "I tell you I heard movement up there. On the hill above the driveway."

Unbidden, Vallancourt's mind created an imaginary scene, Nancy up on the dark hillside realizing now what a foolish and terrible mistake she had made . . . Nancy helpless against Keith's strength . . . Keith's arm locked about her throat, his breath hot against her ear as he warned her not to make a sound . . .

"I don't hear a thing," said Conway.

"Neither do I, now," Hibbs said. "But I know damned well I did a minute ago."

"Probably a dead branch blowing off a tree."

"We'll have to make sure," Vallancourt said. He raised his voice again: "Keith, we're not armed. We have not brought the police. Let's have a word with you, that's all."

"Hell, John," Conway said, disgusted, "he isn't up here. He's probably getting wrapped up by a roadblock while we stand here like idiots talking to the wind."

"We'll have to make sure, Howard."

He walked quietly forward, then stopped with a jerk. His flashlight ray had fallen across the MG. The car sat empty. It looked like a toy.

The light probed, swung, stopped, swung back to the MG.

"At least we know he was here," Hibbs said. "That means the two of them are in Nancy's car."

Vallancourt crossed the driveway to the MG and aimed the light. The key was not in the ignition. A glint of gray metal in the farther seat caught his eye.

"Howard, Ralph, will you come here?"

His tone brought Conway and Hibbs lumbering over.

"Take a look."

"Looks like a cashbox."

"The one Dorcas kept in her study, Howard?" Vallancourt asked.

"Could be."

"Its disappearance was discovered right after her murder. The city detective seemed to consider it an important find."

"Don't you?" Conway asked.

"I'm not sure. We reached her place at about the same time, Howard. You were passing the MG when I pulled up. Did you get a look inside?"

Conway knuckled his chin. "I think I did. It's natural to glance inside a convertible when it passes with the top down."

"Did you see the cashbox?"

"No, John, I think there was a coat or jacket lying on the seat. Trenchcoat, maybe."

"The cashbox might have been under the coat," Hibbs said. "Anyway, the police can lift fingerprints from the box and determine if it really is . . . was Dorcas's."

"Yes," Vallancourt said, "I'm sure they can. I'm sure they will."

I'm equally sure, he thought, that Keith didn't have the cashbox with him when he went out the window of the Ferguson living room. He was in there with a murdered woman, and the box was outside, in his car.

Why didn't he keep going when he carried the box out? Why should he return to her lifeless body?

9.

From the advantage of the cottage porch, Keith watched Nancy's sedan crawl along the lake and disappear into the distant woodland.

It would be getting dark soon now. The lake was as peaceful as a church.

Keith told himself he should be feeling better. He knew the worst now. He knew what he had to do. Always in the past, when he realized the full extent of his predicament, a strange calm had come over him, an ability to crouch down within himself, watchful, ready.

The old man used to say he had a streak of bulldog in him.

Maybe I do have, Keith thought.

He scuffed at the porch floor with his toe, remembering.

It was some consolation to know how many times he had denied his father victory. The experiences went as far back as Keith could recall. The old man would freeze him out, cut his allowance, humiliate him, pile ridiculous chores on him. Like the time he'd made Keith spend a Saturday carrying leaves from the front yard a bucketful at a time.

And then the resort to physical violence. Keith would vomit in private, but facing his father he was stolid, prepared for pain, knowing whose endurance was the greater. The ending was always the same, with his father sweating, backing away finally with a curse. And the boy carrying a heavier load of hatred and contempt.

Keith walked to the top of the porch steps and sat down.

Of course, it hadn't been uninterrupted war between him and the old man. Mother was an angel, he thought. Vague, helpless, unable to cope with the old man; but she was jake, george, and number one, all put indefinitely together in a little woman everybody called Maggie.

Elbows on knees, hands knotted, he rubbed his forehead against his knuckles.

Mom, I'm glad you don't have to wonder and worry. About this thing now . . . and that Cheryl Pemberton mess in Florida.

They thought they had me. But I knew I could stand it. The nerves all dissolved, leaving nothing for them to get to. Like with the old man. Sixty hours of it. One after another of them. I worked them in shifts, Mom. And there weren't enough of them . . .

He jerked his head up, jumped to his feet, grabbed the porch post. A fluttering went through his chest. Too soon for Nancy. She hadn't had time to get to the drive-in and back.

He stood listening. He was certain the breeze had

carried the faintest sound of a car down the trough of the long, shallow valley.

He vaulted the porch rail, dropping like a cat to the yard. After a moment's hesitation, he ran toward the lake.

They've got her, he thought. They've made her talk. I should have gone myself, the way I wanted to. Why did I let her talk me into her going?

Far down the lake, twin shafts of light stabbed across the water.

Keith faded across the road into the shadows. He stood breathing hard, studying the dark hills behind him, the road ahead.

He had to decide quickly.

He jumped a drainage ditch with an easy flow of movement and started dog-paddling parallel to the road, in the direction from which the car was coming.

He could hear it quite clearly now. Far ahead of him, the car's lights danced, closing the distance rapidly.

He reached a cave of darkness beneath a giant spreading oak. He dropped in a crouch, hands spread on the rough bark.

He recognized the Continental as it surged past. John Vallancourt was driving. He wasn't sure how many people were in the car. Three, he thought. At least one man in the suicide seat, and an impression of another in the rear.

Howard Conway and Ralph Hibbs, he decided.

Join you for golf, fellows? A smile twisted Keith's mouth as the taillights of the car dwindled.

His grim humor was brief. He was again in motion. Vallancourt and his cronies would go to the lodge, look around and, when they found the place deserted, return this way.

She'll meet them head on, he thought. I've got to reach her before that happens.

Off the road, underbrush and rough stony terrain impeded his progress. He slipped to the edge of the road, looked back. The taillights of the Continental were far down the lake, almost to the driveway, he judged. Even if they looked down the road from there, at this distance they wouldn't see him.

Keeping to the side of the road, he moved at a ground-eating pace, loose and loping, getting his second wind and breathing through his nose.

He reached the woodland, stumbled over a shallow pothole in the shoulder of the road. Still no sign of Nancy's compact. Had Vallancourt and the others left the cottage yet?

His lungs began to pain at last, and he had to stop for a brief rest. He gulped deeply. Then he saw giant fireflies through the trees. Up around the next curve.

He stepped out into the middle of the road, gambling that he had correctly identified the sewing machine-like whirr of the small sedan's engine.

He began waving his arms as the headlight glow enveloped him. The sedan stopped, and he ran over to it. Nancy's face was white mist under her blonde hair.

"Keith . . ."

"Move over," he said, "quick."

He opened the door of the car and threw himself under the wheel. His body slammed against hers. She slid over.

"Hey," she said with a taut laugh. "I'm making mush of these hamburgers I got at the drive-in."

"Never mind that. Listen!"

He had turned off the headlights and engine. Nancy pulled the bag of hamburgers from between herself and the door.

"Keep it quiet, can't you?" he snarled.

Her face snapped toward him, shocked. "Keith . . ."

"For God's sake, shut up!"

She eased back in the seat, suddenly pressing away from him, from his voice, so cold and hostile.

He poked his head out. Down below the trees, the lake as an effective sonar, catching and echoing all sound.

"Oh, God," he chattered, "they're coming!"

"Who, Keith?"

"Your father and a couple of other men. Maybe a carload of them."

He knew there was no chance of getting the sedan turned around and beating the Continental in a race. He kicked the parking release, threw in the clutch. The sedan began to roll forward. He set the ignition key and put the gear shift to the third position. When the sedan had rolled several yards, he slipped the clutch out. The engine caught without the grinding of the starter.

Through the foliage he was now able to see the big car's headlights. How far away were they? Second or third curve?

He felt naked, disarmed, on the narrow road. Underbrush on either side formed hemming barriers.

He tried to unroll a mental map. The cottage

belonging to the Florida people . . . Harkleroad, that
was their name! . . . right after this next curve . . .

Or the curve after? The one that would put him
in full view of the approaching Continental?

He kicked at the accelerator. The sedan shot
forward.

He followed the heavy darkness of the trees and
thickets, headlights off. *Come on!* A century later,
there was a break in the dense shadows, a lighter
patch, the gravel of a driveway twisting up behind
the dark house.

Keith twisted the wheel, sending the compact into
the driveway. It jackrabbited upward, vanishing in
the shadows of the deserted house.

The Continental purred past on the road below.

10.

———◆———

Keith didn't like the looks of the proprietor. The motel had seemed made to order, an older one, clean, inexpensive. Not a fancy place, and not a seedy dump a rat would run to, either. Just an everyday, run-of-the-mill motel. The kind of place he'd told the taxi driver he wanted for himself and his sister.

"Say you had car trouble?" the proprietor said.

Keith nodded, looking at the registry card he was signing. Why was the old bird quizzing him? The story he had told was perfectly plausible: He and his sister . . . driving downstate . . . car trouble . . . the need for an overnight repair.

"I guess you want adjoining rooms," the lanky, wrinkled man said.

"If you have them."

"Sure." In a wise tone.

Keith let his breath out cautiously. This map-cheeked character with the granite eyes . . . did he think he'd spotted a couple of college kids shacking up for the night?

He handed the man the card. The eyes shifted. It made Keith want to reach across the registry desk in the dingy office and tap the old man on the chest and ask him what the hell was bugging him. Instead, Keith jammed his hands into his pockets.

"You'll have to sign a card of your own, honey," the man said, smiling at Nancy.

Keith pictured himself backhanding the old punk, wiping that wet, wise smile off the withered lips.

Nancy bent over the card. The eyes met Keith's across her shoulders. The eyes turned stonier, and the old man got two keys from a pegboard behind the desk.

"Just the one bag?" he asked.

"Oh, yes," Keith said. "Left the rest of the luggage in the car. It'll be locked in the garage until the mechanic gets started on it tomorrow morning." He reached down and picked up the bag. It was heavy. Her trousseau kit, Nancy had called it when they'd planned the elopement.

The heft of the bag, the sight of her blonde head bent over the registry card, caused an ache to spread through him. He was almost overcome by a feeling that it was useless to keep running. They were unreal people stumbling through a nightmare. Cold, greasy hamburgers for their dinner. Her compact abandoned on the other side of town. A ride on a municipal bus. A taxi to here. We're making progress like a turtle backing his rear into a pot of water the cook has got boiling, he thought.

"This way," the motel man said. Keys in hand, he started around the waist-high desk.

"Newt?" a shrill female voice called.

The man glanced with irritation at the open doorway beyond the desk. "Heather," he called toward the living quarters, "we got . . ."

"I have to go out, Newt. None of those crummy friends of yours while I'm gone, hear? I'll only be . . ."

A woman appeared in the doorway. She was thin and sallow, an arrangement of slats in clean, threadbare clothing. "Oh."

"You never give me a chance to tell you," her husband said. "This is Mr. and Miss Lonergan, Heather. They're staying the night. I'm putting them in three and four."

The woman glanced at Nancy's left hand.

Keith looked frankly into the narrow face with its pinched mouth and anxious eyes.

"We're not from the college, ma'am," Keith said with a forced smile. "Brother and sister, on our way downstate because of sickness in the family. Our car broke down and we can't get it fixed until tomorrow morning."

"Sure. Well, you'll rest easy here. We have a nice place." She brushed by Newt, took Nancy's bag, and led the way outside.

Keith glanced over his shoulder as he followed the woman across the parking area. Old Newt was standing in the doorway. Stiffly, watching.

The woman opened a door, switched on a light. A small, commonplace room was revealed.

"There, now," the woman said. "The young lady can have this number three. New print curtains, see? Like them, miss? I work my fingers to the bone keeping this place up. If I had to depend on that

sorry husband of mine . . . Here's the bathroom.
And a nice big closet. My father built this place, you
know. When he and mama passed away, I made up
my mind I'd keep it as nice as they left it. Respect-
able, too. We don't take in the trash some of the
older motels do nowadays."

She crossed the room, threw a bolt. "This is your
room, young man."

Keith followed her in. "Fine."

"I'm glad you like it." She moved about quickly,
like a sparrow. "I own up, when I first saw you two,
I thought to myself, uh-uh, a pair of those college
hellions. They do try to register here, you know. But
I took one look at you, young man——"

"Why, thank you," Keith said. And get the hell
out, he thought.

He looked through the window. Old Newt was still
in his doorway, watching.

The woman paused as she started from the room.
"Oh. We always collect in advance."

"I paid your husband."

"Oh, excuse me. By the way, you'll find extra
blankets in the bottom drawer of that bureau. Nights
still get chilly this time of year."

"Thanks very much." *Get out!*

Finally, she left.

He shut the door behind her, leaned against it.
Nancy was standing in the middle of the room, looking at him.

"Keith." She took a couple of steps toward him,
noticed his change of expression, came to an in-
decisive halt. "You're very tired, aren't you?"

"No," he said, "I'm not a damned bit tired. I can last for days. Weeks. I know how not to get tired."

She was turning slowly toward her own room, stricken. He felt a savage frustration. Something was happening between them. It had begun back there on the lake when Vallancourt's car had almost cornered the compact. It was getting worse. It was all that suspicious sonofabitch Newt's fault.

"Nancy . . ."

She shivered. Then she came across the room deliberately, put her arms about him, stood thigh to thigh against him.

"The only way you can hurt me, Keith, is to close the door against me."

"I don't understand why you bother with me."

"Why try?"

"I need to. I want to. If you were a plain Jane or a cripple, I might understand. But you could have your pick."

"Why do you keep running yourself down, Keith?"

He passed the back of his hand across his forehead. "You mix me up. Worse than hell, Nancy."

"Everything is mixed up right now. But we've reason for hope."

"Give me one."

She stood looking up into his face. "You really don't know how to hope, do you, Keith? You just know how to survive."

"I've made it for twenty-two years," he mumbled.

"Then you can keep on doing it."

"Nuts," he said.

"All right, I'll give you another. You think whoever killed Dorcas Ferguson is lying on a bed of roses while you're loose? While the case remains wide open?"

"His nerve won't break. I'm on the run. Why should he walk in and confess?"

"I didn't mean that, and you know it. But he's trying to cover up a murder. He'll make a slip. As long as the investigation goes on, we've plenty of reason for hope."

Outside, a rough-running old car started with a backfire.

Keith slid away from Nancy.

"Kill that light!"

She jumped for the wall. He eased up to the side of the window.

He saw an old sedan leaving the parking area. It stopped at the street's edge, and in the light of the street lamp he saw that the woman Heather was driving. She got the bucking jalopy into the street and disappeared.

Keith glanced back to the office of the motel. Newt was still standing in the doorway.

"That old guy suspects something!"

"Keith . . ."

"Damn it, don't use that patronizing tone to me, Nancy! I tell you, he thinks we're up to something. He's a canny louse, living off a woman who does all the work."

"Keith, you've got to control these suspicions."

"I know what I'm talking about. I could feel it in the old man. That Newt and my father . . . They carry the same stink in their eyes."

Across the parking area, Newt had come to life. He was at the telephone, dialing quickly.

Keith pushed Nancy aside. As he burst out of the cabin, she ran after him, caught his arm. "Keith!" she said in a sharp whisper. "You mustn't!"

He shook her loose without taking his eyes off the lighted window of the office. Newt was acting furtive. Any fool could see it. There could be only one reason why. The old man had given his wife time to get out of harm's way . . .

Newt spun about, guilt written all over his cunning face.

"What the devil . . ."

Keith jerked the phone from his hand.

Newt stood staring as Keith lifted the phone to his ear.

"You sure you want it that way, Newt?" a voice said. "The whole ten bucks on Sandy-boy in the fourth tomorrow at Gulfstream? Well, it's your dough, but if your wife finds you've been laying more bets . . ."

In a panic, Keith let the phone drop on its cradle, killing the voice.

Newt was pressed against the wall, studying Keith nastily.

"Boy, who'd you think I was calling? The cops, maybe?"

"Forget it," Keith muttered. "I'm sorry. I didn't mean anything."

"You acted like you meant plenty, busting in here this way. You know, you look damned familiar to me. You ever do time at Prison Farm Four? Nah, that ain't where I seen you . . ." Newt stopped, his mouth slack. He went mud-colored. He tried to recover, to move non chalantly across the office toward the sanctuary offered by his apartment.

But, Keith was there, grabbing a handful of sleazy shirt-front.

"Okay, let's hear it. Where have you seen me before?"

"Boy, I ain't. I swear."

Keith pulled the man up on tiptoe. "You're a liar. You've seen my face on every TV newscast today, in the newspaper. Isn't that it?"

Newt swallowed, his Adam's apple jerking. "Boy, why didn't you just stay in that cabin? I had my mind so set on calling the bookie soon as my old woman was out of here, I wouldn't of remembered you from Adam . . ."

11.

———◆———

Ivy Ferguson Conway was waiting when the three men returned.

"In the living room, Mr. Vallancourt," Charles said quietly. "Mrs. Ledbetter has been keeping her company, and I've left word at Mr. Conway's home, in case you dropped him there."

They went into the living room. Mrs. Ledbetter was standing beyond a high-backed brocaded chair. Vallancourt dismissed her with a nod. She slipped out of the room.

Ivy was sprawled in the big chair, very drunk. All her girlishness was gone. She looked like a surly, vain old crow.

"Home the hunters," she said in thick mockery. "Did the great big mans make heroes of themselves? I don't believe they did. The nasty delinquent is still at large."

"Ivy." Conway's voice was full of phlegm. "You've no business coming here in this condition."

"Dear boy, I had to welcome the shining knights. John, get me a drink."

"You've had enough, Ivy!" her husband said.

"This is John's house, and John can do as he likes in John's house, can't you, John? Poor John ... thought you knew her so well, didn't you? And Nancy turns out to be just another female with the usual streak of bitch."

Conway towered over his wife. He seemed about to strike her. Vallancourt caught his arm.

Ivy was staring at her husband's broad hand. Then he shook himself and moved backward, and she giggled. "We never never never strike little wifie before friends, do we, darling? Only in the privacy of home sweet home."

"Please, Ivy. We'd better go."

For an instant, his tone reached through the fog. Her eyes deepened briefly with suffering. "Home is where the heart is, Howie boy. So I have no home. Because you don't have a heart."

Conway took her arm. The glaze hit her eyes. She pulled away from him.

"Don't touch me, Howard!"

He straightened, standing heavy and miserable, not looking at either Vallancourt or Hibbs. "Ivy, John has more than his share of trouble without you ..."

"The devil with John! What do I care about John?" She clutched the arms of the chair. When her eyes refocussed, it was on Hibbs.

"Poor old Ralph. Good old Ralph. Here, boy." She puckered her lips in a whistle, producing a dry, gusty sound. "And what are you, Ralphie? With your heart lying in a funeral home? Big man of the auto business! Big front to everybody—"

"Ivy," Howard said distinctly. "We are going home."

Blearily she swiveled her head, looked at him. Then she crumpled and began to cry as he helped her to her feet.

"John . . ." Conway began.

"It's all right, Howard," Vallencourt said.

"Thanks. If you need me, call."

"Of course."

"Well. Good night."

Watching them leave, Vallancourt remained the self-possessed image in silver and tan. But Ivy's words stuck in his mind like knives. *She turns out to be just another female with the usual streak of bitch.*

Ivy's drunkenly candid assessment of Nancy, my daughter. How close to the truth?

His belief of a short time ago, that he understood his daughter better than most fathers, now seemed fatuous. He had also guessed wrong in at least one other respect. She had not postponed the seriousness of the relationship.

He pushed aside the temptation to dwell on the error. The truth went deeper. She was a healthy young female, designed by nature to desire and arouse desire. But physical need alone would not have caused her to take the plunge with Keith Rollins. Vallencourt knew beyond any shadow of doubt that she was not that variety of bitch.

She had gone to the lake cottage before the murder of Dorcas Ferguson, since she had not reported for any classes. Keith had homed in on the same spot. The meeting was therefore prearranged.

The nature of their dialogue was obvious, Vallan-

court thought. Thinking of what he had said, Nancy
had wanted to stall him, to wait. He had reacted in
the only way possible for a father, taking it as a re-
buff. And so she was in the dilemma of either pleas-
ing her father or doing what her love for Keith
Rollins demanded. Not an easy decision. And not
the kind of marriage she would have wanted. A load
on her conscience because of dear old dad. But, up
to that point, a spunky rightness in her actions.

Then, he thought, comes the crucial moment
when they meet at the cottage. Keith would have to
tell her that he is in trouble. It had to have been that
way. Otherwise there was no sensible explanation
for their actions, running, hiding, switching cars, not
heading for the nearest justice of the peace.

It was Nancy's last opportunity to turn back, and
she had let it pass. Either Keith had made it physi-
cally impossible for her to return, or she had been
convinced of his innocence and the decision had
been hers.

And Keith. Guilty and doomed, he was dangerous. Innocent and doomed, he might well turn
deadly.

The sound of a running car invaded the room.
That was Conway, taking Ivy away.

Vallancourt lit a cigarette and turned to Ralph
Hibbs. "Will you stay to dinner?"

Later, Hibbs rode with Vallancourt toward the
apartment building where Keith had been staying
with his father. When they were near the place,
Hibbs stirred. "Terrifying, isn't it, the way the world
can turn upside down? Like a ship breaking up

under your feet. I'm trying to recall the steadiness of the deck, John. Am I being a coward?"

"I think not."

"Just a matter of hours . . . I spend the morning showing a car, a big expensive one. I go back to my office with a big fat sale in my pocket. And all the time . . . Ivy wasn't the only one who leaned heavily on Dorcas, John. Maybe Ivy was right. I'm not sure how I'll get along without Dorcas's business brain."

Vallancourt glanced at him. "Are you sure you're not underrating yourself, Ralph? You built up the agency."

"Not alone."

"True, but maybe Dorcas didn't make as many of the decisions as you thought."

Hibbs subsided into silence.

Vallancourt pulled up at the curb.

"Will you need me?" Hibbs asked.

"I think not."

"Then I'll wait. I have no particular yen just now to look at a man whose son has a murder rap hanging over his head."

"It's you." Sam Rollins's sharp face caught light on its ridges. He was carrying a beer can. "What do you want?"

"May I come in?" said Vallancourt.

"Sure the place is good enough for you?" Rollins kicked the door closed. The living room of the flat was a mess. "Make yourself comfortable. You ought to feel right at home here. We're in the same boat, aren't we? My son. Your daughter."

"Have you heard from Keith?"

"You out of your mind? That young punk call on me? Not that it'd do him a damn bit of good."

"I was hoping . . ."

Rollins flopped into a chair. He grinned evilly. "Hoping. You would. You live in such a nice, hoping sort of world. Where everything is set up for you."

"Shouldn't we stick to the subject of Keith and Nancy?"

Rollins gulped the rest of the beer and sat with his arm dangling, the empty can touching the floor. "The fine home, the comforts, the whole bit. And she runs off with the first crummy thing in pants!"

"You think so little of him? Or of anyone who would have anything to do with him?

"Let's face it, Vallancourt. He's scum."

"He's your son."

"I wouldn't claim the bastard if he had the key to Fort Knox."

"You know," Vallancourt said, "twice I've heard that epithet tacked on him. By Ivy Conway, the first time we discussed Keith, now by you. Maybe it isn't an epithet at all, but the literal truth."

Rollins turned wary. "You're nuts."

"It would explain a few things. Ivy's aversion to him. Your attitude. Afraid of losing your link to his inheritance if he were proved guilty of that rape-murder in Florida."

"You've conducted too much business in foreign capitals, Mr. Ambassador," Rollins said, heaving out of the chair. "You should have brought along your cloak and dagger."

"I'm giving you a chance to level with me."

"Level? What the hell have I got to hide?" Rollins pitched the beer can toward a wastebasket and went into a small kitchen. Vallancourt followed him as far as the doorway. He stood watching as the man opened the refrigerator and took out a quart bottle of beer. "You wouldn't know how it's been with me, Vallancourt. All my life . . . nothing ever going right. And that damn kid hating me through it all."

"And Maggie?" Vallancourt said. "The lost middle sister of the Ferguson girls? She finally lay down and died to get out of it?"

"Listen, you can't accuse me . . ."

"I'm not accusing you of anything, Rollins. I'm merely saying that you'd never let go of Maggie and her bastard son."

"If what you think is true," Rollins said, fumbling with a bottle-opener, "I'd have given her the boot years before she died."

"Maggie had a wealthy sister who loved her, and who loved her illegitimate child as well. After all, there was Ferguson blood in the boy's veins. Your wife and Keith—they were your ticket to an easy life."

Rollins returned to the living room, Vallancourt following. "He won't see no light from the bottom of this hole he's in. This is one time he'll get the stubborn streak kicked out of him."

"What have you told the police?"

"The truth. I think he's guilty. He's got an extra switch in that brain. I ought to know, I've seen it. The switch clicks, he turns into Mr. Hyde. Just one thing the cops have to do when they corner him, and that's take no chances. Cornered, he'll kill, quick, like an animal." Rollins sucked at the beer, looked at Vallancourt, laughed. "Doesn't it give you the creeps, knowing your daughter's with a rat like that?"

"I can't share your pleasure in the situation," Vallancourt said coldly.

Rollins shrugged, dropped into his chair. "I did what I could for the kid. Tried to beat that streak out of him. Now it's up to the cops. And it ain't a teenager he's killed this time. It's an important woman, a business and social leader. The meat grinder is hungry, and the cops ain't looking for nobody but him."

"Who was his father, Rollins?"

"Me."

"I think you're lying. You've known the truth and hated him from the day he was born."

"Pal, you're boring me." Rollins tilted the bottle and took a long swallow.

"I suppose it was the one act of rebellion against you Maggie ever allowed herself. And you made her pay and pay and keep on paying, didn't you?"

"Look, Vallancourt, you got no proof of anything. So why don't you quit wasting my time?"

Vallancourt took hold of the man's soiled shirt front and yanked him to his feet so abruptly that his head snapped back. The beer bottle flew from his hand, spewing foam on the floor.

"One word of advice, Rollins. If Keith should get in touch with you, think twice before you set him up in a way that will cause shooting. Stray bullets and my daughter are incompatible quantities. Are we clear on that?"

Vallancourt let him go and went to the door. He looked back at the sprawled man. "I hope I don't have to come back, Rollins. Think about it."

Vallancourt's breathing was not quite normal when he reached the car. He got under the wheel. Ralph Hibbs stirred, clicking off the car radio.

"Anything on the newscasts, Ralph?"

"No, except that he's still at large."

"Then he's beaten the odds and slipped through. Or he's still in town, which is more than likely. He knows he can't trust either the MG or Nancy's car. He'd pick a place with care. Not a dive where he and Nancy would stand out. Not a fancy place, where questions might be asked. And certainly not a downtown hotel, with the city hemming him in. He'll want space around him for maneuverability."

"You've described a type of motel, John."

"Yes," Vallancourt said.

"There aren't so many we can't check them out."

"I know." Vallancourt started the car.

12.

———————

Keith herded Newt from the office into the drab little apartment at the rear.

Now what? Keith asked himself. No more kookie stunts. You've already fouled it, tipping this guy to your identity.

The motel man was recovering from the shock. He backhanded a drop of spittle from the corner of his mouth, leered as if he sensed Keith's indecision.

"The girl with you," Newt said. "She's the big shot's daughter, ain't she?"

Keith made no useless denial.

"Ought to be worth plenty to him, a kid like that," Newt mused.

His movements were casual, but his eyes betrayed him.

The old man had worked his way to a cheap knee-hole desk that occupied a corner of the room. As his hand shot to the top drawer, Keith threw himself across the distance between them.

The impact slammed Newt against the desk,

closing the drawer on the old man's hand. He screamed, eyes watering.

Keith took him by the shoulder and yanked him clear of the desk. The proprietor reeled against the wall, cradling his injured wrist and whimpering.

Keith pulled the desk drawer open. A tingle went through him. He reached slowly, and his fingers touched the cold metal of a .38 revolver.

The gun was cheap and old, but the heft and balance of the weapon seemed good to him. He had the oddest feeling that the gun had been designed to fit his hand.

As he turned, holding the gun, the old man looked at the young face and forgot the pain in his wrist. He began sliding down the wall. His knees touched the floor.

"Listen, kid, you can't . . ."

"What's to stop me? When you get right down to it, there's not a damn thing to stop me. And if the gun was all right for you, why not for me?"

"My God, boy—"

"Come on, you creep. Explain it to me. Who makes the rules? Punks like you? Politicians on the take? Cops who look the other way when some Mr. Big gets behind a steering wheel stoned to the eyeballs and takes the chance of killing somebody? Then why not me?"

"Kid, I figured you for real smart the minute I saw you. Too smart to get himself in a worse jam."

Keith laughed. "Worse? They say I raped and killed a girl in Florida. They claim I knocked off the most respected woman in the state. Now if I step on a worm, it's going to make it worse?"

"You got to give me a break, kid! I won't talk! I swear! It ain't even my gun, kid. Heather . . . she got it while she was here alone, when they had me in prison. It's her fault, not mine."

"You make me sick, Newt, you know that?"

"I know a little what you been through, boy. You're keyed up tight. Only don't do nothing while you're nervous. It's the first thing you got to learn."

"As a teacher, Newt, you miss like a junkyard jalopy."

Newt's head slumped. Keith's interest in him became less immediate. He stood thinking. Then he said, "You'll take us out."

The old man raised his head, began inching up the wall.

"When your wife gets back with the car," Keith said, "we'll borrow it. You, me, and Nancy."

"It won't work, kid."

"Why not?"

"The car . . . It's junk. Just use it for errands. Get it on the open road and it heats up. It won't run for beans."

"We'll make it run."

"You're wrong, kid. It ain't the car you need. You'd be better off stealing one."

"I'd still be behind the wheel. No, you'll drive us out, Newt. They're not looking for your face. Certainly not for a car like that."

"Kid—"

"How'd you like this gun barrel right where the teeth meet the gums, Newt?"

The old man whimpered. The racket of a noisy car in the parking area drifted in to them.

"It's your wife," Keith said. "Remember the girl in Florida, Newt, and the big-shot woman. You've got snake brains. You'd better use them. Now let's get going."

He slipped the snub-nosed revolver in his trousers pocket, keeping a grip on it. With his left hand, he gave the old man a shove.

They were several feet into the parking area when the man's wife met them.

"Ma'am," Keith said gently, smooth-cheeked, innocent in the dim lighting, "I phoned our relatives downstate to let them know about our car breaking down. The sickness there is worse. Our relative may be dying. We want to rent a car and push on tonight. Your husband said he'd drive us to the car-rental agency."

"I don't give no refunds!"

"That's all right. We put you to a lot of trouble. We don't mind you keeping the night's rent."

"Ain't that I mind doing a favor. But I'm not one to borrow, or lend."

"Just your husband and the car for thirty minutes or so. We'll never forget the favor, ma'am." Keith edged closer to Newt and touched him with the gun through the fabric of their trousers.

Newt coughed. "These people are strangers, Heather. Not somebody I've hatched up a party with."

"If I knew you'd come right back—"

"I will, Heather. Sure to goodness, you can't turn them down."

"All right." She opened her purse, handed him the keys.

The old man's eyes were bugging, trying to get across a silent message. Keith's stomach bunched in knots.

But the woman's mind was elsewhere. "Now, Newt, don't you be a minute longer than you have to."

"I won't, Heather." It was a croak of defeat.

Keith crowded old Newt into motion. Heather stared after them a moment, then went inside.

Nancy was standing in the open doorway of the cabin.

"Bring the bag," Keith called. "We're not staying."

"What is it? What's happened?"

"Just bring the bag!"

Nancy moved out of sight. The two men reached the car.

"You're doing fine, Newt," Keith said. "Buying the smartest insurance in the world."

Nancy reappeared. "Over here," Keith said. She came across the parking area in a very fast walk.

"Keith," she began worriedly.

"No time," he said. "I'll explain later. Newt's going to drive us."

She stood there for an exasperating minute.

"For God's sake, Nancy, get in, will you?"

The menace in his voice galvanized her. She opened the door quickly and got into the car.

"Under the wheel, Newt. I'll ride in back."

The car crept out of the parking area with rattles and bangs.

"Just baby her along," Keith said, "and she'll run all night."

He slumped in the rear seat, letting out a long

breath as the lights at the edge of town fell behind them. Fenced farmland, woods and meadow, all dark and silent, slipped past.

"How far are we going, Keith?"

"All the way." He studied the pale sweet blur of her face. "He knows about us, Nancy."

She glanced at the old man, who was driving doggedly, hunched over the wheel.

"How much are you paying him?"

"Paying me?" Newt choked.

"Forget it, Nancy. He's doing us a favor."

"No, Keith, I want to know why a stranger should run the risk of helping us. I want to know what you've promised him."

"Promised me," Newt sniveled. "Lady, talk to him, talk to him!"

Nancy lit a cigarette. Keith glimpsed her face in the brief flame. The change in her eyes, the set of her mouth brought a dryness in his throat.

"Or is promise the wrong word, Keith? Would threat be a better word?"

"Nancy, we'll be out of this in a little while."

"I haven't wanted to think about it, Keith. But I can't help it. Will we ever be out of it? I keep telling myself nothing matters, so long as I can believe in you."

"You can! You know you can!"

"But this man . . . And his wife—did you say you'd hurt her, Keith?"

"I said nothing of the sort! Look, Nancy." He jabbed Newt's bony shoulder. "This punk doesn't care about his wife. He's an ex-con. She's just somebody to keep him in food, a roof over his head, in the motel she inherited. If he had the guts he'd probably cool her."

"Don't rile him," the old man choked. "I've seen his kind in the pen, lady. They look like Joe College, but they carry a short fuse. Let it lay! He's got a gun."

Keith saw the rigor invade her shoulders. He expected her to say something, to turn on him. But she merely sat there. He was prepared for anything but this utter absorption with the darkness.

"Okay," he flung at her finally. "But ask him where I got the gun."

"Does it matter?"

"He was going for it, Nancy. A man doesn't go for a gun unless he intends to make use of it."

She continued her refusal to look anywhere but at the night through which they moved. "Does that include you, Keith?"

His lips slitted, twisted. She was putting him on a spot. Why couldn't she understand? If he started acting soft, Newt would get ideas. The old man was a hardcase, the kind who gouged eyeballs. You had to put the screws in his kind, and keep turning. Any hint of human feeling and Newt figured you for a blubber-belly.

"Nobody but Newt has anything to worry about, Nancy."

She stirred at last, turning to look at the old man's crooked profile.

"Newt," she said quietly, "I don't care very much for you."

Newt concentrated on his driving.

"But you're a matter of concern to me, Newt."

"Yes, lady," Newt said eagerly.

"I'm concerned, Newt, because you're the next drop of grease on the skids."

"Nancy," Keith said distantly, "I'm handling this deal!"

"Newt," she said, "I want to be rid of you."

Keith inched his way forward. "Nancy, I'm telling you . . ."

"I want you out of our lives, Newt." All feeling was pared from her voice. "Turn into the next side road. We'll leave you where it will take you a good part of the night to walk back to the motel. We must have a little time."

"You can trust me, little lady! I know trouble first hand. And I hate the fuzz. I won't say a word. I hope you make it."

"You're a liar," Keith said. He sensed that Newt was hovering on the brink of a decision, balancing risks, tempted by the thought that his chances might be far better now than at any time in the future.

A break in the woods ahead marked a dirt road that meandered over deserted countryside toward the hills.

Newt slowed the car.

The gun came out of Keith's pocket. Nancy screamed his name and threw herself backward.

Her body pressed against Keith. The gun was smothered. He struggled to free himself. His arm flailed and struck Newt. The car veered onto the soft shoulder of the road. Newt's foot struck the brake too quickly. His shoe slipped from the edge of the worn pedal and jammed against the accelerator. The car bucked across the shoulder. The right front wheel crunched into a shallow ditch as the engine died.

Instinctively, Keith grabbed Nancy. The car smashed to a stop, lurching, almost tipping over.

Keith's head crashed against the door frame. He had only a dazed awareness that old Newt was getting out of the car; that Nancy, unharmed, was pulling herself back across the top of the seat.

He heard the thud of the old man's footsteps. The pounding was faraway, unreal. He made a herculean effort to force will into his muscles.

Keith half fell when he got out of the car. He squinted through fog. Newt's running figure was a weaving blur. But after several reeling steps, Keith's senses began to clear, his stride steadied, Newt became a sharp image. A frozen look snapped over the dark landscape, as if a giant clock said *tick* and then waited, refusing to *tock*.

Keith had no authentic sense of movement. Newt seemed to be rushing backward toward him, the weasel face turned to throw a look over the bony shoulder, the eyes desperate, the etching mouth gasping for breath . . . The sight gave Keith renewed strength. He knew the old man would not escape. All uncertainty left him.

Newt ducked, twisted, darting away from the empty road toward the heavy thickets and trees.

Keith's rush carried him past the old man. He wheeled, laughing. Let the punk sweat. Prolong the agony.

Newt jumped the ditch. As he came down, Keith hurtled into him. With a wild cry, the ex-convict spun and threw a looping punch. Keith raised his shoulder to take the blow. He launched his fist like a piston and felt the stringy musculature of the old man's middle quiver and collapse.

Grabbing his abdomen with both arms, Newt reeled in a senseless circle. Keith punched him on the nose. Cartilage flattened, a black fountain spurted. The color carried no bloody meaning for Keith.

Newt's knees struck the weedy earth. As he pitched forward, Keith struck him again in the face, and the old man flopped on his back. His fingers clawed and dug as he slewed himself around. He looked like an overturned turtle.

Keith was reaching for his collar when Nancy flew against him. "Stop it, Keith! You'll kill him!"

He struggled to pull away from her as Newt blindly burrowed his way into the thickets.

Nancy seemed to have eight arms. "Let him go, Keith—for your own sake . . ."

Keith suddenly grew quiet. He stood without docility or penitence, spent. Nancy clung to him; almost gently he disengaged her arms.

He walked to the car, examined it. He squatted near the right front wheel, picked up a bit of dirt, flicked it at the car.

"Spindle's broken," he said. "When this crate moves again, a wrecker will be towing it."

"Keith, a moment ago . . ."

He rose; his face was remote. "I don't want to talk about that creep. If you're ready to cut out on me, Nancy, go ahead."

"Is that what you want?"

"You know I don't. But I was wishing instead of

thinking. I was fool enough to think you would stick. It's the same old story. But don't let it worry you, Nancy. I'm used to going it alone."

Twin lights appeared in the darkness. Would the oncoming car stop? Sooner or later some curious motorist or a highway patrolman would see the wrecked jalopy and apply the brakes.

Keith dog-trotted across the highway, glancing down the road as he crossed the shoulder. The shadows of the trees closed over him. A dim trail of sorts pointed toward emptiness and silence.

Behind him on the highway the car swished past. His tension lifted. That one hadn't been stopped by the sight of the junker. Nor by a girl standing alone.

Keith stopped and turned. Nancy was no more than a dozen yards away, closing the gap between them.

13.

———◆———

Vallancourt sensed Ralph Hibbs's growing discouragement. He was not strongly affected by it. By training, tradition, and experience, he and Hibbs were very different. The attempt to anticipate their quarry's moves, to track down a course of action as if a mistake would not have terrifying consequences —these were factors in a milieu strange to Hibbs. Vallancourt was the hunter.

With Hibbs standing disconsolately beside the door, Vallancourt tapped the bell on the motel desk and waited.

Although their search had so far proved fruitless, Vallancourt was not discouraged. Against big game there were no rewards for impatience or discouragement. You followed the trail and your hunches. He had never felt more vitally alive.

A woman came through the doorway beyond the desk. She had a spare frame, a dry-skinned face. Her mouth was plotted in lines of strain, her eyes snappish.

Vallancourt felt himself tighten.

She looked surprised at Ralph Hibbs's prosperous portliness and the well-cut excellence that was Vallancourt.

"What can I do for you?" She seemed to take it for granted that such men would not have chosen her place for lodging.

"We're looking for a young couple," Vallancourt said with absolute assurance, "who registered here this evening."

"We only had one young couple. Don't get much calls here nowadays. Folks have gone soft on fancies —swimming pools, air conditioning."

"One couple is all we're after," Vallancourt smiled. "The boy is husky, with black hair in a widow's peak—good-looking youngster, twenty-two years old. The girl is tall, blonde, with a golden tan." He added, "Pretty."

The woman's eyes flickered. "My husband registered them. What have they done?"

"Which unit are they in?"

"They took two cabins. Registered as brother and sister."

Bless you, Nancy, Vallancourt thought. And bless you, woman, for telling me.

"They said they wasn't from the college," the woman said. "We're careful here, we don't break no laws. They told my husband they was on the way downstate to see a sick relative and their car had broke down."

"They gave you a plausible story," Vallancourt said. "But they're runaways."

"I didn't know."

"Of course not."

The drab, pale pink of her lips curled inward until it disappeared. "If they're what you say, I want them out of here."

"They're what I say. Where are they?"

"You the girl's father?"

"Yes."

The woman sniffed like a wolverine. "Probably give her a nice home, car of her own, all the advantages. Kids nowadays are going to hell in a basket."

Vallancourt held himself in. It would do no good to rush her. A glimpse of his inner suffering would probably cause her to keep him dangling.

"You might as well sit down over there and wait," she said. "They ain't back yet."

"They checked in and went out?"

"Practically right away. I just had time to do a little shopping and come back. They was ready to leave when I drove in."

"Did you notice the car they were driving?"

"It was Newt's and my car. Newt's my husband. They came here in a taxi."

Dumped Nancy's car, he thought.

"May I speak with him?"

"Newt went with them. I let him talk me out of the keys. Should have knowed better." Her lips curled. "They didn't make even a show of going to the car-rental agency, like they said. Instead, they turned right on the state road. If you ask me, they're over in Tuscawana by this time, lapping away in some gin mill. With Newt sitting next to your girl so's he can let his leg bump hers now and then. When that old lech gets back . . ."

"Will you describe your car?"

"An old one. Packard, about the last that was made. Black and gray; the gray part is on top."

"Now if you'll give me the license number, please."

"I don't want nothing to happen to my car."

"Shall I call the police?" Vallancourt asked pleasantly.

"BD-4418," she said quickly.

"Thank you." Vallancourt jotted the number down. "Come on, Ralph."

"I just don't like trouble," she said. And when Vallancourt reached the door, she called, "Better watch out for Newt. He's got a mean streak a mile long, 'specially when he's been drinking."

"We'll be careful."

"I didn't know, remember," she said. "You can't law me. Newt was the one registered them."

"You have nothing to worry about."

"Mister, with Newt you always got something to worry about."

They went outside. When they were in Vallancourt's car, Hibbs said, "A rented car, John? I mean, after he ditches the Packard?"

"I think we can rule that out, Ralph. He'd have to identify himself, show his driver's license." Vallancourt studied the highway briefly. "He means to make his try tonight, in the jalopy with the other man driving."

"Newt sounds like an unwholesome character," Hibbs said. "Keith might have bribed him. He was pretty well heeled with the money from Dorcas's cashbox."

"The primary question is direction," Vallancourt said. "The right turn on the highway might have been a deception play. But we'll have to play the odds. He was under pressure and in a hurry, conditions that don't make for complicated thinking."

A block from the motel Vallancourt turned into a filling station. While the Continental was being gassed, he used the station telephone and called police headquarters.

A desk sergeant had to say hello three times before Vallancourt could bring himself to answer. Let him go through, he was thinking. Hang up and don't throw Nancy into the danger of what might happen at a roadblock.

But let him through, and you make him drunk with triumph. It might be catching.

Stop him?

Surely by this time Nancy has begun to think, to be her old self. Whatever her feelings for him, she must know now that this route is inexorably downward. At this very moment she may be praying that you'll do the best thing for both of them.

On the other hand . . . play the ostrich and you make the showdown tougher. The moment of truth you and Nancy will have to face some time, somewhere . . .

"John Vallancourt speaking."

"Oh, Mr. Vallancourt. Have you heard from your daughter?"

"Not directly. But I've run across their trail." Vallancourt gave the desk sergeant the motel woman's story about the Packard.

He hung up, the steadiness of his hand a passing mockery. He went outside, paid for the gas, and got into the Lincoln.

As the car hissed onto the highway, Hibbs said sulkily, "I'm still here, you know."

"The roadblocks are ready for him, Ralph."

Hibbs looked at him a moment longer; than he shifted his gaze to the highway ahead.

The big car pressed over the outer edge of the speed limit.

Suddenly Hibbs jerked forward in the seat. "John! Off there in the ditch!"

Vallancourt had already seen the wrecked car. He eased off, letting the Continental roll onto the shoulder before bringing it to a stop.

He had the door open and was out before Hibbs could hitch himself around.

Vallancourt had swung in several yards past the ditched car. He had completed his circuit of the old Packard by the time Hibbs came puffing up.

"Looks like the one," Hibbs gasped.

"It is. The license checks."

"Is she . . . Are they . . . ?"

Vallancourt shook his head. His eyes were probing the darkness.

Ralph had lumbered around to the front of the jalopy. "Doesn't look as if they hit anything—until the ditch." He glanced from the car to the road. "It's a straight stretch. Funny place for a car to go off the highway. Unless an oncoming car forced them off."

Or there was trouble inside the car, Vallancourt thought.

"Might as well notify the men at the roadblocks."

Vallancourt nodded absently. His brain was busy trying to put itself behind the dark, brooding eyes under the fine forehead and widow's peak.

Newt is driving, he thought. And I'm sitting beside him. . . . No, that would leave Nancy alone, out of my line of vision, in back. I am in the rear seat where I can watch Newt and lay a steadying hand on Nancy's shoulder.

Everything is going well. We have the car and Newt to drive us out.

Then it begins to go sour. How? Why? Perhaps Newt wants more money. Or gets cold feet. No . . . won't do. It's something more than a sudden, irrational dissatisfaction with a deal.

Back up . . .

Newt is driving. He wrecks the car? Deliberately? If so, it was certainly not from greed, but from fear. The only explanation. He's afraid of what will happen once he's past the roadblocks. He'd rather take a chance on running the car in the ditch here and now . . .

Vallancourt moved to the hood of the Packard and laid his palm on it. The metal was still warm.

He suddenly thought, Keith, you haven't had much time. You may be watching every move I'm making.

Any of the thickets offered a shelter. For Keith— and what else?

"Ralph . . ."

"What is it?"

"You've expressed a desire to be of service."

"Anything I can do. You know that."

Vallancourt took the keys from the ignition, moved to the trunk of the Packard, opened it. From the welter of old papers, oil cans and junk tires, he salvaged a jackhandle.

"Turn the Lincoln around. Find a phone and get the highway patrol out here."

He watched the Continental swing full circle. Then, as the red taillight glow dwindled in the darkness, he stepped off the road to stand in the thickest shadows, listening, waiting.

He won't like the waiting, Vallancourt thought. He's an aggressor, not a counterattacker.

Stepping very carefully, inches at a time, he drifted several yards further from the Packard. He carried the jackhandle loosely, ready for instant launching in any direction.

The silence became a heavy question. Had some unwary motorist stopped and found himself impressed into service as a chauffeur? If so, where was Newt?

In the stand of trees ahead, a twig cracked. In the silence, it sounded like a shot.

"Keith," Vallancourt said quietly. "Before you make a move, listen to what I have to say. You've a chance, understand? The cashbox, Keith . . . the box that belonged to Dorcas Ferguson. I question the way it showed up after it disappeared from Dorcas's study. It's a detail that makes me want to hear what you have to say."

Nothing.

"Nancy—if you're there with Keith, convince him

that I mean what I say. By itself, the cashbox isn't enough. But it's a starting point." Vallancourt's tone took on an edge of anger. "Keith, you young fool! I'm trying to tell you I don't think you're guilty. And I want to help you."

He held his breath. Twigs cracked. Undergrowth swished somewhere ahead.

And then a human form stumbled into view. The shadow was too tall and rawboned to be Keith's.

Vallancourt moved quickly to the other man. The man was old, and his face was clotted with blood. He saw that the old man's nose was broken.

"Are you Newt?"

"Yeah. Where is he? Where is he?"

He took the trembling arm and helped the old man toward the highway. "I don't know. Neither he nor my daughter was around when I got here. Did he do this?"

Newt cursed steadily and horribly. "If I was younger—so help me I'd break his back. I'd rip—"

"You've no idea where they went?"

"No," Newt stumbled; Vallancourt supported him. "I laid low, scared he was still looking. Then I heard your voice." He hawked blood from his throat. "The way he hit me . . . Nearly killed me. I think he busted something loose in my gut."

"We'll get you to a doctor, then you'll have to tell the police what happened."

"Sure," Newt croaked. "I'll tell! One time I got nothing to hide from the fuzz. He made me haul them off. Used the gun."

Ice water coursed down Vallancourt's back. "Gun?"

"Belonged to my wife. He took it. Even money they bury the first man catches up to that sonofabitch."

14.

———◆———

Stabbing between the slats of the Venetian blind, a strip of early sunlight lay across Keith's forehead like a scar.

The downward creep of the band of light measured the rising of the sun. When the light touched his lids, his eyes opened. He blinked, moving his head away from the dazzle.

He sat up quickly, immediately remembering the long stumbling hike through the night to the lake cottage.

In the familiar surrounding of the lodge's living room, he sprang from the couch. He had intended to rest, not to sleep. But exhaustion had overcome him.

Noiselessly he moved from the stone and timbered room to the pine-paneled hallway. He stopped at the first door and inched it open.

He stood in silence, looking at Nancy. She was still here; she hadn't run away. Fully clothed, she was sleeping relaxed, her young body curled like a child's, one slender arm outflung. He looked at the firm lines of her thighs; the swell of her hips, the

119

cups of her breasts warmed and thickened his blood. He took a step into the room. But then he turned and moved away.

In the stainless steel kitchen, he boiled water for instant coffee and opened a can of condensed milk from the generous supplies that Dorcas Ferguson had always maintained in the lodge.

He sat down to the coffee, playing with his thoughts. What would it be like with her—the long smooth body naked, the lips in fever, the buttocks writhing, demanding? Coffee slopped as he picked up the cup; he had to steady it with both hands. A picture leaped to his mind, of his hands undressing her, the slipping of a button, the slide of a zipper, the tantalizing peeling of each garment. . .

He kicked his way back from the table. The light wooden chair tilted and fell as he jumped up.

He moved to the window, fumbling through his pockets for a cigarette. Why not? he thought bitterly. You've been kidding yourself. There's no way out for you this time. In a little while it will all be over.

So why not?

You've already lost part of that wonderful miracle the two of you possessed. Admit it. It was too fine to last very long. She's beginning to doubt you. You sensed it last night, after you slugged the old creep. You knew, as you brought her here, that regret and fear were building in her.

She didn't run away because she was so damned tired; both of you were caved in when you finally got here. She must have fought sleep, waiting for her chance, thinking of Cheryl Pemberton, listening for a sound from the living room. In the end, exhaustion had slugged her, too.

He dropped his cigarette and ground it underfoot on the kitchen tile. Quickly, he passed through the cottage to the bedroom door.

She had heard him this time, swung her feet off the bed. She was sitting up, warm and wobbly from sleep.

An instant change came to her eyes. She was afraid, all right. Terrified. His lips twisted. Move a few feet, he thought, and you can confirm every rotten thing they've ever believed and said about you.

"I've got some coffee, Nancy, if you don't mind the instant kind."

"I'll be right out."

He turned away from the doorway, went back to the kitchen. He had coffee steaming in two cups when she came in.

The terror was still in her eyes, her smile.

"Went beddy-by as if I were drugged," she said.

Small talk, he thought. She's going to cut out. So it's the same old story. He could have throttled her as she stood there.

She picked up her coffee and sipped it, moving about the kitchen opening cabinets, refrigerator, freezer.

"Eggs?" she asked. "Some cereal?"

"Toast will do."

While Keith smoked and drank his coffee, she made toast, got out butter and marmalade. They ate silently. The food was tasteless.

Like, man, you counted on a first breakfast together once, he thought.

"Scram," Nancy said. "Get some sun on the porch while I KP."

Her bright pretense was touching, but transparent. He walked out of the kitchen, knowing that the decision was crystallizing in her head. He wondered how she would tell him and what he would do when the moment came.

He swung over onto the porch railing and sat hunched, legs dangling. It would be different now, being alone. He had glimpsed what it was like not to be alone.

He heard the hiss of water, the clatter of dishes. Why the hell hadn't she sneaked out during the night?

She'd had her chance. She hadn't taken it. She should have realized how the prospect of again being alone would hit him now.

A breeze soared through the hills, across the long surface of the lake. It carried sound within it.

His back straightened. He grasped the porch post beside him. His head tilted to one side.

Then he swung around and dropped to the porch floor. Nancy was at the sink when he ran into the kitchen.

"We're leaving," he said curtly.

"I haven't dried the dishes."

"Never mind the damn dishes. We've got to get out of here! A car's coming around the lake."

She stood planted at the sink as if she were paralyzed.

He crossed the kitchen and grabbed her arm.

"Don't you understand? We came back here because I figured they wouldn't expect us to take cover in the same place twice. But it hasn't worked out. Could be the police coming. Or your father. Somehow, he digs the way my mind works."

"Keith, it's no good."

"So what?" he cried. "It's never been any good. But we have to keep trying. Come on. Let's go!"

She arched away from him, looking at him with pity and fright. Resentment boiled up in him.

"I should have taken you last night!"

The words brought no lessening of his pain, merely the turning of the invisible knife inside.

"It isn't me you're striking at, Keith. You don't mean that."

"I said it, didn't I?" He started to pull her with him. "I don't want to be alone, Nancy. Not now. You'd better hope we get out before your father walks in here."

"All right," she said quietly. "You can let go of me. I won't run away."

He chose the back door. The yard was on a grand scale, with redwood patio furnishings and a barbecue pit. They ran to the stone retaining wall. He jumped up on it, reached for her hand, hauled her up beside him.

"This way!"

They fled across the narrow stretch of open hillside to the cover of the woodland. The shade of the trees fell over them, soft and cool. Against the quiet of the lake and the woods and growl of the approaching car came to them distinctly.

Keith loping ahead, they moved through the trees

for about two hundred yards. Nancy was breathing heavily.

"Okay," he said. "We'll rest a minute."

She sank to a patch of moss beneath an oak tree, folded her arms about her knees. Her head drooped.

Keith said, head cocked, "The car's stopped." That brittle clarity struck him again. He thought of the dishes she had left stacked on the sink drain, the cigarette he had crushed out on the spotless floor, the rumpled bed where Nancy had slept. He felt for the short-barreled revolver hidden beneath his shirt.

"I wish I knew for sure," he muttered, "who's in that car."

She raised her face. "You said dad . . ."

"A guess. But I can't take chances on a wrong guess."

Tears came to her eyes. She made a gesture, as if to reach for his hand. Then her hand fell to her side, on the moss.

He was looking in the direction of the cottage.

"Could be Aunt Ivy, or her husband. Even Mildred Morgan, the housekeeper, up to ready the cottage so the town house can be closed for a while after the funeral." Murmuring his thoughts aloud was no help. He was unable to evaluate the risk of returning quickly to the cottage and trying to make off with the car.

"We'll wait," he said finally. "It's safer. Get up."

Nancy got to her feet. They worked their way along the spacious curve of the hill, the lake to their left, visible occasionally through breaks in the foliage.

When they had reached a position beyond and

around the end of the lake, Keith veered their course downward. After several minutes of walking, they came in view of a house.

The place was smaller and less elaborate than the Ferguson lodge. It was a squat, stout log structure, the woods growing close at the rear, the lakeside road passing to the front of it.

Keith helped Nancy down an embankment. He had already noticed the lack of tire marks in the dirt driveway and the unflattened bunched leaves and pine needles which had drifted onto the back porch.

He inspected the hasp and padlock securing the back door. Nancy watched stolidly, leaning against the porch rail. He slipped the gun from his shirt, inserted the tip of the barrel in the hasp, and snapped the lock. He flipped the flange back and turned the knob. The door opened with a rusty sound. A smell of must flowed out.

"Lots more of the niceties than when the Indians were prowling," Keith said mirthlessly. "But we don't use them. Catch? The place is deserted. We keep it looking that way."

He motioned Nancy inside. When she was in, he shut the door.

At the same instant, Ivy Ferguson Conway was rattling her key in the front door of the Ferguson lodge, not noticing that a key was really not needed.

The bulky shopping bag in her arms made her entry an awkward one, and she reached with a spike heel to nudge the door shut. She went down the paneled hallway and fumbled under her burden to open the door to the furthermost bedroom.

She set the shopping bag carefully on a bureau. Then she kicked off her shoes, unbelted her expensive polished cotton dress and, consulting the mirror, fluffed her short brown hair with a touch of her fingers.

She saw a trim, girlish woman with rather empty eyes and a haughty expression. She made a face at herself.

She picked up the bulky bag and carried it to the bed. Here she sat down, setting the bag on the floor.

The deserted silence of the cottage caught at her. That Keith . . . They said he had taken refuge here after Dorcas . . . after what happened to Dorcas. If somebody had walked in on a boy like him . . .

Ivy shivered and made an effort to put such ghastly thoughts out of her mind. She stopped and opened the shopping bag. It held a half dozen fifths of Scotch. She babied the first bottle from the bag and opened it.

She held her breath during the first long swallow. Gagging, eyes watering, she placed the uncorked bottle on the nightstand and stretched full length on the bed.

The rebellion in her belly was gradually quelled by the Scotch. A wry smile lifted her lips. Why was the first drink always so damn difficult?

She reached toward the nightstand—toward temporary oblivion.

15.

Vallancourt returned to his home from police headquarters in mid-morning. Ralph Hibbs was waiting in his study.

"I heard a newscast," Hibbs said. "The search is now state-wide."

"The police think Keith got hold of a car and slipped through. An incident downstate caused the waste of several hours."

"What incident?"

"A man was found badly beaten, unconscious, near some dive of a bar early this morning. He was lying in a ditch at the rear of the parking lot and it looked as if he had been there for some time. While he had a driver's license and auto registration, he had no keys. Looked promising, but turned out a dud—some sordid business involving two men, a prostitute one of them had picked up, and a drinking bout. The man talked readily enough when they finally brought him around."

"Nancy may phone you, John."

"I'm hoping so, but I'm not counting on it. There

are a number of reasons why she may not." Reasons he did not care to think about. For the byways of hindsight, Vallancourt thought, are the hiding places for anxiety, and anxiety saps a man. God knows, he thought, I need everything I've got.

"Have you heard from Howard this morning?" Hibbs asked.

"Early. He came by police headquarters. He was on his way to discuss arrangements with the mortician."

"Later, he called me. Looking for Ivy. Seems he got back home and found her gone."

Vallancourt offered cigarettes from the carved box on his desk. "You've known the Ferguson women a long time, haven't you, Ralph?"

"Why do you ask?"

"Dorcas trusted you. I've always had the impression," Vallancourt struck a match, "that you were more than just her business associate."

"We all need a father-confessor at times," Hibbs smiled sadly. "Even Dorcas."

"Strange that she never married. I wonder why. Dorcas was made for a husband and children."

"The one man she might have married was killed years ago when his hydroplane flipped during a Miami regatta."

"I didn't know that," Vallancourt said thoughtfully.

"She rarely referred to it. I don't know the whole story; never pressed her for it—picked it up by bits. I do know that afterward she went away for a long time to try to forget."

Idly, Hibbs spun the world globe that stood near

the vast desk. He watched continents and oceans spin by under his fingers. "She was a rare woman, John."

"All people are rare to you, Ralph."

Hibbs looked up slowly. "I suppose they are. Even characters like Sam Rollins." He made a queerly appealing gesture. "I know how people feel about me. They see a bumbling, naive sort of slob —good old Ralphie. I don't really mind. I can't help the way I feel about people, and it doesn't cost me anything. In fact, if you believe the best of people, you get the best out of them more times than not."

"How long ago did that hydroplane accident happen to the man Dorcas was in love with, Ralph?" Vallancourt asked slowly.

"I'm not sure."

"Twenty-two, three years ago?"

"Just about," Hibbs said with an odd hiss.

"Keith's age," Vallancourt said.

The other man stopped the spinning globe with a sudden slap. "So you suspect, too," he said softly.

"I'm reasonably certain Sam Rollins isn't Keith's father. Sam's always known it. So he's hated the boy, refused to assume any measure of responsibility. But he never broke the relationship, because Keith is his meal ticket.

"If it had been Sam's wife, Maggie, who had borne a child by another man, Dorcas could have taken care of her sister and nephew and cut out a brute like Sam Rollins. But she didn't. It adds up, Ralph."

Hibbs was pale about the lips. He said nothing.

"I'm speaking of a good woman who was young and full of life and loved a man. It happens every day, Ralph. Dorcas was carrying his child, and they intended to marry—I don't believe she would have given herself to any other kind of man. But he was killed, and she was building an outstanding business career. She was afraid of scandal and disgrace. And she was human."

Hibbs stirred. "So you figure that, rather than give the child to strangers, she turned him over to her sister and brother-in-law." He looked unhappy.

"It would explain several things," Vallancourt nodded. "The strong physical resemblance between Keith and Dorcas. Same hair, same eyes, same quick intelligence and fighting spirit, which in the boy has been battered and misdirected.

"It would explain Dorcas's undiscourageable interest in Keith, her providing for him indirectly all these years, even bringing him here after the Florida rape-murder thing. It would explain Sam Rollins's following Keith here. It would explain Sam's inside track even after the boy came of age and Maggie died. Need I go on?"

"No," Hibbs said. "I thought I was alone in suspecting. My case was built on watching Dorcas with him, her eyes, her expressions, little things she said about Keith, the way she said them."

"You were never sure?"

"I didn't think it my business to try to confirm my suspicions." Hibbs wiped his face with a damp handkerchief. "I don't think Keith suspects at all. Sam Rollins was too solidly real in Keith's life for the boy to dream he was another man's son."

"So what we have done," Vallancourt said, "is reduce this affair to matricide."

Hibbs shuddered. "What a ghastly word!"

"It's in every dime-store dictionary, I'm afraid, Ralph."

"But John, the boy didn't know! Anyway, how sure are we that he's guilty?"

"Not sure at all," Vallancourt said. "But that's damn little comfort. The fact is, guilty or innocent Keith is on the run, with the whole world chasing him. With his temperament, that could make him try to bring everything down with him."

"I know," Hibbs said miserably. "That's what I'm most afraid of, John. It keeps haunting me."

"And time is working against us," Vallancourt said. "If he did get hold of a car, he's probably out of reach. If not, we have a chance. He may have returned to the lake cottage."

"We knew he was there earlier. We almost caught him. It's the last place he'd choose."

"Which would make him think of it as the first," Vallancourt said.

When they reached the lodge, Vallancourt recognized the two cars in the driveway.

Ralph did also. "Howard's and Ivy's," he said. "So Howard's run her down." He seemed depressed.

They approached the cottage slowly. Howard Conway had come out on the porch and was waiting, gray and tired. His eyes, however, reflected annoyance.

"She's in there drunk." Conway's heavy lips pulled themselves into a mockery of a smile. "Family skeleton, boys, secret of the country club queen. Once in a great while, when the accumulated pressures of living get too heavy for her, Ivy goes for the bottle. She'll be fine in a day or so. She always is."

"It isn't news to me," Hibbs said gently. "But I've never found it worth talking about."

"Good old Ralph," Conway said grimly.

"We were playing a long shot," Vallancourt said, "coming out here."

"Keith and Nancy?"

"Any sign of them having returned here?"

"Someone has been here."

"Are you sure?"

"There are used dishes and a rumpled bed in the first bedroom off the hallway. Butts in an ashtray near the living-room couch. I started noticing after I'd found Ivy and calmed down."

"Only the one bed mussed up?" Vallancourt asked with an effort.

"I think he spent the night on the living-room couch, John. They both smoked a lot. The butts in the bedroom ashtray show lipstick smudges. Those near the couch don't."

Vallancourt gave silent thanks. For the first time he began to realize that he was an old-fashioned father. If they had gone to bed together, did it really matter? All other factors excluded, they were in love with each other—or had been.

"I was searching the place when I heard your car," Howard Conway said.

"As he must have heard Ivy's," Vallancourt said, taking himself in hand. "We can guess his choice of direction. Away from the lake road. An incoming car would present a threat."

"He must have left fast," Conway said, "before he found out that it was a lone woman driving the car."

Hibbs looked around at the hemming hills. "He may be in shouting distance this minute."

"Not necessarily. He's got several thousand acres to hide in. It's my opinion he's long gone. If he'd stuck close, he'd have made a try for Ivy's car."

"But he likes cover," Vallancourt said. He had been deep in thought. "A cottage. A motel room. An attic." He started from the porch. Conway glanced inside the house, then fell in beside him.

"Ivy will be out for a long time," Conway said. "She isn't going anywhere, and I'm needed here like a boil on my secretary's fanny. You staying, Ralph?"

Hibbs shrugged. "I've been with it this far, Howard. I'll keep going."

Vallancourt stopped at the top of the porch steps.

"Let me go, Keith," she was saying again. "Let me

"Let's keep one thing in mind. If Keith's taken shelter in an unoccupied cottage, we want him to know we're coming. We have to move openly. Otherwise he may panic and do something foolish."

Both men nodded.

"Think he'll bargain?" Conway asked.

"I don't know. But I want him to have the chance to warn us off. I want talking room. As long as there's talk, hotheads don't fight."

"Isn't it stretching the law," Hibbs asked, "giving him a chance to get away?"

"Nancy's welfare is my law at the moment," Vallancourt said.

"We need luck," Conway said. "The motel man wasn't very lucky."

"He was luckier than he knows," Vallancourt said grimly. "Keith didn't lay a finger on the man until he became a threat . . . Keith might have killed him, but didn't. His overriding thought is to hide, to get away. No doubt he's felt a sense of nemesis, a lack of choice in everything that's been forced on him."

"You sound as if you're defending him!"

"We need to understand him, Howard, if we're to keep from triggering him. He has a need to rationalize a rightness into everything he does. I want to direct the process until Nancy is safe."

"He's been under pressure quite a while now," Ralph Hibbs said. "What if he's slipped over the line?"

16.

In the living room of the log cottage, Keith stripped a muslin dust cover from a big chair. He glanced at Nancy. In the gloom created by the shutters and the drawn blinds, her face and hair gave a blurred impression of loveliness with details obscured. He could look at her without enduring the sight of the changes in her.

"Might as well cradle it," he said. "The chair's for free."

She came to the chair and sat down. He watched her, yearning.

"You don't have to do it like a robot," he said savagely.

"You offered me the chair, Keith."

"And you're so damn obedient!"

He turned away. His eyes stung; he was going to jelly inside, he thought. Time had grown teeth, grinding him to shreds. He wouldn't break suddenly; nothing in him would snap. He was just being picked to pieces, taken apart. Like a worm being cut into sections.

He looked over his shoulder at Nancy. She sat gripping the arms of the chair, head turned, staring at the floor.

Why in hell did I ever meet you? Keith thought. Then there would have been none of this almost-having, nearly-winning, having it end up slipping through my fingers.

"Big devil cat got your tongue?" he sneered.

She shook her head, bit her lip.

"Okay," he said, making a flat gesture with his hand. "Okay, oh-oh-kay!"

He walked across the room and sat down on the floor, back against the wall.

"Anything special you'd like to hear? Want me to tell you what a hot-looking dish you are, doll?"

She looked at him then.

"Maybe you'd rather hear about me," he said. "Cops all over the state looking for me. I've crowded the politicians out of the headlines today. They're spending thousands of dollars this minute trying to find me. Cool, hey? My old man always said I'd make the grade. 'You bastard,' he'd say, 'you'll end up on the business end of a police bullet one of these days.' Damn dutiful making your old man's predictions come true. Don't you think so, chick?"

"You're convinced you have to go that way," Nancy said.

"My God!" he said. "It talks! You see any alternatives?"

She turned her face away again. He snapped his fingers, hard, rapidly.

"Come on, doll, you can do better than that. You're a sexy piece who happens to have brain to go with the equipment. Why don't you give me a bookful of alternatives? Let me pick and choose."

"Maybe there aren't any, Keith. Not for you."

"So I should be somebody else. Everybody else has alternatives."

"Let me go, Keith," she said like a little girl.

"Cut out? You? You're the babe that came on the joyride of her own free will. I didn't hold a gun to your head."

"Let me go, Keith!"

"But I've got a gun now," he said. "Full of bullets. Bang, bang, bang! They make holes in people and the blood runs out and they fall down dead."

She raised herself from the chair. He watched her almost sleepily.

Nancy was reminded of a big black and white cat she had once had. It would crouch over a bug for endless minutes, only its tail twitching. The day the cat had killed a bird, she had asked her father to give it away. That night she had cried herself to sleep over her lost, loved, hated cat.

She took a step from the chair, then another. She was halfway across the room.

Magically, he was standing before her, blocking her way.

"What's the rush, doll? The party's just starting. In another couple of days it'll really jazz. We're bound to snag a crate by then. We'll go crashing out."

"You'll go alone, Keith."

"The hell I will. I like this togetherness kick. I find it the greatest. How could I dream of doing a solo?"

"You won't make it, Keith," she said. A great sadness was in her voice.

The sadness reached out and touched him. Almost he let it go through. But then he forced himself to laugh. "Why not? Other cats have made it."

"But not you, Keith. Even if you were within reach of it, you wouldn't let yourself stretch that last inch."

"So what's the diff, a hundred years from now?"

"No difference a hundred years from now. But we don't have a hundred years. The difference is today and tomorrow."

She was so right that a sense of doom overwhelmed him. It had lain buried in him all his life. He recognized it now. He had glimpsed it before, many times, in a dream, or in his father's eyes. At last he was face to face with it, and the face of doom was no stranger.

"Let me go, Keith," she was saying again. "Let me take what I have left with me. Don't destroy it all."

"They'll know where you came from."

"No. I won't tell, Keith."

"What's to stop you?"

"Don't you know?"

"They'll make you tell."

"They can't."

"They've got ways. They'd work on you. I know. It happened to me for sixty hours in Port Palmetto, Florida."

"My father wouldn't let them."

"*He'd* get it out of you."

"No more than they would." She put her hands

on his shoulders. "Can't I make you see? Don't you understand at all?"

Close to her, he could not avoid the details of her face, that precious, lovely, hated face. His brain pulsed and pumped in his skull.

Why couldn't she see through his talk? he wondered. See the desolation inside him? Understand that he couldn't stand the thought of being alone at the end? He'd been alone most of his life, knowing that he was different, that there was something strange about him. Why wouldn't she stay to the end?

Without warning a man's voice cut through the log and mortar walls.

Keith moved first, flinging his arm about Nancy's waist and clapping the palm of his other hand against her mouth.

The voice outside was joined by another. Two . . . no, three of them at least.

They were making no pretense of stealth. He was instantly suspicious. They were looking for him—there could be no other reason for their appearance —and yet they were tipping him off, giving him a chance to get set.

Her father's voice . . . and Uncle Howard's . . . yes, and Ralph Hibbs's. The big, soft man's sermonizing tones were unmistakable.

Nancy struggled briefly, and Keith's hand tightened on her face. He could feel the bones of her cheek and jaw and teeth under his fingers. She rolled her eyes with pain.

The brittle time-suspension snapped into place.

His mind raced. Had they all come in the car he'd heard? If others were outside or on their way . . . John Vallancourt had outguessed him.

They were here. They had seen the signs of disturbance in the Ferguson lodge and Vallancourt had pegged his compass point of flight.

Turning Nancy around, he walked her toward the back door. With Nancy as his shield, the hunters' position would not be so good. He'd warn them to stand clear. He'd take her with him into the timber. When he had sufficient cover, he could make a break for the hills. Good thing he hadn't yielded to sentiment and let her walk out. He really needed her now.

Push back the end minute by minute, second by second, Keith. Damn them all!

Then he stopped. He stood still, with Nancy's back against him.

Don't give in to the first impulse, he told himself. You've really got to cool it this time.

Man, they want you to step outside. It's the thing they're after. They're betting you'll react to pressure and do half their work for them. That's exactly why they've come with the yak-yak, the lack of caution.

Cross Vallancourt up, Keith thought. A rabbit doesn't get hit until he's flushed.

His iron clasp kept Nancy immobile. She heard her father's voice, calm, reasonable, unhurried: "Keith, we know you're in there."

The hell with you! Keith thought.

"Howard Conway and Ralph Hibbs are with me, Keith. But no police. No arms. No threats. We know you have a gun. We'll keep our distance. It can't hurt you to talk to us. How about it, Keith?"

Sweat crept down his face. He was more certain than ever that they didn't *know* he was inside. They were stabbing in the dark. Well, he wouldn't fall for it. Let John Vallancourt deliver his sweet little speech outside every cottage around the lake. By that time, Keith thought, I'll be over the hill.

The voices informed him that they were splitting up. Howard Conway was drifting up the hill around the cottage. Ralph Hibbs called to Vallancourt from below.

Keith stopped breathing as footsteps scuffed on the porch. Then they were going away again. Keith half closed his eyes; dizziness swept over him.

He waited. Nothing was moving outside now. No sounds came to him. The need to know what was happening became urgent.

"Not a sound," he whispered in Nancy's ear.

He eased his grip on her just a little. Pulling her with him, he moved to a front window. Slowly he removed his hand from her mouth and inched a slat in the Venetian blind.

Through the narrow line of vision, he saw them on the road below. They were all there. As he watched, they turned away from the cottage and went on down the road.

When they were out of sight around a bend, Keith let the blind slat fall. He leaned against the wall, releasing Nancy. His muscles were suddenly flaccid, his stomach stirred sluggishly. But he was buoyed by the thought that he had beaten them. Give them time to work their way far down the lake, he thought. Then out the back, across the hills.

It was then that Nancy made her move. She was a flicker, like a bird, in the near darkness. He plunged after her.

She reached the dining room. Without looking back she grabbed one of the cane-bottomed chairs at the rustic table. He saw the chair and heard its clatter, but he was too close to avoid it. The chair fell in front of him and he pitched forward, lunging for the end of the table to break his fall. The house shook under his weight as he struck the floor. He heard the back door open and slam.

Keith scrambled to his feet. Pain sheared through his right knee. He ignored it, trying to reach the door. But the door echoed the slap of metal as she threw the flange over the heavy staple.

He struck the door with his shoulder, grunting. Again the house shook. But the door refused to yield. He bounced back, holding his shoulder.

He stood there gasping. How good it would be to tear the door apart with his bare hands. She had slipped the broken padlock back in the staple, he knew, securing the hasp. The lock was as effective against him as if it had not been broken at all.

He wasn't beaten yet.

He wheeled about, returned to the dining room, grabbed a chair.

With the chair drawn back at full cock, he approached the nearest window.

17.

"The next house is almost a mile," Howard Conway said. "The one up on the Point."

"I think we've drawn a blank, John," Hibbs said. "We've tried three cottages now without luck. I don't think he'd have gone all the way to the Point."

"We'll try it." Vallancourt walked doggedly along the dusty road, studying the stone house set on the jut of land far up the lake. "If we miss there, we'll go back for a car. On second thought, Ralph, maybe you should return for a car now. Bring my Lincoln."

He pitched Hibbs the car keys, and Hibbs started walking hurriedly back around the lake.

Vallancourt and Conway trudged on. They had gone a few yards when Hibbs's voice stopped them.

"John! It's Nancy!"

Vallancourt had already whirled and begun to run.

She had come out of the trees near Hibbs. Slipping, falling, she slid down the embankment formed when the road was cut.

Hibbs reached her first. But Vallancourt shouldered him aside and took her in his arms.

"Nancy, Nancy," he said. He held the trembling form very tightly. She sighed.

After a moment, he held her away from him, looking at her hard and long. That was when Nancy began to sob. So he pressed her against him once more, murmuring to her, as he had done when she was a little girl in trouble.

She shook herself, raised her face, even managed a faint smile. "I'm okay, dad."

"He didn't harm you," Vallancourt said. "No, he didn't."

"There's so much to explain, daddy, to try to make you understand . . ." She touched her father's lean cheeks with her fingertips, turned to the other two men. "And you two . . . it's so good to see you."

"By God, if he had done anything to you," Conway began.

But Ralph Hibbs simply nodded and set about furiously wiping his eyeglasses.

"How long since you got away from Keith, Nancy?" Vallancourt asked.

"I was with him until a few minutes ago."

"Where?"

"The house back there. That log one. We heard you coming. I thought for a while he was going to yell at you, order you away. Then he decided to lie low."

"He's as cunning as a damned stoat," Conway growled.

"He forced me to remain quiet," Nancy said. "After you'd gone by, he let go of me and I managed to get out the back door. I fastened it with the hasp and padlock he'd broken to get in. As I ran from the cottage, I heard him smashing a window."

A breeze off the lake stirred her blonde hair. She seemed older than when Vallancourt had seen her last.

"Dad . . . what I did I did willingly. I went to him because of what I felt for him . . . and I had to leave him because of the same feeling."

"We don't have to talk about it now, darling." Vallancourt glanced at Conway and Hibbs. "Take her back, and wait for me at the Ferguson cottage."

He gave her a quick smile and vaulted up the embankment.

"Alone, John?" Hibbs asked anxiously.

Vallancourt nodded and plunged into the trees and made for the rear of the log cottage. Fifty yards up the hillside a fault had ruptured the earth, thrusting a spiral of granite upward. He began a hunter's noiseless ascent. Then he was looking down, surveying the lay of the land.

Keith at last admitted to himself that he was bushed. He had to rest. He lowered himself to a bed of pine needles and lay on his stomach, gulping air.

He wanted to close his eyes and stay there forever. But closing his eyes was no good. When he did, Nancy's face materialized. How she had looked at him that last time. He shook his head, wincing.

After a while he sat up. Got to get moving again.

He rose, backhanding sweat from his face, thinking of his long circling flight across the face of the hill. He had intended to go straight across, but the steep spine of shale near the ridge had turned him back. From a distance it had looked rough but climbable. Up close, it had loomed perpendicular.

He raised his eyes. Should be able to start upward again, he thought.

He started climbing, working out the stiffness that had settled in his muscles during the pause.

Still no sounds of pursuit, he told himself gratefully. They must have found Nancy. Or she found them.

Okay, Mr. John Vallancourt, have your damn reunion. You've got back everything that matters to you. No more worries, no fears. You can call the state fuzz, the county fuzz, the city fuzz. Tell them where the bull crap is. Mark it on a map for them. Then sit back and watch the fun. God damn you, Vallancourt!

He reached a small clearing where the spreading arms of giant oaks formed a natural arbor. As he took his fourth step into the clearing, a shock rippled over his body. He set his foot down like a man in a dream, with impossible slowness.

A man was standing at the edge of the clearing, to his left—Vallancourt.

"I've been waiting for you, Keith," Vallancourt said, as if Keith were merely late for a golf date.

Keith stood very stiff and still.

"How did you get up here?"

"Walked." Vallancourt's tone was conversational. "I figured you'd made your try across the ridge, and the shale cliff would turn you back. In that case you'd have to swing around this way. So I came here on a straight line, and here we are."

"You think you're so great," Keith said thickly.

"Not at all. But when you've done a little hunting you learn your terrain and the instincts of your quarry."

"I don't like being quarry," Keith said. "I don't like it one damn bit. I don't like hunters. I don't like you."

"I don't blame you, Keith."

Keith was silent. Suddenly he said, "Hunters carry guns. Have you got a gun?"

"I've a dozen very fine guns at home," Vallancourt said. "And I'm reasonably good at using them."

"Too bad you didn't bring one with you." Keith's eyes were roving. He looked very much like an animal, standing there, at bay.

"Why bring something I'd have no intention of using, Keith?"

"That's tough, old man. I've got a gun."

"I know." Vallancourt stood there impeccable, unwinded, not a hair out of place. Tricky! Tricky as hell! Damn him.

"You know?" Keith said. "The hell you do."

"Of course. The gun you took from the motel proprietor."

"And you came anyway? You're a fool!"

Vallancourt did not flinch. "It's your folly we ought to be discussing, Keith. Besides, I'm not really running any risks."

"You think I wouldn't use the gun on you just because you're Nancy's father?" Keith snarled.

"Being Nancy's father has nothing to do with it.

I simply don't believe you're the kind who'd use a gun on a friend."

"Friend! Are you kidding, Vallancourt?"

"Would I come here unarmed, knowing you have a gun, if I didn't trust you?"

"You can't trick me!"

"And how could I trust you," Vallancourt asked patiently, "if I didn't have some measure of belief in you?"

"You're a liar!"

"Nancy believed in you, Keith." Vallancourt took an easy step forward.

Keith bolted.

"Keith!" Vallancourt called. "You mustn't! I want to help you!"

Keith began dodging among the trees. Vallancourt launched himself. He ran easily, with the long stride and kick of the professional runner. The distance between them began to shorten.

Keith glanced over his shoulder. Seeing how near Vallancourt was, he gave a short, angry cry and wheeled to one side. His feet slipped on pine needles, and he lost a tick of time. Then he was upright, meeting Vallancourt's rush squarely.

His full young weight was behind the fist that he hurled at the chiseled face under the silver hair. But the fist never met anything. Instead he lurched off-balance, floundering to keep from falling.

He whirled about to look for Vallancourt. His fist lashed out a second time.

A steel vise clamped on his wrist. He heard Vallancourt's quick hard breath, felt the impact of the older man's surprising strength.

The pull of his wrist carried Keith forward. His body slammed against Vallancourt's hip. He felt the ground give beneath his feet and saw the treetops pinwheel against the blue sky. The earth slammed against his back and shoulders, smashing the breath out of his lungs. He tried to rise.

Vallancourt's knee hit him in the groin. He fell back, nothing real for the moment except the pain. Helplessly, he felt the gun being jerked from his pocket. Then the weight lifted from him. Keith crawled to his feet, lashed out feebly.

"You don't know when you're licked, do you?" asked the quiet, friendly voice.

Useless now. He had the gun . . . Keith stood with arms dangling, slobbering breath.

Vallancourt made no move with either his hands or the gun.

"Son, you have one hell of a fine physique and a lot of potential, but you lack the training," Vallancourt said. "I was a Marine field commander in the war, and I keep in shape. No, Keith. Stand easy."

Keith panted, "This isn't the end. You haven't got me down there yet. It's a long way from here to the lodge."

"The way back is as long as you want to make it, Keith." Vallancourt studied Keith intently. "Yes, you have a great deal of her in you."

"Her? What you are talking about? Who?"

"Your mother."

"My mother?"

"Dorcas Ferguson," Vallancourt said.

Keith glared at him.

"You won't believe it on such short notice,"

Vallancourt said, "but it's true. Your real father was killed in a hydroplane accident before he and your mother could marry. She loved you too much to give you away. She gave birth to you in another city and left you with Maggie and Sam Rollins. All these years she's cared and provided for you. I'm sure she didn't know the full story of the relationship between you and Sam. He cowed Maggie to silence and put on a front when your mother, in the guise of aunt, was around.

"But as she grew older, I'm convinced Dorcas came to realize the wrong she had done you. Your mother, in your time of greatest need, brought you here, and I'm positive that only her death stopped her from telling you and the world that she, not Maggie Rollins, was your mother.

"I know you didn't kill Dorcas Ferguson, Keith, and that's why I've gone to all this trouble to talk to you.

"You can keep running. Or you can come off this hill and take hold of your future—start acting rationally. Which will it be? It's up to you. I'm going back to the lodge."

Vallancourt glanced at his hand, raised his arm, and threw the gun in a high, flashing arc. It vanished from sight with a crash.

Before the sound died, Vallancourt was walking rapidly down the hillside.

18.

———

They were waiting for him on the porch of the Ferguson cottage.

"You didn't nail him," Howard Conway said with disappointment.

"Aren't you glad?" Vallancourt smiled.

"What do you mean?" Ralph Hibbs asked.

"Go inside, Nancy," her father said.

A glance at her father's face was enough. Nancy went into the lodge.

"I mean that the case is still open. A fugitive is still at large. There's still the chance that he'll stop a police bullet and close the book on the Dorcas Ferguson murder." Vallancourt smiled. "Except for one thing. I know who the murderer is—and his name isn't Keith."

Conway and Hibbs exchanged puzzled glances.

"I suspected Keith was innocent quite early," Vallancourt said. "In fact, when the cashbox from Dorcas's study turned up in Keith's car. He was not carrying the box when he broke out of the house. That means it had been put in his car beforehand.

151

It simply wasn't reasonable that Keith would kill her, lug the cashbox out, then return to her lifeless body.

"So it looked very much as if the cashbox was a plant, and Keith the victim of a frame-up—the sacrificial goat being offered up by the real killer to save his own skin. At the time, of course, my principal concern was not Keith's innocence or guilt, but getting Nancy back before she came to harm.

"The morning of her death, Dorcas phoned Keith to come to her home. I'm convinced she was going to tell him the truth about their relationship—that she was his mother.

"When he got there, he found her dead. She had been dead only a short time. Someone had preceded him there. Obviously the murderer. And the murderer, having been informed by Dorcas that she had summoned Keith, and why, had used those few minutes to set his stage. He was desperate. He had nothing to lose at that point, and his neck to save."

"Ralph," Conway said, "you went by Dorcas's house early that morning."

"Even if Ralph did," Vallancourt said, "it was too early, some time before she was killed. At the time of her death Ralph was selling a car to a customer."

"That's true," Ralph Hibbs exclaimed. "I remember mentioning it to you, John."

"And it would have been a silly attempt at an alibi if it weren't true," Vallancourt said. "Too easily checked."

Howard Conway moved to the edge of the porch and leaned against the railing. "So where do we go from here?"

"Police headquarters, Howard. We'll have a matron sober Ivy up."

"Damned poor joke," Conway said.

"Yes, it was. But it's not on Keith any longer, Howard," Vallancourt said. "I don't think you intended to kill Dorcas, but she's no less dead. And to have framed Keith . . . Did you think your own hide worth the lives of a boy and girl, Howard?"

"Afraid you've lost me on the curve, John." But Conway was beginning to sweat.

"Then let's take it from the beginning," Vallancourt said. "You tried to talk Dorcas out of revealing the truth about Keith. Your motive was obvious. If the whole world knew she was his mother, she might then leave everything she had to him. And that would freeze out Ivy, her sister—your wife. You'd counted on that inheritance. So you argued, and she wouldn't listen, and you lost your head and shoved her, and the edge of the table got in the way—and there you were, with a dead woman on your hands.

"You were on a very hot spot, Howard. Keith was due to arrive momentarily. But . . . the boy was already under suspicion of the nastiest kind of murder—that Florida business. Why not let Keith pay for the crime? Make it appear that Dorcas, the doting aunt, had become suspicious of his part in the Florida rape-murder, disillusioned. That he'd knocked her down when confronted, killed her, stolen money from her study, and fled.

"Sam Rollins was the only other person, aside from you and Ivy, who knew the truth about Keith. You figured that, if it ever came to that, you could buy Sam's silence.

"Your more immediate problem was your wife. You had to tell her Dorcas was dead, and you had to force her to pretend to be Dorcas—to make the call summoning me, the needed witness whose additional testimony would wrap it up tight for you.

"Dorcas was dead. Nothing Ivy might do could change that. And you had a prime weapon. You could threaten Ivy with the exposure of Keith as Dorcas's son and heir, if you went to jail. Ivy wanted that inheritance, too. She made the call."

Ralph Hibbs was gaping at Howard Conway as if he had never seen him before.

"You were cutting it thin, but you had luck," Vallancourt said. "But not quite enough, Howard. There never seems to be enough luck for that kind of thing.

"First detail to go haywire for you was the cashbox. I imagine you wanted it to look as if Keith had gone from the living room back to the study, grabbed the box, and opened it on his way out.

"You snatched the box, opening it outside while you waited for Keith's arrival. I'm sure you intended to return the box to any point in the house where it would look as if Keith had dropped it. From your hiding place you saw Keith arrive. A mere matter of minutes for it to fall in place for you now. If I got there late, it wouldn't matter. You could pretend you'd just arrived, too; you'd seen Keith drive away hurriedly; we'd both go inside and discover the murder.

"Instead, I arrived a few seconds early and you had to leave the cashbox in Keith's car. Still, no harm done, you thought. The police would catch Keith and close the whole thing out in a matter of a few hours. The presence of the cashbox in his car would be taken to be plain stupidity on Keith's part. Anyway, so long as Keith's true relationship to Dorcas remained unknown, no one could pin a motive on you for the murder.

"Second detail to blow up in your face was your certainty that Keith would be caught. But he wasn't. He kept fighting, dodging, stayed out of the hands of the police. He strung it out, and the more he strung it out the deeper I got into it. And I got to the truth, Howard. About Keith's parentage, the reason for the fight that led to Dorcas's death, the identity of the man who wanted Keith's true parentage to remain unknown, the only woman who could have posed as Dorcas on a telephone.

"Everything building like a wall around you, Howard. Until the final detail that nails the lid on—with implications that nauseate me!"

Vallancourt's face was iron.

"When we started checking lake cottages earlier today, it was you, Howard, who went to the rear of the cottage where Nancy and Keith were hiding. Nancy later came out that back door, the door through which they'd entered after Keith broke the lock. *You couldn't have missed that broken lock, Howard.* You knew they were in there, and said nothing. *You wanted them to stay.*

"Why would I want that, John?" Conway asked blindly.

"I think you meant to go back there later—alone," Vallancourt said. "I think you were so deeply corrupted by what you'd already done that you intended for the police eventually to find a young murder suspect in that cottage who, in despair, had apparently killed himself. And—God help you!—if Nancy was still with him when you went back, I believe you could have nerved yourself to making it appear a murder-suicide pact. Right, Howard?"

Conway wiped his forehead.

"It's a nice tale, John. But you spent too much of your life in countries where intrigue is a way of life. This isn't a foreign country. Here, you have to have proof."

"I don't have to prove a thing, Howard. That's the job for the police. I don't think they'll have much trouble. How long do you think Sam Rollins will hold out? And Ivy—you can't delude yourself into thinking she'll last very long when the questions start coming—and she has no Scotch to fall back on."

Howard Conway rolled over the porch railing. He struck the ground and was off running toward the road, the hills, anywhere.

And then Conway stopped dead. Keith was coming along the road, toward the lodge.

"Keith!" Vallancourt shouted. "Howard Conway killed her. Do you understand? Howard is the guilty man, Keith. Take him!"

Keith stood with face raised toward the cottage for an instant, intently. Then he looked at Conway.

Conway scrambled about and started running in the opposite direction.

Vallancourt watched a young tiger gather himself and spring. He nodded soberly as Conway crashed to the road. No more mental block, Keith, to bar the final act of winning, Vallancourt thought.

Nancy was back at her father's side. From below came the sounds of turmoil.

Nancy touched her father's arm. "Dad . . ."

"Going rather well, isn't it?" Vallancourt said. "Do you have a cigarette, dear?"

"Dad, there's still that Florida thing . . ."

"Keith's claim of innocence down there was the truth, Nancy, or he was acting drastically out of character. I'm not speaking of the first uncertainties and fears I sensed in him. I'm speaking of the basic stuff I've discovered in him, the material that survived the slings and arrows. Do I make sense?"

Her eyes were misty. "You make sense, dad."

"But no more of this elopement nonsense. I want to give you away in style."

"Oh, yes, daddy!"

"And Sam Rollins—don't you think we ought to suggest to him a less hostile environment?"

"Whatever you say, daddy."

Three months later, on a day in late summer, Vallancourt happened upon a wire-story squib with a Port Palmetto, Florida dateline.

A known degenerate, with a long history of sex offenses had been picked up on a molesting charge and, to the surprise of Port Palmetto police officials, had confessed to the sex murder of Cheryl Pemberton.

Vallancourt cut out the squib, sealed it in an envelope, and addressed the envelope to Mrs. Keith Rollins at Niagara Falls.

Other SIGNET Books You'll Want to Read

The Best in Fiction from SIGNET.

Big Bestsellers from SIGNET

☐ **DANIEL MARTIN by John Fowles.** (#E8249—$2.95)

☐ **THE EBONY TOWER by John Fowles.** (#E8254—$2.50)

☐ **THE FRENCH LIEUTENANT'S WOMAN by John Fowles.**
(#E8066—$2.25)

☐ **RIDE THE BLUE RIBAND by Rosalind Laker.**
(#J8252—$1.95)*

☐ **MISTRESS OF OAKHURST—BOOK II by Walter Reed Johnson.** (#J8253—$1.95)

☐ **OAKHURST by Walter Reed Johnson.** (#J7874—$1.95)

☐ **HOLISTIC RUNNING: Beyond the Threshold of Fitness by Joel Henning.** (#E8257—$1.75)*

☐ **THE SILVER FALCON by Evelyn Anthony.**
(#E8211—$2.25)

☐ **I, JUDAS by Taylor Caldwell and Jess Stearn.**
(#E8212—$2.50)

☐ **THE RAGING WINDS OF HEAVEN by June Shiplett.**
(#J8213—$1.95)*

☐ **THE TODAY SHOW by Robert Metz.** (#E8214—$2.25)

☐ **THE LADY SERENA by Jeanne Duval.**
(#E8163—$2.25)*

☐ **LOVING STRANGERS by Jack Mayfield.**
(#J8216—$1.95)*

☐ **BORN TO WIN by Muriel James and Dorothy Jongeward.**
(#E8169—$2.50)*

☐ **ROGUE'S MISTRESS by Constance Gluyas.**
(#E8339—$2.25)

☐ **SAVAGE EDEN by Constance Gluyas.** (#E8338—$2.25)

☐ **WOMAN OF FURY by Constance Gluyas.**
(#E8075—$2.25)*

☐ **BEYOND THE MALE MYTH by Anthony Pietropinto, M.D., and Jacqueline Simenauer.** (#E8076—$2.50)

☐ **CRAZY LOVE: An Autobiographical Account of Marriage and Madness by Phyllis Naylor.** (#J8077—$1.95)

☐ **THE PSYCHOPATHIC GOD: ADOLF HITLER by Robert G. L. Waite.** (#E8078—$2.95)

*Price slightly higher in Canada

"WE ONLY HAVE ONE TEXAS"

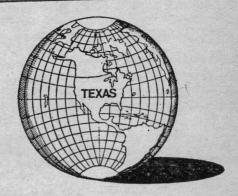

TEXAS

People ask if there is really an energy crisis. Look at it this way. World oil consumption is 60 million barrels per day and is growing 5 percent each year. This means the world must find three million barrels of new oil production each day. Three million barrels per day is the amount of oil produced in Texas as its peak was 5 years ago. The problem is that it is not going to be easy to find a Texas-sized new oil supply every year, year after year. In just a few years, it may be impossible to balance demand and supply of oil unless we start conserving oil today. So next time someone asks: "is there really an energy crisis?" Tell them: "yes, we only have one Texas."

ENERGY CONSERVATION -
IT'S YOUR CHANCE TO SAVE, AMERICA

Department of Energy, Washington, D.C.